Rebecca spent most of her teenage years sneaking into gigs, trying to befriend cool people, drinking $4 jugs of beer at the Empire Tavern, and dreaming of working in music.

After a brief stint in radio, she moved to London and spent her career travelling the world making Music TV for MTV and Channel 4, and creating award-winning digital content for Cartoon Network, the BBC and ITV. She's worked with diverse talent; from Scooby Doo and The Powerpuff Girls to Iggy Pop, Sonic Youth, Jack White and Laura Marling.

She now lives between London, Austria and New Zealand with her young family, freelances in TV, and writes YA novels and horror movie scripts.

D0418204

Also by Rebecca Denton

This Beats Perfect
A Secret Beat

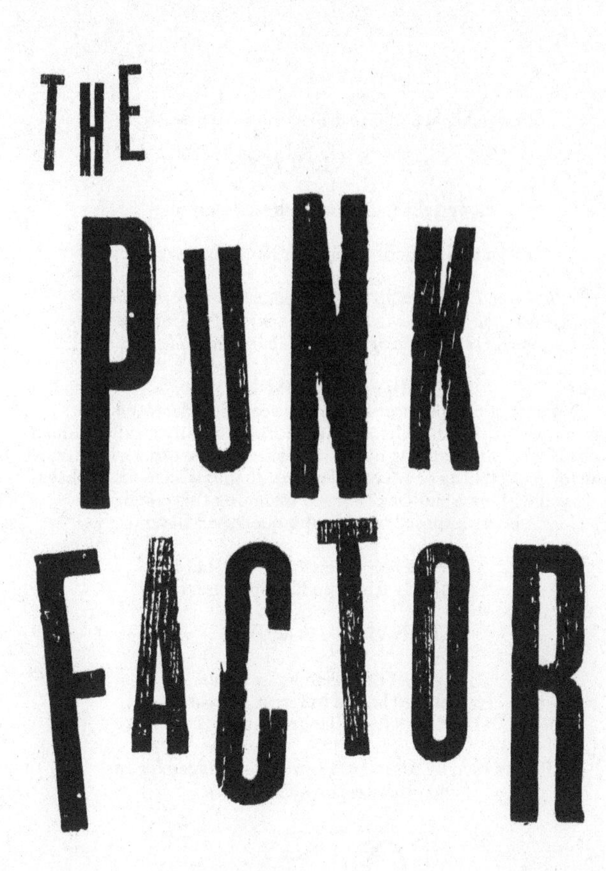

REBECCA DENTON

ATOM

First published in Great Britain in 2018 by Atom

1 3 5 7 9 10 8 6 4 2

Copyright © 2018 by Rebecca Denton

The moral right of the author has been asserted.

All characters and events in this publication, other than those clearly in the public domain, are fictitious and any resemblance to real persons, living or dead, is purely coincidental.

All rights reserved.
No part of this publication may be reproduced, stored in a retrieval system, or transmitted, in any form or by any means, without the prior permission in writing of the publisher, nor be otherwise circulated in any form of binding or cover other than that in which it is published and without a similar condition including this condition being imposed on the subsequent purchaser.

A CIP catalogue record for this book is available from the British Library.

ISBN 978-0-349-00312-2

Typeset in Janson by M Rules
Printed and bound in Great Britain by
Clays Ltd, Elcograf S.p.A.

Papers used by Atom are from well-managed forests and other responsible sources.

Atom
An imprint of
Little, Brown Book Group
Carmelite House
50 Victoria Embankment
London EC4Y 0DZ

An Hachette UK Company
www.hachette.co.uk

www.atombooks.co.uk

This book is dedicated to Celia Mancini.

Track List

1. Rebel Girl – Bikini Kill
2. Surface Envy – Sleater-Kinney
3. Tenant – Siouxsie and the Banshees
4. Little Liar – Joan Jett
5. Happy House – Siouxsie and the Banshees
6. Morning Dew – King Loser
7. Germfree Adolescents – X-Ray Spex
8. Gigantic – The Breeders
9. Break It Up – Patti Smith
10. High School Never Ends – Mykki Blanco
11. Call Me – Blondie
12. Cherry Bomb – The Runaways
13. I Want to Grow Up – Colleen Green
14. Trying – Bully
15. Yuk Foo – Wolf Alice
16. Typical Girls – The Slits
17. Baggage – L7
18. Bad Girl – The Detroit Cobras

19. Kool Thing – Sonic Youth
20. Army of Me – Björk
21. Edge of Seventeen – Stevie Nicks
22. (Ooh Yeah) Cool in the Cool – Bebe Ray Gains
23. Volcano Girls – Veruca Salt
24. Cool Schmool – Bratmobile
25. Cannonball – The Breeders
26. Hot Topic – Le Tigre
27. Spare Me – Ayo Nako
28. Close Up - Peaches
29. Hey Baby - Spazzys
30. Bad Apples – Pussy Riot
31. Wild is the Wind – Nina Simone
32. Bad Girls – M.I.A.
33. Top of the World – Shonen Knife

THE PUNK FACTOR

Chapter 1

Rebel Girl

Frankie slammed her cheap, black, fabric guitar case down on the small, wonky stage at the London Fields Primary School Community Christmas Market, and tried to calm her irritation. The guitar hit the stage with a thud. *Probably another bloody dent*, she thought. Sure, she was so wretchedly hungover she didn't want to play, but it was a far worse state of affairs that nobody had turned up.

'Fucking useless. What a disaster of a gig, what's the bloody point?' she muttered to an audience of no one.

'Come on, Haruna!' she shouted at her best friend who was lip-locked on the swing with her newish squeeze, budding grime DJ, Cheq.

'Chill out, Frankie,' Haruna sang dreamily. She ran a hand around the back of Cheq's smooth, thick neck as they kissed once, twice then several more times before she grinned and pulled herself away, slowly, stretching out her arm and holding on until the tips of their fingers were just touching. Finally she turned to Frankie and floated across to join her. Frankie could not hide her contempt for this nauseating coupling.

She glanced over at the second-hand record stall, and narrowly avoided locking eyes with the red-haired girl who was sorting display items ready for sale. Her hair cascaded down her back in a glorious sea of bright dye, and her T-shirt emblazoned with *Le Tigre* was, to Frankie's mind, a cocky, self-conscious signpost, ensuring that all who saw it were dazzled by her knowledge of feminist electro-punk.

'You're not the first couple to ever fall in love, you know,' Frankie snarled at Haruna when she finally made it to the stage. 'Maybe get a room, and spare us the sideshow?'

'Some of us are not burned by the fire of past experience, and can love with brave abandon,' Haruna teased, pressing her hands together in prayer. 'Speaking of love, Jules is here somewhere. What do you think?'

'I think all boys are losers,' said Frankie.

'Okay. Well, when you're ready, maybe?' Haruna said. 'Let's just take a breath. It's our first gig and it's not like we're going to disappoint thousands of waiting fans by not playing the three cover songs we don't really know.' She pulled herself up on the stage. 'Now, are you ready to be marginally less angry? Look what I did.'

Haruna unfurled the huge canvas sheet she had hand painted with the band's name – SEVEN – in punk pink typewriter lettering. 'What do you think? Where shall I put it? There's nowhere to hang it.'

'Why isn't our website on there?'

'Thanks for staying up all night secretly painting the new logo, Haruna. Despite the risks. I really appreciate that you probably had many other things to do, like studying for your History exam, but you took the time to do this instead. And you know, we don't even have a website.'

'We have a holding page. And you know I love it,' said Frankie, pulling out and waving her phone around. 'I'm even trying to Instagram it. Look!'

'Thank you, Haruna,' Haruna said, arms folded, waiting.

'Thank you, Haruna. Where're Aimee and Greer?' Frankie asked, checking over the piecemeal equipment left by the organisers. She shook her head.

'Aimee will be here. Frankie, please, can you be a bit more chill?' Haruna pulled her hair back into a ponytail and yanked two drumsticks out from the waistband of her trousers. 'And what's with the top?'

'Irony,' Frankie snapped, pulling her oversized chunky cardigan closed to obscure the huge *introvert* emblazoned across the front of her T-shirt.

Eight years they'd been friends. They met at the dance studio where Frankie's mother worked, and where Frankie was forced to help out on weekends. And also every bloody Wednesday after school. It was a place so full of pink and sequins and tulle and ribbons that Frankie had quickly developed a chronic and life-long aversion to all things ultra 'girlie'.

Haruna came strutting through the main doors of the studio one afternoon with a full face of stage make-up, hair pulled back into a severe bun and wearing a dance tuxedo with black-and-white tap shoes. Her mother stood quietly next to her, head slightly bowed, probably in embarrassment, as Haruna announced she had 'arrived' and had an appointment with admissions.

'You're here for tap class?' Frankie asked.

'Tap, commercial and street,' she declared. 'And world, if there's still space. But no ballet. Mum says I'm too tall. Am I too tall?'

'No, we take literally anybody,' Frankie said reassuringly. She pulled out a sign-up sheet and a pencil. 'You'll have to fill this in,' she said as she handed them to Haruna's mother. 'We have a special going for the term, but she will need *some* experience. It isn't for beginners.'

Haruna looked perturbed for a moment, then turned up her chin, tapped her toes in near perfect rhythm on the tiled floor, before spinning on her heels and coming to an abrupt stop with a sweep of the arms and a dazzle of jazz hands. It was an impressive display of spirit, if not skill.

'I'll catch up,' she insisted. And she did. Haruna was a great dancer, and she had an amazing natural rhythm – something that Frankie seriously lacked (but made up for with what her mother always described as 'exceptional confidence in performance'). At school Haruna was the only girl to learn percussion and drums, and so became the best drummer a three-piece girl punk band could ever hope for. Admittedly, she was far better than Frankie deserved – she herself was not exactly dedicated to the practice of her crappy guitar.

'Frankie! Haruna!' Aimee cycled up at considerable speed and gracefully dismounted. Today, her long, pale purple hair was in pigtails and fixed up with wire like two ski jumps jutting out from her head. Aimee was whip-smart and kind to a fault and although the least musically trained – she couldn't play a note on bass, really – she made up for it with cheery enthusiasm.

'Sorry I'm late; studying since dawn. Ugh, my parents are all over me right now because of that bloody B in Physics. Wow, there's, like, literally no one here except the stall owners. Oh, and isn't that the girl from the party . . . the redhead? The girl that was with—'

'I don't know,' Frankie snapped, before quickly conceding, 'Yes, that's her.' Then, giving her a half hug and staring up at the grey, damp London sky, she said, 'I know the crowd is thin. It's the rain, I guess.'

'Sure, Frankie.' Aimee gave her a cheery, supportive grin. 'It's gonna be great. What time did you leave last night? I didn't see you go? Was it cos *he* turned up?'

'Where's Greer?' Frankie interrupted, ignoring the question since she didn't know the answer. Also, it was possible it might lead to other embarrassing questions about last night. Her head pounded, and she suddenly longed for a large, cold glass of coke.

'Oh, I thought she called you. She said she called you?' Aimee's eyes darted to Haruna and then back to Frankie. 'She can't do sound today, she had to go Wick Rooms, there's some issue with one of the bands. I don't know. I thought she called you?'

'It's cool. We'll manage,' said Frankie, vaguely remembering some conversation from the night before. Her frustration was quickly turning to anger. 'I mean, there's not even a mixing desk, so—'

'Let's just do a sort of improvised, unplugged set,' Haruna interrupted. 'As it's our first gig, I'm guessing no one will feel misled? I've got brushes in my backpack.'

'We. Are. A. Punk. Band,' said Frankie.

'Then. We. Can. Do. What. The. Hell. We. Want,' replied Haruna. 'Do you even get punk?'

'It's okay, Frankie,' said Aimee. 'We can figure it out.'

'I only have my electric guitar, anyway. There must be somewhere I can plug my amp in,' Frankie said, lifting a cable and following it along the stage to find its source. 'Surely this leads somewhere?'

'Look, it is what it is.' Haruna sighed. 'We can work with what we have.'

'I can't play in these conditions,' Frankie moaned as she realised there was no actual power connected to anything, and that the extension lead had been pilfered for use by the stall selling split pea soup.

'To be fair, you can't really play anyway,' Haruna said, now laughing at her frustration. 'Come on, babe. This was just for a bit of fun. Stop taking it so seriously.'

'I'm done!' Frankie said dramatically.

'Let's just do what we can and call it a live rehearsal.' Haruna sighed, shooting Aimee *the look*. Frankie knew the look. It was the *Frankie is being an unreasonable pain in the ass* look.

Frankie checked her watch and gazed out across the playground. Alongside record stall loser, there were about a dozen others set up in a semicircle – cheap jewellery, crochet booties, dry cupcakes, Christmas decorations, second-hand tat, some old lady trying to get signatures for a petition to save the local theatre, and an unusually chic stall on the end selling gourmet pies for £8 a pop.

Frankie counted about twenty adults, six children and three dogs; it was as big a crowd as they could expect for their first gig, in a school playground, in the middle of winter. 'Fine.' She shrugged.

Aimee gave her the thumbs-up and they began to get themselves organised when a man dressed in a bright yellow suit, piano tie, tattered red wig and large green top hat climbed up on stage.

'Hey, darling, mind if I ask you to clear the stage so I can get blowing?' he said with a big grin.

'Ha. I get it. Blowing,' Aimee giggled, 'blowing bubbles. That's cute.'

'It's Frankie, not darling. And you're what?' Frankie said. 'Who are you?'

'Mr Bubble, if you please,' he replied, pulling a huge plastic bubble wand out of his travel trolley and decanting some liquid soap into a Tupperware container. 'And I'm on first.'

'Oh. But we're just about to go on,' Frankie said. 'And they said two p.m. to me.'

'Well, I'm on before you, and I have to be, I have another gig in an hour.'

'Two in a day?' said Aimee, wide-eyed. 'Wow. That's impressive!'

Frankie scowled at Aimee, and made a mental note to discuss 'how to be cool' with her. *Must she give everything away?* Mr Bubble handed Frankie a limp, creased, black-and-white flyer, which read: *It's Christmas at London Fields Primary School.* And down the side in bold Comic Sans font: *Entertainment from Mr Bubble, Girl Band Seven, followed by Joshua King.*

'Who's Joshua King?' Frankie demanded, shooting a fiercely irritated look at Aimee and Haruna.

'Oh, it's that handsome new Labour candidate delivering his manifesto on urban development,' said Mr Bubble.

'Why is he under "entertainment"?' Frankie huffed. 'And this is not a running order, it's a list. There's no times. Where's the organiser of this shit show? And why are we called *girl* band? What the hell is wrong with just *band*?'

'Frankie . . .' Aimee whispered, putting a hand gently on her arm.

'Look, if you just hop off the stage and let me do my thing, you'll be on in thirty,' Mr Bubble chirped. 'Go have some hot tea and a sit-down. My audience awaits.'

Frankie turned to the audience of three – a young mother with a baby strapped to her chest and a toddler who was twisting like a pretzel to escape her hand.

'There's no power,' Frankie snapped at Mr Bubble.

'And that's why the good lord gave me a voice.' He smiled, nodding at her to step aside.

Frankie surrendered, climbing down off the stage and placing her guitar back into its case. 'Show's off,' she said plainly to the girls. 'I give up.'

'Frankie, wait!' Aimee said, grabbing her arm. 'Come on. Don't be dispirited.'

'*Dispirited*?' Frankie said. 'I'm royally pissed off.'

She yanked her arm away and stomped across the fake grass, ducked under the monkey bars, huffing and puffing as she parked herself on one of the picnic tables tucked away behind the stalls. She crossed her arms and closed her eyes and sucked in a deep breath. She could hear the thump of her heart as she reached her fingers up to her mouth and chewed on the edges of her nails, tearing the skin away at the sides until she felt a sting.

She ran her hand through her black bob, and shook it out so it fell across her face. Then she sat back and propped herself up on her arms, staring up at the drizzly London sky. Why was this so hard? It had been so much work to harass the school to let them play, and now this? Could she even be bothered?

She sat glumly for as long as she could, knowing her dramatic departure needed a good fifteen minutes to have any impact on Aimee and Haruna. Her head was pounding and all she really wanted was her bed. Her phone buzzed. It was Aimee, who wasn't more than 100 metres away, but was clearly too afraid to come over. Frankie felt a satisfied surge of power, there was a part of her that liked the way she could create reactions in Aimee.

'What?' She turned her head to see Aimee standing by the stage holding on to her bike with her free hand.

'Um. Well, Mr Bubble is wrapping things up here . . . so . . . '

'I'm not playing,' said Frankie as plainly as she could.

'Okay,' said Aimee, pausing. 'Well, can I go? Only, I'm supposed to meet Greer at the Picturehouse after and I'd love to get changed.'

'Fine,' replied Frankie, 'and tell Haruna she doesn't have to hang around either.'

'She already left,' said Aimee meekly.

'Oh. Okay. Whatever. Have fun.' Frankie hung up the phone and slumped her shoulders forward in complete defeat.

'Hey, Frankie.'

Frankie turned to see where the familiar voice came from. Cheq's flatmate Jules had arrived, guitar in hand, plonking it down next to Frankie. He was almost unrecognisable in a big winter coat with beanie pulled down low. He smiled at her. That *familiar* smile that she wasn't having any of. 'I was on my way to practice and Cheq said you guys were playing. Are you still playing?'

'No,' she said angrily, folding her arms, hoping it would give him the *go away* vibe, then felt mean and unfolded them again.

'No? Damn, what happened?' he asked, blowing into his palms and rubbing his hands together before shoving them deep in his pockets. 'Man, it's cold.'

'I wasn't happy with the set-up,' Frankie said, spinning the situation. 'I told them I wasn't prepared to go on.'

'Fair enough,' he said, sounding impressed. 'Nice ink, by the way.'

'Cheers,' she said, tugging at the sleeve of her cardigan, feeling suddenly shy about the new vagina-shaped blood-red orchid she had tattooed on her forearm.

'Don't suppose you'd fancy a beer, then?' he said, picking his guitar back up.

Frankie almost wretched at the thought of drinking, flashes of the night before flooding her brain. *Why did I have to get so drunk?* She looked at Jules's fairly attractive – if somewhat babyish – face, that open, flirtatious look that boys get when they're hoping for some kind of engagement, and Frankie wondered if she could ever be taken in by that kind of look from anyone else ever again.

She had to get this band to work.

'No,' Frankie said. 'Sorry, Jules, I'd love to stay and chat, but . . . '

He stared at her for a moment then shrugged his shoulders, smiling. 'Cool,' he said, nodding at the stage. 'I was really here to watch Mr Bubble anyway.'

Frankie couldn't help half a grin, which she hid behind her hand as she stood up. 'He's prolific,' she replied, tossing him a wry smile. She jumped off the table, her black Converse hitting the ground a little harder than she would have liked. She snatched her guitar and marched over to the main stage just as Mr Bubble was creating a cow-sized bubble to the sound of cheering from his crowd of half a dozen.

'Seven are no longer playing,' she shouted out across the playground. 'But you can stay in touch with us online at sevenband.me or @sevenband on Instagram or @sevenbanded on Twitter and Snapchat. If you want news about any upcoming tours or recordings you can visit—'

'Oh, shut up!' yelled a father in double denim, shaking his head at her as Mr Bubble was nearing the end of his monster bubble act.

Frankie couldn't help herself: she walked around the back of the stage, looked a visibly rattled Mr Bubble in the eye and thrust a fist through the centre of his enormous creation, which exploded in a fountain of soapy mess across the floor. She shrugged at him, slipped her guitar over her shoulder and marched off, catching eyes with Jules who was almost doubled over in laughter.

As she turned the corner out of the playground and on to Mare Street she felt her frustration and anger start to dissipate. She paused, staring down Tudor Road at the row of terraced flats at the far end. And then, the internal battle began.

Don't do it, Frankie.

Oh, come on, just one last look won't hurt.

It just makes you feel like shit.

You're awesome.

You're an awesome disaster.

No, no. Just awesome. And you look really great today, so ...

Like a moth to the flame she was compelled. She turned down the road by the petrol station, making the simple four-street detour that would take her right by his flat.

CHAPTER 2

Surface Envy

Frankie walked carefully between the brick walls of the terraced houses and the roadside line of naked cherry trees, ensuring that anyone who might be peering out from the balcony of apartment 27 would see nothing. She found her spot and peered up. Up, with the heavy eyes of a girl on three hours of drunken sleep. It was quite an effort, but if anyone knew she was doing this, they would be surely impressed with her dedication.

Am I still writing this stuff down? she thought and she gazed across the dull new-build apartments' beige walls to the recycling bins that were bursting with rubbish and broken furniture. The lampshade she'd accidentally broken and tossed off the balcony was still wedged behind the bin.

Frankie pulled out the black notebook Haruna had given her last Christmas – a gift intended to 'capture her creative musings' – and flicked it open to the dog-eared page, frowning at her diary of shame.

Oh, she knew that technically she was stalking him, but since he had no idea, and no one was really being hurt, she preferred to call it *stalking-lite*. Or, a kind of semi-detailed staring. Really, she was just looking at his house. With notes.

But there was nothing interesting today. He was probably still in bed, anyway. Was her hungover, deep self-loathing worth noting? she wondered. Why had she come past today? Was she here because the gig was a catastrophe? I mean, the whole band thing was because of him.

Samuel James Ruddock, or Doc as he was known, was the love of Frankie's life. *Was*, mind. She was definitely, publicly, over him. For almost four months they'd been in some kind of relationship after drunken snogging in the toilets at a gig. The attraction was instant and intense and blinding, turning everything else in her life grey in comparison.

He introduced her to politics: he was anti-establishment, anti-military, anti-government, anti-capitalism, and anti any kind of authority. He was anti all sorts of things, really. Even things like Danish cheese, iPhones and *Bake Off*. He spoke at length most nights about vast conspiracies, none of which she really cared about. In fact, if she was honest, his passionate diatribes were riddled with hypocrisy and sometimes actual lunacy – but it was great watching his jaw move as he spoke.

He played her Dead Kennedys and Ramones records, smoked roll-up cigarettes and drank French red wine while all the other boys drank Red Stripe. He had posters of punk girl icons like Kathleen Hanna and Siouxsie Sioux on his wall and taught her about feminism and the patriarchy and gender power structures.

He held her face in his hands and called her 'baby' and didn't go to school any more and was old enough to get into pubs without fake ID.

And to make matters even more attractive, he was the lead guitarist in one of the hottest bands in town. Blood Flame Riot, were, admittedly, *very* underground, but they had some real buzz if you knew where to look.

Loving Doc was a bit like turning on a forever tap to her heart, a constant stream of pleasure that became insatiably addictive and increasingly desperate as he cooled. Which he abruptly did.

Yes, Doc was a beautiful, willowy, clever art student drop-out with thick spiky black hair and a kind of Teddy-boy-meets-punk swagger that made him utterly irresistible to everyone, and unable to tie himself down for too long. And that was why she was dumped, and why she had to exact a twisted revenge by being the coolest girl, in the most successful punk band in London.

'Frankie? Twice in two days.'

She swung around, stuffing the notebook in her pocket, and there he was, standing before her. *Damn! Of course he was out on a Saturday morning getting his bloody takeaway Americano and fresh pack of tobacco.* This hangover was really muddying her judgement. But oh boy, he looked glorious. Black tattered jeans clung to his skinny long legs, and his white Cure T-shirt hung loose over his hips. She noted with pained pleasure that his hair was longer, its thick dyed black mass spiked in a subtle fan. A faux-hawk, if you will.

Oh, how she missed those summer days when he would hang outside school waiting for her looking like *this*.

'We didn't get to say hello last night,' he said, curiously. 'You look really different, I wanted to say.'

She did look a little different. Since the break-up she'd lost a bit of weight. Not a huge amount – she was still pretty curvy – but enough to make her clothes hang off her differently. She'd also cut her long brown hair into the short bob, and dyed it black too. And there was the orchid tattoo she'd convinced her cousin's best friend to do for her. And maybe a bit more eye make-up. And the large ear cuff. Yeah, in the five months since she'd seen him, she had changed quite a bit.

'Your clothes . . . ' he continued, eyeing her appreciatively. 'I dig it.'

There may have also been a slight wardrobe update. But it was a bit rude of him to keep pointing these things out. She felt her cheeks redden.

'You look totally different,' he said plainly, but when Frankie just stood there, unable to reply, he quickly added, 'I mean, *good* different, but different. What are you doing here?'

'Hi, Doc,' she said with resigned humiliation. 'I'm just heading home, thought I'd take a detour to see the Banksy.'

She pointed at the huge stick figure street art outside the medical walk-in centre at the end of the road.

'That's not a Banksy, though.'

'Oh, really?'

'Yeah. Looks nothing like one,' he smirked. 'Anyway, nice to see you again. How you been? I heard you started a band or something?'

'Yeah, it's nothing. Just a girl punk band. A bit DIY, a bit kind of a rough. Just wanna make some noise, you know.' She shrugged and looked at the ground, feeling self-conscious as hell.

'Sounds cool.'

'How's *your* band going?'

'Awesome. We're actually waiting to hear . . . ' He paused, looking past her wistfully. 'I'm actually not supposed to say anything, but whatever, they don't control me.'

He looked her right in the eyes, the intensity of which almost gave her vertigo. 'We got a slot playing The Hackney Crawl in March.'

He dropped the news with a sturdy, serious tone, before tilting his head back and drawing a more self-effacing picture. 'I mean, not that it's Glastonbury, but it's a solid start.'

'Oh,' Frankie said, impressed because she knew she should be, and made a mental note to look into The Hackney Crawl when she got home. 'That's cool.'

'Yeah, maybe your band will get there one day. Have you been gigging?' he asked, somewhat supportively. Frankie tried to ignore the mental image of London Fields Primary School,

Mr Bubble and the tiny number of middle-class mums and dads she'd just walked out on.

'Oh yeah. Just starting to,' she said, shrugging.

'Where do you practise?'

Okay, time to lie, there's no way she could say the school music room. 'Wick Rooms.'

'No shit? We're there too now, just moved into the second floor. What room you in?'

Panic. 'Um, I dunno. My bandmate Aimee looks after all that. Her girlfriend does the bookings.'

'Who do you mean? Greer?' he said, eyes brightening at the connection. 'I know Greer; she rented our room to us. She's cool.'

This quick detour home was fast becoming a disaster. Frankie wished she could eject herself out of the conversation, away from Doc, and to her brown corduroy sofa to watch reruns of *Glee* and eat big chunks of cheese. She had always been an embellisher, but this lie was really stupid and easily verifiable. 'Yeah, I mean, we haven't done much there yet, not much at all really. I mean, but we should be there properly soon.'

'So you're not actually practising there yet.' He nodded, looking somewhat relieved. 'I mean, I'd have been impressed if you'd gone from not knowing how to strum a single chord when we were together to being *that* set up in, what, three months?'

'Five.'

'Well, five. Anyway, you were never interested in playing. That's all. I'm surprised.' He shrugged. 'Good surprised.'

And just like that, the veil of disinterest fell across Doc's face. She knew it well. The audience with Doc was up. He had another thing. He breathed out, thrust his hands into his pockets and pulled a tight-lipped smile. 'Well, I better split.'

'Sure, see ya.' Frankie took a wobbly step around him, wondering if they might hug. I mean, they did have sex five months ago, why was it so weird to hug or even shake hands? But all he did was pat her shoulder as they passed, and send her a crooked half-smile.

She waited a few steps, heart pounding in her chest, before peering back over her shoulder, and everything felt utterly shit. What had she been doing? Had he seen her writing in her notebook? Why did he still get to her?

Frankie pulled out her phone and called the emergency hotline.

'Rooney. It's okay, I left too. Are they home or are you alone? Can I come? I've just seen Doc. I need a talking-to.'

'Shit, Frankie, hang on.'

Frankie heard a muffled sound, followed by a semi-concealed groan of irritation – from Cheq, she guessed – then silence. 'Sorry,' Haruna said at last. 'Of course you can. Come right over.'

CHAPTER 3

Tenant

Haruna saw the call come in and *really* wanted to avoid it. There may have been many years of friendship but truth be told, her patience was wearing thin with the dramas. She knew that Frankie had struggled to let go of Doc, but this was getting seriously boring.

'You better go,' she said to Cheq, pushing him back. 'I have to see her.'

'Ah, not again . . . ' He leaned in and tried to push his tongue against her lips, willing her mouth to open.

'I know,' she said as she stood up, wiping her mouth and reorganising her crumpled tee, tucking it into her high-waisted black jeans. 'And can you just back up a bit? I mean, I dig you and everything, Cheq, but I'd rather be alone than suffocated. I'm not going to sleep with you, so would please quit trying to wear me down? I hate it.'

'Damn. I wasn't trying to do that at all. Sorry,' he said, standing up next to her and shuffling slightly, unsure and awkward. 'You can be so harsh, Ru.'

She looked at him, this tall, broad, apparently brilliant lyricist with his tightly shaved head, creeping-vine neck tattoo and silver nose ring. He was hot. Hotter still, as he made this hard, aggressive music that Haruna found an insatiable turn-on. But he was also impossibly sweet sometimes, and vulnerable.

'I didn't mean that.' Haruna shrugged. 'I don't really hate it. You know I love it. But Frankie is on her way, and . . . ' Her voice trailed off. She shrugged again. Frankie came first, and he knew it.

Her mum's kitchen was a 'mess' by her standards, and she resented the amount of work needed to return it to its usual pristine state. 'Can you take the pizza box and the empties with you? Mum will kick my butt if she sees them in the rubbish. Quick quick.'

'When am I going to meet her?'

'Probably never,' replied Haruna, watching as Cheq pulled his sneakers on by the door. 'Pizza boxes!' she reminded.

'I know! Got it. Pizza boxes. Get out of here, Cheq. When will I see you?'

'Next weekend. No texts, remember?'

'I know, I know. Take care, Ru. I love you. You know that?' he said, snatching the boxes and rolling his eyes as he shut the door behind him.

'Yeah, yeah,' she rolled her eyes back, and grinned, 'I know.'

Haruna rushed upstairs to clear up the mess that Cheq had made in her room: crisps packets, a receipt from the corner store; and the toilet seat was up in the bathroom. She huffed and puffed, pulling out the toilet cleaner and giving it a quick once-over. She leaned into the shower and plucked out a couple of hairs from the drain. Then she stripped off, jumped in, scrubbed off her basic make-up and washed her hair. She stepped out of the bath and wiping the steam off the bathroom mirror, she inspected her eyes. Bright enough, despite the lack of sleep.

She ducked into her bedroom, stuffing the clothes she'd had on to the back of her wardrobe and picking out some plain blue jeans and a crew-neck sweater in pale green. She smoothed down her long black hair and tied it back with a simple band. She looked in the mirror and scoffed. *At least that should keep any fuss to a minimum.*

Maybe it was overkill but she couldn't risk her mother finding out she'd been entertaining, not when she was this close to the finish line. Soon she'd be eighteen, finished school and out of this goddamn prison cell, off to university with a pocket full of cash and her freedom.

She skipped downstairs, dropped her iPhone into the dock and put on The Slits. She had been on a bit of a personal musical journey through kick-ass women in music, and The Slits were her current obsession. And a damn sight more fun than Tchaikovsky.

As quickly as she could, she ran the vacuum over the carpet by the door, wiped down all the surfaces except the framed photo of her mother and her stepfather Greg. She felt the burn of hate stab through her at the sight of him, and she turned the frame slightly around to face the wall. Her own little act of rebellion.

She went around to each of the cushions on the sofa and gave them a good fluff, arranging them exactly as her mother liked. Then she went to the hook at the back of the door of the under-stairs toilet, fishing for her school bag which she heaved on to the kitchen island, carefully arranging her books and stationery, creating the appearance of a weekend of studying.

With nearly everything done she started on the dishes and then, of course, the door went. Frankie.

'Welcome, and God bless,' said the electronic doorbell in Greg's throaty voice.

'Hi, Greg!' shouted Frankie, giving the CCTV entrance camera the finger, as was her custom.

Haruna smiled, pulling off her Marigolds. She swung the door open, and Frankie looked her up and down, taking in her squarest of square outfits

'Hey-lo, normcore,' Frankie said with a frown. 'When are they back?'

'An hour or so, I think. Everything's ready, though. Hey – sorry about the gig.'

'I'm already over it,' said Frankie as she gave Haruna a kiss on the cheek and pushed into the kitchen. She went straight to the fridge and pulled out the orange juice, which she proceeded to drink straight from the carton.

'The hangover. I just want all the juice, you know?' She took another big gulp, finishing at least a third of the carton. 'When are you out of this crap hole? Makes me want to break things just being here five minutes.'

'Six months,' Haruna said. 'Oh man, I cannot wait.'

'Have you done all your uni applications?'

'Yeah, but I was actually thinking I might take a trip. You know how Mum has this money put aside for me, from Dad? Well, it's for uni but I was thinking of doing something a bit reckless.'

'How reckless?'

'Frankie levels of reckless.'

'Oooh, tell,' Frankie said, brimming with delight. 'I can't wait to see you free and cutting loose at last!'

'I was thinking of going travelling for a bit. See Japan? Maybe see my dad.'

'Japan?'

'Yes, you know, where half of me is from?'

'But it's so far away!' Frankie said, suddenly in a panic. 'What if you don't come back? I couldn't cope without you. I'd end up in jail. Or pregnant. Or in a cult. Or dead.'

'It's only ten hours. I looked it up. And I've been kind of syphoning off a little of the shopping money to get myself a passport.' She grinned, feeling proud of herself.

'Oh really?' Frankie said, surprised, before suddenly frowning.

'But have you spoken to your dad? Like, does he want to see you? You should email him first.'

'We email a bit. I think he might want to see me,' she replied. 'I don't see why not. Mum left him, he didn't leave me. You know he used to be in touch a lot. Letters and presents when I was smaller and I dunno, it's just been going over in my mind ... What if he's worth a visit? Maybe I might stay for a while.'

'But the band!' Frankie cried, bringing her hands to her face. 'Oh no! Just when we're kicking off.'

'Is that really your first thought when I tell you I'm thinking of going to see my dad for the first time I since was ten?'

'Sorry,' Frankie said. 'I mean, that's heavy. I think it's good, though. You should see him and maybe punch him in the face for leaving you with your mum and her asshole.'

'Yeah, well, it's just a thought,' Haruna said lightly, realising she should have picked another less Frankie-centric moment to bring the subject up. 'It wouldn't be for long. Maybe the summer or something. Anyway, forget it. What's going on with Doc?'

'We urgently need to be a better band.'

'Huh? What's that got to do with Doc?'

'Oh my lord, he looked good. And he spoke to me for about fifteen minutes, I reckon, and he asked about the band. He *knew* about the band. He seemed *interested*. Have you got anything to eat? I'm starved.'

'Did he?' Haruna doubted it. When Doc had ruthlessly

blindsided Frankie by break-up text five months ago, there was no room for misunderstanding.

SorrFrankles. It's overI've met someone else. Plesetcc.

The drunk text came in at around 3 a.m., so he'd obviously *just* met that someone.

'Yes, he did,' Frankie huffed at her. Haruna could tell she was irritated at her lack of enthusiasm, but the whole Doc thing was such a goddamn drag.

'Okay, so start at the beginning, where did you bump into him?' Haruna dug through the pantry, pulling out some old rice crackers, and sliding them across the table to Frankie. 'You can take those.'

'I'm starving. Need to get home to mum,' said Frankie, stuffing two in her mouth, paying no mind to any manners. 'She's not doing the evenings at the studio any more, so Dad's off dinner duty. Thank God.'

'How will you ever manage flatting?' Haruna said, shaking her head. 'You need to learn to cook, girl. Preferably like your mum.'

Haruna loved Frankie's parents. Their family home was warm and loud and full of energy. Her little brother Hamish was sweet and annoying in the perfect way a little brother should be. Her Dad, Eddie, bald as a snooker ball (his description), was boisterous and opinionated, and her mum was a kind but stern Scottish dance teacher, who had taken a deep shine to Haruna. Those evenings at Frankie's parents' place were the best, not least because they took her away from her own oppressive home.

'So, tell me. How did you *bump* into him?'

'Okay, but you mustn't judge.'

'Honestly, I'm already secretly judging.'

Frankie laughed, and then, clearly feeling comfortable enough to spill, dropped an absolute clanger. 'I bumped into him on the way home from the gig. Our failed gig. I was feeling all down and bad, and, I was . . . you know, outside his house.'

Haruna felt a sudden sense of unease. She folded her arms and looked Frankie right in the eye. 'You need to tell me absolutely everything.' She swiped the juice off the counter top, putting it back in the fridge in silence before returning to clean the counter of orange juice drops. Frankie was nodding. '*Everything*, mind. Why were you outside his house?'

'Well, sometimes I take that route home, and you know, just look up at his room. I dunno . . . ' Frankie was scratching her nose and looking everywhere but at Haruna. 'And sometimes, you know, I record what's going on.'

'What the fuck do you mean, *record*?' Haruna said, with frustration starting to rise. 'You film it?'

'No no. Not really. I mean I *have* filmed, but only once.' Frankie hesitated for a moment, then pulled the notebook out of her jacket. 'Here. Here's the book of shame. Welcome to my world.'

Haruna spied the notebook she'd bought for Frankie and for a brief moment was delighted to see she hadn't lost it. The first page had some scrawled lyrics from Frankie's first attempt at penning a song but what followed was page after page of perplexing scribbled notes.

'What is this?'

'I just go past his house and write stuff down,' Frankie admitted. '*You* wanted to know why I was there. Anyway, who hasn't done a spot of light stalking? It calms me.'

'Um, most people,' Haruna said, dumb founded. 'Me.'

'Says the girl with the secret life and the secret boyfriend,' Frankie said, lashing out. 'Sorry. I know that's not your fault. Anyway, the point is that Doc was passing by today and he stopped me for a proper chat.'

'He caught you hanging around outside his flat?'

'No, it wasn't like that. He was just coming home and I was, you know, passing by.'

'Of course he was passing by. He lives there!!'

'Look, what I'm trying to say is that we need to be a better band because he seemed really impressed that I was in a punk band, and I *think* that he felt a little differently. He kept saying I looked good. Well, he said, different – good different – but you could tell what he meant. That's good, right?'

Haruna looked at her friend. 'Frankie, this is pretty on the edge.'

'No no no, it's not.' Frankie shook her head frantically, folding her arms. She was trying to normalise her behaviour, but it wasn't going to work. Haruna didn't speak for a minute; she just watched Frankie who started to look caged and vaguely panicked. 'It's not like that. It's just not like that.'

'Let's put the creepy stalking to one side for a moment. I thought you'd finished with Doc? You told me this obsession was over.'

Haruna had been here with Frankie before: there was always a story that came before the real story, and the real story was nearly always something that Frankie was ashamed or embarrassed about. And unfortunately, because this was Frankie Taylor, there was often good reason to feel embarrassed.

'It is,' Frankie said, brushing away the dark hair from her eyes, which were ever so slightly glassy, signalling the break was coming. 'Don't be so harsh on me, Haruna. It's not as bad as it seems.'

Haruna looked at the clock. 'Look, I've got about thirty minutes.' She held up the notebook. 'Let's go out into the yard and burn this – because, Frankie, this has to end.'

Frankie nodded, biting her lip. 'But the band . . . I thought maybe we could—'

'I'll do anything you want with the band! I'm totally on board. I love that you want to get it going, I've been hassling you for ages to start a band. But you do need to take it more seriously.' Haruna sighed, 'Oh God, I should have known. It's all been about him, hasn't it? No wonder the gig was more important than actually doing any music.'

'No, that's not right,' Frankie insisted. 'I mean, it's like, the band is first, but Doc being impressed and falling for me all over again is like a bonus.'

'Jeez,' complained Haruna, 'you could try to lie a little?'

Frankie squeezed out half a smile and uncrossed her arms. 'I want to do the band. I've wanted to be in a punk band since for ever.'

'Well,' Haruna was dubious, 'we do really need to talk about the fact that you're still not over that dickhead, because you are clearly still *all about* him.'

'I don't actually feel like I still care about him,' Frankie replied, looking sheepish. 'That might sound weird, but it's not like I cry or anything.'

'That's because you're the queen of denial. There are walls upon walls of denial to break through with you to get to the actual problem. And this whole Doc thing is a problem.'

'You can be a real asshole, you know?' Frankie said, shoulders hunched as she followed Haruna outside. Haruna then unceremoniously flung her notebook into the pizza oven.

'Don't do it again. Like, really don't. For one thing, it's probably illegal, or potentially illegal or something. Plus, Frankie, I just really want you to know how awesome you are. He's a loser, and you're just such a good woman.' She peeked at the time on her phone and felt the anxiety begin to fizz.

'Babes, we have exactly twenty-one minutes to come up with a plan for you to move forward. And if you don't listen this time, don't expect *me* to, next time.'

'Got it, Nana,' Frankie said, resigned.

After Frankie left, Haruna felt the room deflate like the life had been vacuumed out of it. Cheq was gone, Frankie was gone, and in a moment her other life would return.

She readied herself on the kitchen island, opening her school book and staring at her notes, waiting for sound of the key in the door.

CHAPTER 4

Little Liar

'So anyway, Aimee, here's the thing: I need you to ask Greer if we can take a spare room up at Wick Rooms.' Frankie smiled her fullest, warmest smile and slid a herbal tea across the table to her friend. Aimee had been brought here under false pretences; Frankie had no intention of discussing Haruna's surprise birthday party with her. That wasn't even a thing. In fact, Frankie's birthday was next.

No, Frankie had hatched a plan, and Aimee was the poor mug who would be strong-armed into helping. This was how Frankie got things done, just like her dad taught her. 'You gotta hustle the hell outta life,' he used to tell her. 'No one's going to hand it to you.' He also told Frankie that the moon landing never happened, that Elvis was still alive and that the government was poisoning tap water with fluoride. But over the years you learned to pick and choose your advice from Eddie Taylor.

It was basically Haruna's fault. She had been the usual stern rock the day before and Frankie had been unable to stop herself from talking. Her emotional stability was no match for that hungover run-in with Doc, so as Haruna showed a smidgen of her signature cold practicality, the tears flowed and Frankie confessed more than she would have liked.

Well, Frankie couldn't undo the confession about her extra-curricular activities in that regard, and anyway Haruna didn't seem particularly surprised, though she was definitely unimpressed. When she saw the notebook of shame, it was promptly confiscated, and then burned in her mother's pizza oven. It made Frankie twitch to see all that precious data go up in smoke. *If only I had that kind of dedication for school work*, she mused.

In the end, Haruna once again gave her some choice recommendations for moving forward and on with her life, free of Doc, and Frankie did a moment of real, honest soul searching and decided she needed to do the following:

- Stop stalking Doc. (At his house, at least. Off-the-cuff run-ins at his favourite hang-outs were still on the cards.)
- Get a space at Wick Rooms so he wouldn't think she was lying about that, and also, helpfully, she could bump into him there.

- Probably practise guitar a bit more.
- Make Seven the greatest punk band in the world so that:
- Doc fell in love with her again because she was an enigmatic, wild and successful singer, and as a bonus –
- Haruna wouldn't go away

Of course, this was not quite the advice Haruna had given her, but they'd been best friends so long, Frankie knew when to listen to her and when to wilfully ignore her. And so her first port of call this bright Sunday morning was to the person who could get her what she needed most.

'So, what do you think?' she asked, beaming. 'Will you ask Greer?'

'Oh God, this is why you asked to meet Greer there?' whined Aimee, eyes darting about with anxiety. 'Frankie, it's like 265 quid a month for the smallest room, and we'd probably need to soundproof it. I think you have to pay a bond too. Do you have that kind of money? You quit that job at the Jack the Ripper museum, didn't you?'

'Sexist,' Frankie interjected.

'But also, none of us could legally do it, since we're all seventeen, we'd have to get one of our parents to do it.'

'I was thinking of a more, um, cost-effective way. Like free?'

'What? I don't think Greer could do that. I couldn't ask that of her. And she's only a part-time assistant, for goodness' sake; she can't just give us a room. There's probably a manager or a book-keeping person or something that monitors this stuff.'

'Imagine wanting to do book-keeping,' Frankie pondered, before refocusing. 'Surely there's a band who are on tour for a few months who could sublet? Oh my God, it's Cheq, hide.'

'I can't hide . . . hide where?' Aimee said, flustered. 'Under the table?'

The café door opened and Cheq, with a red beanie and a scarf wrapped tightly round his neck, came in, laughing, his voice raised in excitement. He was with his flatmate – the guy who everyone was constantly trying to set her up with – Jules. Jules was also in a band, though she didn't know what they were called, or frankly really anything about him, other than that he was *nice*. Frankie always tuned out when Haruna tried to talk to her about Jules. *You should really think about dating him. He's so nice.* Nice. NICE?

'Who wants to date nice?' Frankie muttered under her breath.

'I didn't pay anything,' Cheq was saying to Jules. 'I dunno how, man, but he sold me the mixer and was like, "Yeah, you can take it." For nothing!'

'That's amazing,' Jules replied, clocking Frankie, who was trying to hide behind a menu.

'Hi, Cheq,' Aimee said brightly. 'Hi, Jules. Merry almost Christmas!'

'Hey!' Cheq leaned in and gave Aimee a kiss on the cheek, but luckily the table separated Frankie and Cheq so she didn't befall the same fate. 'Hi, Frankie.'

'Hi,' she replied sourly, before nodding at Jules, who took his own beanie off to reveal tousled mousy-brown hair, cut short at the sides. 'Hi, Jules. How was Mr Bubble?'

'Seminal,' he replied, with that slightly amused look he always had. 'How's things? You playing again soon? Got to get back on it.' *Ugh. Ignore.*

'We'll see,' Frankie said, feeling annoyed and avoiding his gaze by pulling the menu up to cover her face.

'Cheq, what you having? Coffee?' Jules said, before turning back to Frankie and tapping on the edge of the menu. 'It's easier to read if it's the right way around.'

Frankie blushed, her eyes flickering up to Jules whose amusement had blossomed into a full-blown laugh. She rolled her eyes and dropped the menu on the counter, resigned to the interruption.

'What're you guys up to?' Cheq asked, while Jules headed over to the counter.

'Having a tea,' Frankie replied flatly.

'Great to see you last night,' Aimee said cheerfully. 'You were amazing. I think you've sent Greer down the rabbit hole. She only listens to hip-hop and grime now.'

'Well, that's cool. I'm super glad you came,' Cheq said, before looking at Frankie's rude expression with irritation. 'Guess I'll catch you guys later?'

He wandered off to join Jules at the counter. They were a bit of an odd couple really, but they were old friends.

'What did you do last night?' Frankie asked quietly, so as not to give away any sign of interest to Cheq.

'Oh, we went to his gig. He's really great. I mean, *really*.'

'Is Jules in his band?'

'No, no. You know Jules's band? Come on. Everyone knows them. They're really taking off.'

'Why wasn't I invited?' Frankie said, half-jokingly.

'You hate that music. And you kinda hate Cheq ... so ...' She lifted her left shoulder slightly, with half a smile, letting Frankie know that it was her own fault she'd been left out.

'Whatever, anyway, back to Wick,' she continued as Cheq and Jules left with their takeaway bacon sandwiches. Jules glanced back, catching her eye and nodding at her as they pushed through the door into the cold. There was something about the way he looked at her that made her uncomfortable, like he could see all the corners of her. *Damn it, Frankie, why did you look at him?*

'Um ... what I was saying was, what if a band was away, on tour or something?'

'What do you mean?'

'You know, an empty room that's already being paid for? I mean, what good is it having a girlfriend that works there if we can't take advantage a little bit,' insisted Frankie, with twinkling eyes. 'Am I right?'

'Um, well, maybe. But, gosh, I'm not really sure.'

'Well, look, good news. I've arranged to meet her and Haruna there in a few minutes.' Frankie stood up, she wrapped her red tartan scarf snugly around her neck and tied it into her oversized men's tweed coat just below the chin. 'Can't hurt to ask?'

'Ah, Frankie, I wish you *had* asked me first.' Aimee sat back, staring up at her aghast.

'You would have said no. Come on!' Frankie said. 'She'll be cool. She'll love my idea. Especially when it comes from you.'

'Good God!' Aimee protested as she stood up and pulled on a dazzlingly bright yellow pea coat and flicked out her long hair. For a moment Frankie stared at her. Aimee was pretty but she could look absolutely model stunning some days and this was one of them. 'It's vintage. Isn't it amaze? Another Greer find.'

As they ventured outside, the brisk cold wind came thundering around the outside of the café and burned the naked skin on their cheeks. The café was a new addition to Hackney Wick, a place that until the 2012 Olympics had been a bit of an industrial wasteland east of the A12. Now, incredible street art seemed to fill each unclaimed wall, and new-build apartments were springing up in every vacant lot.

They walked the narrow cobbled road round to the former Victorian brick factory, Wick Rooms, six floors of music-practice rooms and art studios. As they approached the entrance they spotted Greer standing just outside, arms folded, stern-faced.

'Okay, bollocks. What's this about?' she asked suspiciously, but kind of smirking too. Like she knew. Greer had just had the sides of her head shaved, and her new tight black braids were pulled into a high bun. Her lips were bright orange and a delicate chain hung from a ring in her septum to her ear. Round her neck, an extraordinarily detailed beaded choker in yellows and greens sat just above the round collar of her captain's coat. Greer always looked extraordinary and Frankie was not just impressed by her amazing style – she absolutely fancied her.

'Hey,' Haruna said, nodding her head as she arrived at the same time. Coat buttoned up high, pink cheeks, shivering. 'What's this all about?'

'Aimee has something to ask you,' Frankie said to Greer, nudging Aimee, 'on our behalf.'

'Hmm. Okay?' Greer said, glancing at Frankie and then back to Aimee. 'I think I can guess.'

'Frankie wanted to know if we could borrow a practice room for a bit,' Aimee said, biting her lip, before whispering to Frankie, 'You owe me.'

'I thought as much. Well, lucky for you there're a few free,' Greer said, pulling out her keys, 'but there will be rules.'

'Oh, thank you, Greer,' Frankie said. 'You're the best.'

'Don't thank me yet,' Greer replied, frowning. 'And to be clear, you guys better not screw this up for me.'

'This better be worth it,' Haruna whispered to Frankie.

They all rubbed their boots on the grating by the entrance

to try to remove some of the filth of the wet, sleety mud. They needn't have bothered, really: the place was a goddamn tip. Greer handed a key to Haruna and motioned towards a room down the hall on the left.

'Why does she get the keys?' Frankie complained.

'Because *she* will look after them,' Greer said, crossing her arms before inviting a further challenge from Frankie as she pushed 20p into the power meter and the lights sprung on. 'The meter's just for the shared spaces,' she explained.

'Is there heating?' asked Frankie. 'It's Baltic.'

'There are some radiators but not all of them work, I don't think. This isn't a hotel.'

On the cork board by the door there was a list of occupants written in varying pens and pencils, half crossed out, scribbled. A bloody mess. Frankie was annoyed to see that Blood Flame Riot were not on there. Some bands were listed by people's names.

'Come on!' Greer said, pushing open the door to room 3.

Frankie gasped.

It was a huge room; the walls were covered with egg cartons and grey foam, and there were band posters upon band posters, pasted on top of each other, peeling at the corners. The wooden floor was almost completely concealed by several old rugs, and a couple of brown extension chords snaked, discarded on the floor. A deep, springy, burgundy velveteen sofa sat on the far wall under two small barred windows.

It was glorious.

'Oh my God, take a photo of me here now,' Frankie demanded, thrusting her phone into Aimee's hand. 'I'll lie on the couch. No, better still, I'll lie on the floor. Take it from above.'

Frankie sprawled out on the floor, head back, eyes rolled back with a pained expression plastered on her face. 'Quick. I look waaaaaaaasted. Oh my God! Look, there's a Patti Smith quote on the wall. THIS IS A SIGN FROM GOD, IF THERE WAS A GOD!'

'Wow, this is awesome,' Haruna said. 'It's certainly, absolutely, one hundred million per cent better than practising at school with Mr Laurendet watching.'

'Timely too, since I've handed in my notice at school,' Frankie announced, looking at Haruna. 'What, you thought you were the only one with plans?'

'Oh, you did it, then?' Haruna said, tugging on the edge of her purple turtleneck and looking to the floor. 'That's great.'

'You could leave too . . . ' she said to Haruna. 'Come flatting with me or something?'

'Yeah,' Haruna said, irritated, 'it would be that easy for me.'

'You what?' Aimee said, putting a hand on Frankie's shoulder and turning her. 'You're really leaving? But what on earth will you do?'

'I have some ideas.' Frankie shrugged. 'I can't take another term of that place.'

Epic-nerd Greer, a first-year engineering student, stared for a moment in either disbelief or awe. 'You're not going to finish school? There's only six months left.'

Frankie wavered for a moment before nodding her head. 'Nope. I'm done.' She snuck another peek at Greer's stunned face, revelling in the shock value of it all.

Greer seemed poised to offer advice for a moment, and then seemed to think better of it, continuing her monotonous instructions instead. 'So, you need to load your gear in and out of here, before and after every session. It needs to be empty in case the manager wants to show someone around the room. There's a storage area at the back there next to the kitchen, and the key is on that same ring, Rooney. The big one.'

'Got it' replied Haruna, nodding her head.

'You have to be, like, really careful, guys. Like, no one can get a sniff of this, got it? I'm getting a tea,' Greer said, rolling her eyes at Aimee who still looked utterly aghast at the plan. 'Keep them under control.'

Their second ever gig was fast approaching, a thirty-minute set at a bingo hall, where they had promised to play rock 'n' roll hits from the 1960s. Her dad had wangled it for them, although Frankie didn't give him any credit, but with the date getting nearer and nearer she had turned up the heat on the band. Two practices a week, Tuesday and Thursday, for two hours. If anyone wasn't interested in committing their time to the greatest punk band in the world, they needed to say so now. It didn't matter that Frankie herself rarely practised. At least she was getting a new guitar for Christmas. That was proof of real commitment right there.

'There's one critical issue here, Franks,' said Haruna. 'I

don't own a drum kit, and I can't bring the school one here twice a week.'

'Ah ha! I've thought of that already, my sceptical friend,' Frankie said, pulling out her phone and skimming her photos until she reached the one she was after. 'Here we go. Presenting the very best in pawned goods, direct from my Uncle Chester's store to here.'

'What?'

'Look at the photo!' Frankie exclaimed, holding up the image of a shiny black drum kit in the storage area of Frankie's uncle's pawn shop. In the photo, Frankie was standing next to the kit with a wide smile on her face and her arms outstretched in presentation. 'Ta da!'

'A pawned kit?' Haruna said. '*That's* your answer?'

'Yes, it's ours for all of January – that's when the owner said he'd be back for it. But Uncle Chester thinks not. We do need to look after it, of course, but it's pretty nicely worn in so I doubt they'd notice an extra bonk or two. My uncle wanted to store it at Sackhead's but there was no room in the basement and so I came up with the perfect solution. And we can always buy it if the owner doesn't come back. Don't look at me like that. Where do you think my parents will get my new guitar and amp from? Pawn shops are full of musical instruments. It's universally known that musicians are really bad with money.'

'Or they don't earn much,' Haruna suggested. 'I feel bad. That's some poor person's favourite thing in the world and they probably pawned it to pay for—'

'A new one,' Frankie interrupted. 'Who knows what? Don't presume the person was a desperate gambler or an alcoholic or something. That's discrimination.'

'Oh God, Frankie, we're illegally using a practice space—' Haruna began.

'Semi-illegally,' Frankie reassured her, before whispering, 'I mean, it's really Greer that will get in trouble.'

'We're basically stealing a kit.'

'Borrowing,' Frankie corrected.

'You don't really play guitar.'

'I've been learning.'

'Aimee would rather be anywhere else.'

'That's not true. I'm mostly having fun. It's a welcome break from studying, anyway,' Aimee said meekly. 'I'll feel better when we can legitimise this arrangement. I'm so worried about being caught. Aren't you?'

'This is a goddamn house of cards,' said Haruna, looking from Aimee to Frankie, before bursting into laughter. 'And I'm fully on board. Oh God, Frankie, I so need this in my life right now.'

'I know you do!' Frankie said, grinning at her friend. 'All those years hassling me to start a band and now here we are! Properly.'

'You should leave school more often,' Haruna joked.

'Well, to be honest, I need *something* to do.'

Frankie tried to ignore the sense of anxiety rising inside her. Doc was in this building, somewhere, a few days a week and one day she would bump into him, and on that day she had to look perfect, seem perfectly relaxed and cool, and play in the perfect, most kick-ass three-piece punk band.

She looked over at Aimee, who she had completely bulldozed. For a very brief second she felt bad, so she threw her arms around her. 'Aimee, you're amazing. I just knew you'd come through for me. For us. Come through for *US*.'

CHAPTER 5

Happy House

Christmas at Frankie's house was always a drunk, cheery, sweary and chaotic event.

Every single inch of their two-bed flat was decorated with tinsel, fake plastic candles and sweeties on a string, and the stereo was permanently fixed on *Michael Bublé Sings Christmas*, or some other prosaic wallpaper. Her mum loved to sing along to the big-band numbers like she was Ella Fitzgerald.

'... baby it's cold out-siiiiide,' she trilled, sashaying on her toes while stirring a large saucepan of chilli con carne.

'That song's a bit rapey,' said Frankie shaking her head in disapproval.

'Ridiculous. It's sexy,' replied her mother.

Her mother dyed her hair platinum blonde, and like most of the ladies at the dance studio, she wore an awful lot of fake tan. Now she caught sight of Frankie's garish Christmas jumper and smiled.

'Thanks for making the effort pet.' Her eyes were bright, lined with a royal-blue liner which sat just under her eyes, missing the water line altogether, and as usual there was too much mascara. It sat in clumps on her lashes like invasive mistletoe.

'No worries,' Frankie replied. 'Can I make the guac?'

'Your father's off avocado. Thinks it's causing his irritable bowel syndrome.'

'Yuk.'

'Well, it's hereditary,' she teased, pulling out an extra chopping board. 'I'm just saying.'

There was a commotion at the door as her grandfather arrived. He was eighty-three, but fit as a fiddle, drank like a fish, smoked like a chimney and everyone called him Sackhead because he was bald and his wrinkled head looked like a ball sack. Apparently.

'Frankie, you look like a boy,' he said, kissing her on the cheek. 'What happened to all that lovely long hair you had? She looks like a boy,' he said to Frankie's dad who was on his second Red Stripe and already had the vape out.

'At least one of you does,' her dad replied and both he and Hamish roared with laughter.

Hamish was fourteen, and spent almost all day on his Xbox, but ventured out when there was food or Granddad was here to cause offence. Sackhead certainly knew how to bring the family together.

'Where's your gin, Diane?' he said now, planting a big wet kiss on her mum's cheek. Her mum rolled her eyes in a playful way. They had good banter, those two. Everyone in the family did.

'Not for me tonight. I'm saving myself for tomorrow,' her mother replied.

'Mum, I want to talk to you about something,' Frankie began as her grandfather went through to the lounge to settle in front of the television with the others.

'Shoot,' she replied, wiping the grease off her hands and on to her Christmas apron. 'Apple crumble time. Fancy cutting some apples?' She reached up into the cupboard for the flour and brown sugar and handed Frankie the bowl of apples and the peeler.

'I'm not going back to school.'

Her mother looked up at her curiously. 'Right. And why?'

'As you could probably tell from my last few glittering reports, I'm just not that into it.'

'Aye, pet,' her mother responded, 'well with, what was it, fifty-three per cent attendance, we were not expecting a brain surgeon. Not that you're not capable. But school's not for everyone.'

'You're not mad?' Frankie asked. 'I mean, not really mad?'

'Of course not. I didn't finish high school, neither did your father, and we turned out okay.'

Frankie should have felt happy about this, but she wasn't. Her parents had both left school at fifteen, her dad had worked in a butcher until he was old enough to become a cabbie, and her mum worked in a dance studio very similar to the one she now helped run. While both lived a happy enough life, and certainly Frankie had no complaints about her upbringing, she wouldn't have considered either of her parents to have really reached for the stars.

'Well, yes, but I don't want to just get a job in a shop or something,' she explained. 'I couldn't bear it.'

'It's a decent living. No shame in shop work. Take your Aunt Di. She runs the best hairdresser on the Roman road.'

'Best hairdresser?' Frankie said dubiously.

'You don't seem to mind the free cuts,' her mother reminded her.

'Well, Mum, it's not for me. I want to do something big. I want to be someone. School is holding me back, and I want to get out of there and get on with *living*.'

'What do you want to do, then?' Her mother turned to her with a wry smile. 'Don't let this be the part where you tell me you want to move to Australia like your cousin Ben. I couldn't take it. Hot weather or not, I don't see the appeal. All those spiders.'

'You'd love it,' Frankie smiled, 'just like Malaga but with English.'

'I go to Spain for the flamenco,' her mum insisted, though Frankie had only ever seen her sunbathing.

'DIANE! Can you bring me another beer?' roared her dad from the other room.

'They're watching *You've Been Framed*.' Frankie said, by way of explanation. It was her dad and brother's favourite show, though neither really watched it if the other wasn't there. 'I'll take it through.'

She dashed out of the kitchen and into the lounge where her brother, dad and grandfather sat, tucked snugly into the three-seater couch, the TV casting a bluish light which was interrupted intermittently by the bright white flashing lights of the Christmas tree.

'Three generations of misogynists all in a row. We should write a nursery rhyme,' Frankie said, opening her dad's beer for him, as he muted the commercials and made room on the coffee table in front of them. Frankie gathered the empty cans, and bowl of pistachio shells which her grandfather had put a cigarette out in.

'Can you tell your mother to turn that music down, your brother's starting to like it,' her dad said with a wink.

'I am not!' Hamish complained, looking up at his dad before maintaining, 'There's only one real band.'

'That's right, lad,' he laughed.

Her dad only listened to The Beatles. They were the only band that ever existed according to him, and his record collection was only Beatles albums, plus, curiously, a Belinda Carlisle LP.

'So, Mum, I was thinking about maybe taking a course in Radio,' Frankie said as she returned to the kitchen. She was sounding out her idea, since she had only come up with it a few hours earlier. The plan was to hit them with the idea of dropping out and follow up with the plan of what to do next. Even if she wasn't entirely sure herself what that plan was. 'I'd love to be a DJ, or something like that.'

'Radio, now? I thought you kids didn't listen to the radio any more.'

'We do, you know,' Frankie said, warming even further to the idea once it had been vocalised. She cut a satisfying single ribbon from the final apple, and jabbed the core out with one twist and a satisfying crunch. 'Here you go. I'm gobby enough to be a DJ, don't you think?'

'You're certainly gobby, pet,' her mum replied with a grin. 'I can't think of a better fit. I always wanted to be a weather girl, you know? My friend Shireen was the local weather girl for Inverness and the Highlands, and she was ever so cool. There's no need to hurry into a decision, though. You're young. Besides, there was talk of catering college last month, so you might change your mind again.'

'I wanted the uniform.'

Frankie sat for a moment watching her mother gently rub butter, brown sugar and flour together with her fingertips, the sugary crumbs falling into the bowl below. This conversation had gone exactly as she'd expected – easily – and she couldn't complain, but still she felt a sliver of disappointment that there had been no fight. Haruna's mother would have hit the roof.

'So, how do you become a radio DJ, then?' her mum asked.

'I'm guessing you can't just walk into Capital FM armed with a CV?'

'Well, there are a couple of courses that start in the New Year. Not sure I can take out a student loan, though; I need to do more research.'

The mere thought of researching something was enough to dull her excitement for a moment, when happily her phone rang, and it was Haruna.

'Rooney!' said Frankie. 'How's Christmas Eve at the house of grim?'

''Tis the season to be bloody bored and lonely,' Haruna said quietly. 'Can I come round?'

'Hell yes, Mum would love it.' She looked enquiringly at her mum who responded with an understanding nod. 'Chilli con carne and apple crumble. Not your standard Christmas Eve feast, I admit, unless you're at our house where it's traditional.'

'I need to sneak out after they've gone, so I'll be round at about eight?'

'Perfect. We'll wait.'

'Thanks, Franks.'

'Oh, I'm glad she's coming,' her mother said. 'I've been meaning to ask you if I could talk to her about something.'

'Gawd, Mum, you know she's not allowed to do dance any more,' Frankie said with an exaggerated sigh. 'I mean, I know I let you down in the dancing daughter department, but Haruna isn't the answer.'

'Well, maybe, but there's this audition thing; I thought it would be right up her street.'

'What audition thing? Why didn't you think of me?' Frankie was only semi joking. Her mum's adoration of Haruna was mostly lovely, but sometimes made her a little bit jealous.

'Well, it's all very hush-hush and exciting, actually,' her mum said. 'You know what, I'm going to have a wine.'

She slid over to the fridge and pulled out a half-empty bottle of white wine, tipped it into a long-stemmed wine glass and tossed in a few ice cubes. Then she took a sip and let out a deep breath. 'Oh, that was a good idea.'

'What's the audition?' Frankie was now very intrigued, and, as she was not invited to have a wine herself, retraced her mother's footsteps to pour her own.

'It's for a girl band.'

'A what?'

'A girl band. You know, like that band Little Minx,' her Mum said, eyes dazzling. 'The production company have been enquiring about holding auditions at the studio. They want dancers as well as singers. Or singers that can dance. And so I thought of Haruna. Couldn't you just imagine her in a girl group?'

'It's Little Mix – but Jesus, Mum. No. Absolutely not. I can tell you now, Haruna won't be interested.'

'Well, perhaps she can make that decision.'

'Mum, you know what it's like at her house.'

'How are things with Linda? Actually, I nearly picked up the phone and tried again the other day, but your father talked me out of it. I do miss her at times.'

'Well, you have nothing in common now, I can promise you.'

'Hmm,' she replied, looking square at Frankie, 'would you like to audition, darling? I'm sorry I didn't think to ask you, only you were so disinterested in dance I just assumed this wouldn't be your thing. Haruna, on the other hand, loved it. Surely, at seventeen her mother would reconsider letting her do *some* dance? It's so harmless.'

'Haruna does everything by stealth now,' Frankie said, 'and I don't think she'd choose to come back to dancing. Oh, don't look so disappointed, Mum, we loved our time there, but Haruna is really into pretty different stuff now. She's like a punk culture expert. To be honest, it's kinda boring. I was the one who introduced her to L7 and Bikini Kill and now it's all like, *Frankie, don't get me started on the problems with intersectionality in Riot Grrrl.*'

'Dancing is uncool now, is it?' her mum said, more amused than put out.

'Well, we're in a real band now. She can't very well run off and be in some crappy, manufactured girl band.'

'There's no need to be disparaging of other women's achievements, Frankie darling. We must lift each other up.'

'But they don't realise they're just being used by a bunch of dudes in suits and reinforcing patriarchy by playing into the male gaze,' Frankie declared, unsure whether she'd got the words in the right order, but she was pretty sure that was something Haruna would have said.

'Poppycock,' her mother replied, sending Frankie into a cascade of giggles. 'I mean it, Frankie, that attitude is arrogant. And wrong.'

'It's not *that* wrong. I bet the people making the decisions *are* all dudes in suits.'

Frankie downed the wine in her glass and rounded the conversation back to herself. 'Now, about that guitar-shaped present under the tree. I'm guessing that's not for Hamish, right?'

Chapter 6

Morning Dew

Haruna woke up, fuzzy headed and, for a brief moment, confused.

She was definitely at home. It was still dark outside. She reached for her phone on her bedside table, which was diligently plugged in, and checked the time.

'Six fifteen,' she moaned out loud, then she remembered it was Christmas Day.

She rolled out of bed and switched on her lamp, pulled on her slippers, and reached for her robe, which was not at the end of her bed but lying on the floor next to the cane chair perched in the corner of the room. Haruna must have been a little more drunk when she got home than she'd realised.

She walked to the radiator and tried to warm her cold hands, but really, the only way to cut through this chill was a hot shower and a warm sweater. She grabbed the towel which aired on the hook above her radiator and tiptoed quietly down the hall.

As the hot water flowed, flashes of the night before came back. Frankie getting steadily more drunk and boisterous, fighting with an entire family of boisterous people until it was just a tornado of nonsense and noise. Sackhead passed out on the sofa and was decorated with tinsel and permanent marker. Her dad unveiled the latest conspiracy theory he was investigating – that the earth was, despite all evidence to the contrary, in fact flat. Haruna wasn't sure he really believed the nonsense he spouted but it was fun to listen to his half-baked theories, and to watch him get steadfastly more resolute as the evening progressed and the drinks flowed.

Hamish spent the evening avoiding eye contact with her, which was a new thing, and at one point Frankie whispered that she thought he had developed a crush. Haruna was flattered and charmed.

And Frankie's mum had pulled her aside for one of her chats, heavy in subtext and double meaning. Was she all right? What were her plans after school? How was her mum? Has Greg been kind to her? Her mum and Frankie's had been friends in the beginning, before Greg, but now they didn't talk.

Haruna stepped out of the shower, and tiptoed back to her room to dress. A beige skirt, just below the knee – kind of cool, really, unless it was teamed with the white turtle neck she was currently pulling on.

She crept downstairs and into the kitchen, where she immediately put the oven on and opened the door. Then she made bread. She enjoyed this morning ceremony of flour, water, yeast, oil, and an hour of kneading and rising. Store-bought bread was one of the latest things that Greg had put an end to, and so this had become Haruna's task since her mum and Greg usually got home late from their evening meetings.

They were mega-super-uber religious. And Haruna was not. Not even nearly. Haruna's mother and Greg kept her separate from it all now. Since she embarrassed them at around thirteen by being provocative and questioning in the Church's youth group.

But this was Greg's house now, and his rules must be obeyed. She had pushed the boundaries only twice. Once, at fourteen, she had spoken back to Greg, earning a back-handed slap across the face so hard she'd had to take four days off school until the bruise subsided. And the second time, she had challenged her curfew and when confronted she had slammed the door to her bedroom, and a picture frame had fallen off the wall and smashed. Greg had pulled her out of her bedroom by the arm and dragged her across the broken glass to the bathroom, where he had pushed her so she fell against the cold tile floor, smacking the side of her head on the toilet seat. He had told her to *meditate on her shortcomings*, and locked the door. Three hours later, her mother had come in for her, red-eyed, begging her to just do as Greg said.

'You can always leave,' she'd told her, when Haruna showed her the bloody cuts the glass had made on her leg.

So Haruna had continued to toe the line. The general house rules were that modesty, quiet and hard work were all forcefully encouraged. Haruna could have privacy as long as she didn't interfere with, or disrupt, Greg's life in any way. As she hit fifteen, she found that staying quiet and out of sight actually afforded her a lot of space, and it became apparent that Greg was just waiting for her to finish school so he could kick her out. She became expert at hiding her life outside the walls of this house. And so, on they all went. Two separate lives under one roof. Her mum and Greg going about their business, mostly work with the Church, and Haruna with her head down finishing school, rocking no boats, so she could see Frankie, play in the band, sneak out at night and see Cheq.

Haruna thought about her relationship with Cheq. He had an insatiable desire to please her and to try to protect her. Haruna wanted to be free from 'protection', since Greg claimed to be protecting her too. But at the same time, she wanted to fall into Cheq's arms and be protected. Her heart fluttered at the thought of him. Greg couldn't control those secret thoughts – they were her own. She was not, and would *never* be, subservient to him.

On that thought, her mother appeared. She entered the

kitchen so softly, and spoke so quietly, it was as though she was hardly there at all. She wore a full-length cotton nightgown that gathered in a frill under her chin and at her wrists. Her blonde hair was tied back in a low bun, and her old reading glasses were perched on the end of her nose. She looked like one of those stern Victorian mothers or something.

'Haruna, Happy Christmas.'

Haruna looked at her, mouth open. 'You're up early. Happy Christmas, Mum,' she replied, dropping her voice to a whisper. 'Don't let Greg hear you.'

'Well, he's asleep.' Her mother smiled, and pulled a small box out of her nightgown pocket. 'This is for you.'

'Is it a Christmas present?' Haruna was stunned.

'I wanted to do something. I have been ...' She paused, looking at the ground, then at her tidy short-clipped nails. 'It's been hard for you over the years.'

Haruna moved forward and took the small brown-paper box from her mum and tore off the paper. Inside was a small navy-blue jewellery box stamped with *Hatton's Jewels* in silver, and inside was a ring. It was a curiously bright and cheerful piece in its simplicity, a small blue gemstone sat perched on a delicate silver band.

'Your engagement ring,' Haruna said in awe.

'Your father gave it to me by the lions at London Zoo. A very hot day, as I recall. We'd been to see the panda before it went back to China. Ming Ming I think was its name. It couldn't breed in captivity, and I think they wanted to send it home,' she said plainly.

'Her,' Haruna interjected.

'Her?'

'Not *it* home. *Her* home. The Panda called Ming Ming, it was a girl. She was shipped around the globe for breeding. Poor Ming Ming. We learned about it at school. They tried to get her to breed for a few years at London Zoo but she wasn't having any of it,' she smirked.

'Well, she was quite magnificent.'

Her face showed just a hint of nostalgia as she spoke, but it quickly dispersed. Haruna was left with that familiar empty feeling that she couldn't ask any more questions. The information exchange on her father was based on her mother's desire to tell, rather than Haruna's need to know.

'I didn't know you kept it,' Haruna said, looking back down at the ring.

Her mother nodded. 'I have some things put away. It's time this was out of my possession, and I couldn't donate it to the Church.'

'Oh,' Haruna said, trying to slip the ring on to her middle finger, but it was too small, it only just fitted her pinkie. She looked down at it again, and felt a sting of sadness.

'I bet Dad saved for ages,' she said, examining its blemishes of age. 'It's so nice to have it. I'll really treasure it.'

'Well, I'm happy it's meaningful to you. I guessed it might be our last Christmas together. You will go to university, and it will be harder . . . well, it won't be as easy to see you when you've moved out. I guess it's like that for everyone.'

Haruna paused for a moment, taking in her mother's fixed expression, and decided not to challenge her. It was not like that for everyone. It was going to be different when Haruna moved out. She knew that her mum knew she wouldn't be coming back, even if neither of them were willing to vocalise it.

'I have to finish the bread,' Haruna said as a little timer went off.

'Very well.' Before she shuffled out of the kitchen, her mother turned. 'Make sure you keep that tucked away, now.'

As the room fell silent, Haruna looked out of the small kitchen window to the sky, which was gradually brightening as the winter sun rose. A siren sounded in the distance, but not much else stirred. Everywhere families were still to wake with their hangovers and bickering and brightly wrapped presents. She rolled the bread into a long loaf, and scored the top three times. *When I'm living in a flat of my own, I'll be able to make my flatmates awesome bread*, she thought.

She walked upstairs to her bedroom and gently shut the door, setting her phone timer for thirty-five minutes. She opened her wardrobe and pulled out a small wooden chest from the back and slipped the jewellery box inside with all her other keepsakes. A photo of her father. Concert ticket stubs. A valentine's card from Cheq.

She picked up her sketch book and charcoal and pulled herself up on to the bed. She glanced down at the empty page, frowned for a moment, then she pulled out her laptop, and crawled under her covers, deciding to catch up on *Love Island* and pretend it was just another day.

Chapter 7

Germfree Adolescents

'I'm not sure this is the image we want to project,' Haruna said, studying the poster like it was written in Greek, as Frankie fed a 20p coin into the power meter by the entrance. 'it's a little embarrassing.'

In truth, she was mortified. Frankie had spent all night designing the posters for SEVEN and they were . . . not good.

'It's remarkable, really. Like you tried to do something retro and ironic, but it just looks like you only had your dad's first laptop from 1998 and an early version of Paint,' Haruna went on, studying the pixelated shapes and awkward font.

'Wow, Haruna,' Frankie started seriously, before looking over at her friends and breaking into a grin, 'it's like you were there. Only you weren't. I was the one who worked late doing it. And yes, on Dad's old computer.'

'You should leave the artwork to me,' Haruna said plainly.

'All right, I will. I get it. My design work is rubbish. You're the artist. Et cetera, et cetera,' Frankie replied impatiently. 'I'll let you know next time, okay?'

'Why are we only putting them up at Wick Rooms? And, hang on, why is there no information about our gig on them? Just our, um, website.' Haruna was suspicious, but not for any particular reason, mostly because it was worth being suspicious about almost everything Frankie did. Also, why they would want to direct anyone to that mess of a website was beyond her.

'I want to create a buzz, get people talking, but we don't want anyone to come, for goodness' sake,' Frankie explained, staple-gunning four A5-sized flyers in a row by the front door. 'What glue do they use for these, do you know? I'd prefer to glue them. More permanent.'

'Oh, they'll be talking,' Haruna said, folding her arms. 'So just so I'm clear, we're creating buzz, but just here inside this building?'

'With our friends, yeah. They're, like, influencers, right?'

'Sure, but you know we've never actually hung out with any other band in this building. Everyone practises at different times to us, it seems.'

'It's because we're hamstrung by school,' Frankie said, without looking up. But everything was in the tone of delivery – it was an accusation loosely disguised as a joke and Haruna wasn't falling for it.

'I'm not going to apologise for that.'

'Of course, not,' Frankie agreed. 'Sorry, it's just I'm, like, on the race track ready to run, and you and Aimee are always at the hot-dog stand.'

'A more accurate metaphor might be that we're still training for a bigger race.'

'Well, maybe we're just in different sports.'

Haruna sighed. Frankie had become impossible since she had left school. She had way too much time on her hands and her focus was completely on the band in every which way, except, it seemed, when it came to actual practice, which was too much like hard work for her.

Her look was also evolving, fast. Since being liberated from the rules of the school dress code her hair had been dyed bright red with orange tips, it looked like fire and set off her pale skin remarkably well. She had also had her left ear pierced a third time and was talking about sneakily getting more tattoos. Haruna desperately wanted to get a tattoo. She'd been dreaming of one for a few years now, and she knew exactly what she wanted to get.

'Do you like it?' Frankie said, catching Haruna staring at her hair.

'I preferred it black. But I love black, so . . . It's cool you're playing around, though.' Haruna was unable to be anything but honest. 'Does she charge you, your aunt?'

'We have a deal,' Frankie said.

This could have meant that either Frankie did a bit of work for a free cut or it was totally free, or perhaps she even paid full price. It was her dad's language. The Taylors liked to make sure everyone thought they were on the hustle, but always kept the details a bit vague.

Frankie clasped her hands together in excitement as she stapled the last embarrassing poster to the wall. 'I suppose we should get set up and get on with practice,' she said, with about a quarter of the enthusiasm she had for hanging posters. Haruna couldn't fault her dedication to the idea of being in a band, if not to the idea of making music.

They made their way into the kitchenette, a filthy, stinky place. Haruna hovered over the sink for a moment, wanting to don some gloves and restore the mugs to a hygienic state. Each one was host to cigarette butts, and dark, long-forgotten half-finished teas with their crusty rings and fuzzy mould.

'This is absolutely disgusting,' she said, her nose wrinkled. 'I'm not going to do it today, but dear God, it has to be done.'

'We should complain to Greer. Surely they have a cleaner?' Frankie said, heaving the hi-hat out of the storage area. 'Oooh, I wonder whose mic stand this is. I'm sure we can borrow it.'

Haruna grimaced. It was one thing to blag your way to success, but quite another to be ungrateful to those who helped you get there. Haruna helped her carry through Aimee's amp and they both dropped it against the wall with a thud.

'Holy heck, that's heavy,' Frankie complained. 'Be great when we don't have to move our stuff in and out. That took, what, half an hour?'

'Ten Minutes. And don't push it with Greer, Frankie,' Haruna said carefully as she heaved the floor tom into the room and fixed it in place next to the rest of the kit. 'Just promise me you won't.'

'I'm only borrowing a mic stand, Nana,' she replied, with a tired sigh.

Haruna slipped on to the black leather drum stool and adjusted the height. She was grateful for all Frankie's work with the band, but scoring this kit for her was the absolute best 'Oh baby, it's awesome this kit, much better than the school one.'

'That was a jazz kit. This is the real deal,' Frankie said, beaming.

'I know,' Haruna said, smacking Frankie on the ass with her sticks as she walked past to plug her amp into the wall. 'I've just never played one.'

She tapped the snare once and the sound crackled out around the room. Then she pressed the kick. *Boom boom boom.* Haruna felt a thrill course through her veins and she looked over at Frankie who was watching her with a wide grin. 'Oh, my fucking God.'

She let loose, smashing the drums, roll after roll, beat after beat, louder and louder, each punchy attack on the kit louder than the one before, until she disappeared into herself, closed her eyes and let completely go.

The pace picked up, faster and faster, as she moved through the beat. Something ugly, angry and wild took over and with each smash of the drum, she felt a deep stirring inside of her, until it became almost unbearable. Then, she suddenly stopped.

Sweat was beading on her forehead and underarms, and her heart continued to thump like an echo of the beat deep inside. Her hands were shaking from the force of the attack as she slowly became aware that the room was eerily silent.

'Rooney,' Frankie said, wide-eyed with shock, 'my God. That was amazing. Are you okay?'

Haruna realised she was panting and tried to get her breathing under control. She reached down to her rucksack and pulled out her metal water bottle, sucking down water in desperation. She sat back on the stool, placed her sticks in her lap and smiled up at Frankie.

'I feel incredible,' she said breathlessly, taken aback by the thrill of the big kit, and the freedom of being able to *actually* make noise. 'Oh my God, this is *everything*.'

Haruna sat for a moment, relishing the thrill as her heart-beat slowly returned to normal. She closed her eyes and held the sticks up to her lips. *I need this. Oh God, I need this. Please let Frankie be serious about this.*

'Let's do this,' she said.

Frankie did a little dance, shaking two fists in the air. 'Hell yes.'

The door swung open and Aimee stepped in, awkwardly lugging her bass and her bike inside. 'I lost my bike lock,' she explained, 'it wouldn't last five seconds out there. Was that you, Haruna?'

'It sure was.'

'Wow, sounded really, proper good. And so *loud*,' she said, eyes darting up and down the corridor anxiously, 'so very loud.'

Frankie handed the girls some song sheets that she'd printed up. 'Now, I figured that since we have to play rock 'n' roll covers, but we need to stay true to ourselves, we could just punk them up? What do you think?'

Haruna looked at the pages. 'We're going to punk up "Hound Dog" and "Twist and Shout"?'

'Yes, have some vision, Haruna,' said Frankie, mocking their own music teacher who had, more than once, said those exact words to Frankie. 'Anyway, *three* chords. *Three*. I mean, if we can't manage that, we're screwed.'

'When are we going to write our own songs?' asked Aimee, as she pulled her bass out of its case and heaved it over her neck. 'Also, I still haven't been able to borrow a second mic, so we're gonna have to share, babes.'

'I'm working on both original songs and a mic for you,' Frankie assured Aimee, before adding in the stinger, a gentle reminder that she was the boss, 'I can't do *everything* all by myself.'

'Sure.' Aimee grinned, shooting a quick glance at Haruna who smiled back with a shrug. *That's Frankie*.

Frankie picked up her guitar and placed her fingers on the strings, pressing down and strumming the first, second then third chords. 'Three chords. It's genius. Even I can do this.'

Aimee plugged in her bass, studied the sheet music, which had the bass part written out in full, and turned to Frankie. 'It might be easy for you, but Jeez, I have to remember how to read music to play my part. Ugh. Hello, year six piano.'

'I should start,' Haruna said, holding her sticks above her head. 'Count us in with my sticks, like this: one, two, three, four. That's how these old songs mostly go, isn't it?'

'Okay.' Frankie nodded. 'And then you, Aimee, maybe you come in on bass?'

'Sure.'

'Shall we try?'

'Can you close the door?' Haruna said, pointing behind Frankie.

Frankie turned and kicked it shut, swinging back round and nodding to Haruna.

Haruna clicked the sticks together. 'One, two, three, four.'

It was a goddamn mess – in fact, it sounded like a freight train colliding with a nuclear power plant – but it was beautiful.

Chapter 8
Gigantic

'Yes, Mother,' Frankie said down the phone, 'I'm on time. Yes, I'm wearing the bloody T-shirt. For Pete's sake. I love you too.'

Frankie was sitting in the reception area of the dance studio. She'd not been there since she was fifteen, but everything was almost exactly the same; the bright white round reception desk, trimmed with magenta lighting. The huge glass automatic sliding doors. The reception area itself was large, with well-polished parquet flooring, a long white sofa and about a dozen chairs sat side by side around the walls. Although it was rarely occupied, it was designed to be large enough to manage big groups of dancers awaiting auditions.

Her mother had made her sweep back her hair and tone down the make-up and she had to wear a bright pink T-shirt with the studio name emblazoned across it in silver sparkles. It perfectly matched the logo on the wall above her head.

Earlier that week, Frankie's mum had brought up the decision to leave school again. It was clear she'd been discussing it with everyone here and had decided to take a more 'parental' approach to the move. She had come armed with bloody rules.

'You're my first child to leave school, and I need to lay out some plans for how this is going to work,' she'd explained. 'So, first things first, you'll need to contribute to the house. Not much, but let's start with fifty pounds a week. Don't look at me like that, Frankie, this is what happens when you're an adult. And you'll need to get a job, obviously. I'm not having you hanging around the house messing up my kitchen and taking up drug smoking.'

'No drug smoking. Got it. Can I snort? Inject? And is it all drugs? Or are some okay?'

'Don't be cheeky. And you'll need to do more around the house. I was thinking you could take on the household laundry?'

'I'm not cleaning Dad's undies,' she'd protested.

'Okay, well at least start doing your own.'

Her mother was mostly a pushover, but the weekly rent was non-negotiable, and so now Frankie needed a job. Working at the dance studio was a bit of a pain, but looking for a job had been far more difficult than she had anticipated, particularly when every job seemed to include shift work. Or learning. Or actual work. At least here, she could muck about while she waited for the phone to ring.

'Hello, East Dance Academy, this is Frankie.'

'Hi, I'm Annabelle and I'm calling about the audition for Falls Records.'

'Yes,' Frankie replied, her eyes glazing over with boredom, 'how can I help?'

'I was just wondering, my daughter is fifteen and it says sixteen and over, but I'll be with her. And she turns sixteen in May.'

'I'm afraid it clearly says all applicants must be sixteen at the time of audition,' Frankie replied, checking the FAQ notice pinned above the phone in front of her. This was the eleventh call in the last two hours, and auditions were over a week away. And right when she had a million things to do. She finished cutting a huge 'S' from a headline and placing it neatly on the A4 page in front of her. After twenty-five minutes she'd managed to cut out SEVEN, but at this rate, their press pack wouldn't be published until next year. And without a press pack they would never get a proper gig all of their own.

Frankie spent most of her mornings dicking around on WhatsApp to Haruna, plotting and planning for Seven's future, trying to work out how to use social media (something she detested), secretly printing out song sheets, attempting to write lyrics and sometimes songs (which as it turned out, was really rather hard) and occasionally using the reception computer to online stalk Doc. In truth, the job had turned out to be a bit of a cruise, except today.

They'd been practising for three weeks already and still no sign of Doc at Wick Rooms. Any attempt to covertly locate his practice room had been met with silent, simmering fury by Aimee who saw it as another brazen attempt to break the rules. And of course, Haruna didn't know Doc's band had a room there. *Yet.* Frankie had been planning to either act surprised if Haruna discovered it first and Aimee wasn't around or drop the information one day as a passing comment.

'Frankie, you left school?' enquired Anya in what felt like the nine hundred millionth dance instructor to probe her decision. She sashayed into the waiting area like she was on wheels, leaning over the counter. 'Good for you. You make a decision as a young woman.'

Anya was Russian, but had lived in the East End since she was seventeen and her accent was an almost perfect mix of cockney and Russian. She was sixty-nine now, although she could have passed for fifty with her energy and long, lithe, petite figure. Her face was brightly made up every day with full foundation, caked-on powder and blood-red lips, her eyebrows plucked to nil and then drawn back in like two matching frowns trying to climb up her forehead. The effect was an expression of permanent surprise. Her blonde hair was always a little frizzy at the edges, and pulled back in a black ribbon to match her leotard and wrap skirt. But seventies make-up aside, the only real giveaway to her age were the creases around her mouth – lined like a cat's arse with the unmistakable depth of a hard-core smoker.

'Thanks, Anya,' Frankie said. 'I fucking hated school. It just wasn't for me.'

Frankie had given up trying to sell some story about wanting to chase her dreams. And anyway, it was true. She'd hated school for the last year or so, skipping more and more classes and falling further and further behind until turning up was just an exercise in feeling stupid. She wondered if she would actually have the guts to apply for a radio course.

'You bloody swear too much.'

'You do,' Frankie said automatically, giggling as the phone rang again.

'Hello, East Dance Academy, this is Frankie.'

'My name is Sherise. I'm one of the girls from the street class. Diane's your mum, right?'

'Yep, this is she.'

'Hi. Cool, I heard a lot about you. Look, I'm calling about the audition, and I wondered if I could get a little more information about the day?'

'Sure. How can I help?'

'The audition doesn't say anything about what to wear.'

'It says dress to dance,' Frankie said, rolling her eyes at Anya and deciding to have a little fun. 'Some girls are getting really dressed up,' she added. 'Like as their favourite Spice Girl or whatever. You could do that? Or come in costume. Wonder Woman. That would really help you stand out.'

'You think so? That's a good idea.'

She almost felt sorry for these girls. After she managed to

help poor hapless Sherise, she set the phone to voicemail and turned to a patiently waiting Anya who was doing leg lifts using the reception as a bar. 'You're still here?'

'Why you leave? Too much work to do at school? You don't like work? It's why you don't dance any more. You don't like the discipline. You need to be disciplined to dance. Like a boxer.'

'I'd actually rather be a boxer.' Frankie shrugged. 'I hate dancing.'

'When you were young, you were good at performing. Like your mother. Always in the centre of the room, twirling and twirling, taking home the tutu for dancer of the week. You remember? All the kids wanted to be your friend.'

'I don't remember.' Frankie was growing annoyed. 'I'm in a band, did Mum tell you? She got me a guitar for Christmas. That's what I want to do now. I want to do my band, we're called Seven and we're going to conquer the world. Bigger than the Rolling Stones or . . . who's actually big these days? I don't listen to the charts.' With that she shot Anya a big jovial grin, willing the conversation to end.

'A band?' Anya nodded, evaluating Frankie. Her lips pressed tightly together, she looked up at her hair, down passed the ear-cuff and at the edge of her tattoo poking out from her T-shirt. 'What is this band? A rock band? You don't play an instrument, do you?'

'Punk band, and yes I do, as it happens,' corrected Frankie. 'We've got practice rooms in Hackney, and I just, like, spend all my time working on my music. It's so free. No rules, like dancing. Dancing's full of rules. I'm so over rules.' She felt a small stab of embarrassment at the inauthenticity of this, for really, Frankie was the last person who had suffered under the weight of rules. Apart from this new rent thing, there were no rules at her home. Unlike at Haruna's.

'But you must learn the discipline in order to break the rules,' Anya said logically. 'You can't have a reactionary punk rock sensibility unless there is something to rebel against, no? Punk needs rules. It cannot exist without them.'

Frankie blinked a moment, before quickly reverting safely back to the band. 'We sound like a mixture between Bikini Kill and The Runaways. It's fresh, though. Not retro.'

Frankie liked how that sounded and made a mental note to include this on their website. She had spent the last week painstakingly building this on WordPress – which was easily the least punk rock thing she had done since forming the band. She had decided to include a section of 'reviews' in case anyone (like, say, Doc) happened to google them. The section was nothing but a bunch of made-up quotes designed to make Seven seem bigger than they were. But as her dad always said, 'If you don't shout about yourself, no one else will.'

'You want to be something, somebody. You want to be famous. I know you. But I'm not sure what you want to do. Is there a thing you can be that requires no dedication? I don't think that thing exists, Fwankie,' Anya said, taking leave and moving towards the automatic doors which fired open sending a Siberian-style chill cruising through the reception area.

Goose pimples sprung on Frankie's arms and she hugged herself. She was dedicated. It was true she perhaps needed to spend more time on the actual music, but still.

'Out or in!' Frankie shouted, as her cut-out newspaper clippings of SEVEN were blown in all directions, lost under benches and desks, far too much work to retrieve. 'Goddamn it! *Out or in?*'

Anya sauntered outside to enjoy a cigarette and Frankie sat there for a moment, feeling the wind had been taken out of her sails. She looked down at the newspaper and sighed, then she screwed it up and tossed it in the recycling. She looked at her guitar poking out from under the reception desk, ready to take to practice later that day.

Maybe with all my free time at work ... She unzipped the case and lifted the stark, cream Stratocaster up on to her lap – it neatly sat out of sight behind the desk. She leaned forward over her instrument and typed 'How to play guitar' into Google.

A cascade of dull-sounding websites loaded. ChordBuddy, Guitar for Beginners, Step-by-Step Guide to Being a Guitar Hero. *Ugh, it's just so much goddamn work and why are they all men with acoustics?*

She googled 'Play Guitar Girls' and the tab for Mötley Crüe's *Girls Girls Girls* came up. Followed by The Beatles 'Girl'.

Then, 'How to play punk', and she ended up down a reddit

rabbit hole for twenty minutes. Her only conclusion? She definitely wanted to keep things easy and master three-chord punk, but unfortunately, she probably needed to learn *all* the chords.

Then she googled, 'Why am I so lazy? Why do I hate learning stuff?' And finally went back to Doc's empty Facebook to click through his three profile pictures again.

Just then, she was interrupted by a phone notification. She glanced down at her WhatsApp:

AIMEE: Newsflash, ladies. MID-WINTER BOOZE UP – WICK ROOMS, 8pm Sat. Guess we know what we're doing for your birthday, Franks! ♥

'YUSSSSSSS,' Frankie said aloud, 'the moment Frankie has been waiting for.' She quickly typed her reply.

FRANKIE: I'm busy.
KIDDING! Hell yes I'm in.

HARUNA: I can make it between 8–10/11 prob! Whoop whoop!

Frankie quickly messaged Haruna separately.

FRANKIE: Can't you sneak out for the whole night? Pleeeeeeeease. It's my birthday.

HARUNA: I'm already doing that on Friday night. Date night with Cheq.

Frankie sighed.

Chapter 9

Break It Up

Haruna was buzzing about Seven. For years now, she'd sat in her bedroom, poring over music, her little private escape from her own private hell. Lying on her bed, in her tidy room, with its beige walls and controlled environment (no posters, only approved books) her headphones were like a door to another world. At night she would sit with her sketch book, slip on her headphones and privately rage through the music, finding solace and understanding in the voices of the women who were feeling just as angry as her. And now she had the chance to add her voice. And her sticks.

They'd been practising at Wick Rooms for a while now, and she had to hand it to Frankie, the dedication from her had been awesome. It was indescribable, the feeling she got from those afternoons; when she sat behind that kit and bashed the hell out of it, the constant, rhythmical, primal-ness of it made her feel really alive and free. Something was awakening in her.

And, though Frankie and Aimee were not as precise as she would have liked, they were there every practice, trying ... laughing, sometimes drinking, and making loud, chaotic, liberating noise. It was heaven. Aimee had even started taking bass lessons at school – which was incredible commitment from her, considering the amount of study she already had.

Last Thursday, Cheq had been to watch, much to Frankie's irritation. But during that practice Haruna had also felt a change with Cheq.

Watching him across the room, the soft slope of his neck, the ridges of muscle apparent under his T-shirt, his deep laugh and the way he rolled up a cigarette, slowly licking the paper, his eyes darting up to her, catching them for a moment, a small smile, an undeniable intimacy – for some reason, in that setting, everything was amplified. She wanted to get closer to him.

It was a rare evening at home, with Greg off doing something called 'leadership training', which didn't sound very churchy to Haruna. But then, there was no way any kind of Jesus approved of this nightmare set-up she was living in either.

Haruna sat with her mum at the kitchen island preparing vegetables for dinner. She watched her meticulously peel, chop and discard the tiniest of ends of carrots and parsnip – nothing wasted – and wondered at the thoughts causing the vertical crinkle between her eyes to ever deepen. Today, her mother wore a white turtleneck and a dove-grey cardigan, her blonde hair clasped back in a plastic grip. Her round glasses slipped forward intermittently, and she would push them back with her frail forearm.

She was staring, she knew she was, but her mother had become something of a curiosity over the years, and at times she *would* just stare, unable to strike up conversation, looking for some sign of the mother she remembered from her childhood. The shy, gentle mother who sang her to sleep and told her made-up stories of fairies and elves. Though in truth that memory was fading.

'Okay, Haruna, is there something you want to discuss?' asked her mother, sitting back in her seat and fixing her full attention to Haruna. Her face, while not unkind, had the usual disengagement. It was remarkable, really, the level of disinterest she could show to her only daughter. But somewhere in her heart, Haruna knew their distance had grown from necessity.

'Not really,' she replied casually, unsure whether to approach her subject with forthright confidence or with humble reserve, like a daughter seeking big life advice from a mum. Since she didn't know how to do either of those things it just came out, all awkward, half formed and unsure. 'You know, actually, Mum, I was thinking of speaking to you about when school breaks up.'

'Yes,' she said, putting her paring knife down and rubbing her hands on her apron. 'Yes, it's time we did. Greg has been asking, also.'

A slight shuffle in her seat gave away a hint of trepidation from her mother, something rarely seen in the last few years. Haruna felt just a little nervous: a flutter in her tummy, the quickening of her heart, her view pulling focus on her mother. Now was the time; they were alone together.

'Okay. Well, as you know, I've made my university applications and I wanted to speak about possibly deferring. Not for long,' she added quickly. 'I know that Dad put aside some money for study but I wondered if, maybe, I could use a small portion of it to go travelling. I mean, I know that technically, I'll be eighteen and I don't really need to ask these things, but I guess I need to know how the money will come? Will it be a lump sum or how will it work?'

Her mother blinked for a moment. Did she seem a little puzzled?

'Well, there *was* some money put away,' she said cautiously.

Haruna picked the peeler back up, and focused on the potato in her hand. She skimmed the surface, cutting it in strips, closely, slowly, waiting for her mum to continue for she dared not speak. There was enough money for university, that much she knew. It said so in one of the letters her father had sent and she only wanted a small amount to travel.

'Obviously, Haruna, we've had to use part of that money over the last nearly eight years. Your dad didn't pay us child support ... so ... well, we couldn't expect Greg to foot that bill, could we?'

The 'we' hung in the air for a moment before the faintest of echoes dispersed and nothing was left but cold silence. No one was peeling anything right now. It was funny how you don't often appreciate absolute silence, but here it was, as deafening as people said it could be.

Haruna turned her head away towards the door, the paint only just dry where Greg had tidied up the mess on the small strip of wall between the doorway and the fridge. The *mess* was the little pencil lines and dates marking Haruna's height. She was stirred by a siren sounding in the distance.

Haruna felt her eyes sting, and she looked back down at the peeler, turning the potato over in her hand to do the other side, the sound filling the silence until she found her breath. 'No. I guess not,' she said quietly, before looking up and looking her mother in the eyes. 'So is there any left?'

'There's enough to get you set up in a place of your own,' she said gently, also resuming her cutting, 'plenty for that.'

'I bet there is.'

'Haruna, please. I don't like that tone.'

'I don't like this *news*,' she said boldly, and then bolstered by the safety of Greg's absence, she added, 'Is there *anything* left for me?'

'Haruna, you've benefited from all of that money. We put it towards school clothes, books, living expenses, that kind of thing,' she said, 'all the normal costs a household must find to help raise a child.'

'Right. But still, how much, exactly, is left?'

'I'm not sure, exactly, I'd need to check with Greg, but it's certainly a handsome enough amount. Enough for a deposit on a room, a few months' rent, that kind of thing.'

'A few months' rent,' Haruna said, aghast. 'As opposed to what Dad said: that I had four years of living allowance and uni fees? That's a lot of money.'

'You can take out a loan for university. Many kids do these days, I think. And it's not just vanished. It has gone towards raising you and supporting the home you live in.'

'What does that mean?' Haruna shot back, standing suddenly, the stool screeching on the kitchen floor. She suddenly got it. 'What does it mean? *Supporting the home you live in?*'

Her mother immediately calmed, sitting back in her stool, and squaring off against Haruna, her cool, calm look making Haruna even more ill at ease.

'So how much went to fucking Greg?'

'Haruna!' Her mother stared her square in the eyes. 'Apologise at once, please. Do *not* use that filthy language in this house.'

'That's it, Mum,' Haruna said. 'You can keep what's left of the money. I'm done.'

'Haruna.' her mother was standing now, walking around the kitchen island reaching an arm out towards her. 'Take a moment. You're not in control of yourself.'

'You know what? That's okay,' Haruna said, pulling herself

back and stepping towards the door, 'it's normal to be angry, and to shout sometimes. It's fucking NORMAL.'

She turned, headed upstairs and into her bedroom and slammed the door. She pulled out her iPod speakers and plugged in her phone, skimming the tracks to find something as loud and as obnoxious as she could. But just as she was about to let loose, she stopped herself. This wasn't smart. She urgently needed a sounding board.

'Pick up, pick up, pick up . . . ' Haruna said, pacing her room.

'Sha-rooons,' Frankie said, the *EastEnders* theme fading in the background, as she closed a door and made her way into a quiet spot. 'Ma Ma Ma My Sha-Roona.'

'Hey, I need to talk. I need your help.' Haruna's voice wavered.

'What's happened? Haruna, you sound dreadful. Are you okay?' Frankie stood up, angry, and shouted, 'Has that wanker hurt you?'

'Who? No. No one,' Haruna said. 'Just listen for a moment.'

'Sorry, but you're okay?'

'Yes. Well, not really. I just spoke to Mum and you know how I had that money from Dad?'

'The university fund? Yes, I know.'

'Well, it's gone.'

'What do you mean?'

'Well, Mum says that it was used, like, instead of child support, but whatever. It's so obvious Greg spent it on his work with the—'

'The cult took it,' said Frankie dramatically.

'It's not a cult.'

'Whatever, I can't believe it. That was from *your father* to you. How dare your mum let him spend that money?'

'I don't know. Maybe they're right. I mean, it seems fair that Mum would want some child support. How else do they get their money? Greg didn't have to raise me, I guess.'

'Sorry, Haruna, but listen to yourself. You're actually allowed to be alive and to be cared for by your mother. You have the right. You have the right to be cared for. And whatever choices she made—'

'You know she can't work. I mean, she depends on him. She's as trapped as I am, really.'

'By choice!'

'Is it by choice? I don't know.'

'She *can* work,' Frankie challenged. 'I think Greg would prefer she didn't because he's a violent control freak asshole. I wish Mum had called the cops last time.'

'That was a few years ago now. He's not touched me again.'

'Yes, because you live like a goddamn saint. It's prison. I hate this, Haruna. As your friend it's so hard to listen to. Why don't you leave?'

'*Why don't you leave*?' Haruna scoffed. 'it's not that easy. Where would I go? To live with you guys? You already share a room with Hamish.'

'He wouldn't mind.'

'Be practical.'

'I am. I'm being practical.'

'It's not a solution. I'm struggling. Everything is a fog. Jesus. I just told Mum to fuck off.'

'Good. Pack a bag,' Frankie said. 'Come. Now.'

'Please, Frankie, you know I can't do that.' Haruna sat on the edge of her bed and put her hands up to her face. 'I need to be smart. It's only, what, four months now? I need to stay and get whatever is left of the money, at least. Mum won't make me homeless. Oh God, my mum. She tries her best for me, doesn't she? I have to believe it. The other option is so grim.'

Frankie didn't answer, so she continued, 'Do you know what it's like to face the possibility you could be so completely unwanted? It's pretty dark, Frankie.'

'I can't imagine. My mum would never . . . ' Frankie's voice trailed off. 'Don't get me wrong, I've got problems with my set-up, but she puts me first. I hate this.'

Haruna took that in for a moment, pain rising inside her until she felt the sting of tears beginning again. *She puts me first.* Was that normal? She didn't know that feeling. She took a breath, slowly regaining control of her emotions. 'She did say there's enough money left for a flat – like a deposit on a room,' she said as calmly as she could.

'How much?' Frankie's ears pricked up. 'You should get that money.'

'I know. It could be a few thousand. Frankie, I don't know.'

There was a soft knock at the door and Haruna froze and

whispered into the phone, 'Can you stay on the line, in case it's Greg or something.'

'Haruna, get out of there.'

'It's fine, hang on,' she said quickly, dropping the phone on to her bed, screen side down.

She took the few steps to her bedroom door and leaned in close. 'Mum?'

'Yes, it's me.'

Haruna's hands were shaking, but she opened the door and looked up at her Mum who was, unlike her, fully composed and calm. There was a flicker of hesitation, and she looked down at the carpet, then as if drawing all the will in the world, she drew a deep breath.

'If you want, I will get you what's left of your money, so if you would like to leave, you can go now. I don't want to see you so distressed.'

Haruna started to panic. 'But I can't go now; A levels are coming up. I worked so hard to get this far, there's only a few months to go. I can't go flatting. I'd need a job to pay me so I can live. And eat. I don't even know where I'd get a room since I'm under eighteen. Can you even rent a flat at my age? I need to stay, Mum. It's my home too . . . isn't it?'

'Of course.' She nodded with satisfaction, and something that could have possibly been relief. 'You can stay.'

'Thank you,' Haruna said pitifully. She had nothing to be grateful for here, really, but she felt helpless.

'But, if you're going to stay on, you need to remember that

this is Greg's home too, and we must live by his rules. I've got a good idea what you get up to, Haruna. I know you sneak about when we're away at the weekend. I dread to think what goes on here in my home. I've seen the clothes you try to hide at the back of the wardrobe. I've smelt the cigarette smoke in your hair. You think I wasn't seventeen once?' Her mother's voice was unusually slightly raised, a redness creeping up her neck to her cheeks.

'Mum, I . . . ' Haruna felt ashamed, and lost. 'I try to—'

'I am not interested. Let's get through these next months in peace. You are not going to be saved. You're too flighty, like your father.' She stopped suddenly, regaining her cool, and finished, 'Well, none of that matters.'

'What does that mean? I'm like my father? Help me understand. Please.'

'Stay here, and you will keep quiet. Keep to yourself. Not create any tension under this roof. You will study. You will not talk back. You will keep your sinful business away from Greg and this home. And if – *if* – you can manage that, Haruna, I will make sure you have some money to get yourself set up when you leave.'

'Do you hate me?' Haruna asked flatly.

'No, you're my daughter,' she replied, 'and I'm trying to make the best of the time we have left. For everyone.'

Haruna nodded and shut the door. She didn't believe it, that her mother didn't really care for her. She couldn't. Haruna was in the way of her new life with Greg, and her mother was doing her best to juggle things. That was all. It had to be.

CHAPTER 10

High School Never Ends

Haruna sat at her desk – middle, near the back, the adjoining space next to her empty.

English was never going to be the same without her Franks sitting there telling her how unsexy Mr Greenwood looked in his ill-fitting suits. Frankie made a game out of flirting with him just to watch him squirm. In many ways, it was probably a good thing Frankie had left school: dull as it was without her, at least Haruna could concentrate.

Except she couldn't. There was too much swirling around in her head since the conversation with her mother. For one, everything she'd been working towards with school – to leave her mother and go to university – was now for nothing. She would have to support herself on loans and part-time jobs, and it made the prospect of an Arts degree feel . . . indulgent.

But the thing that kept ringing in her head was her

mother's words: *You're too flighty, like your father.* It wasn't meant to be a compliment, but in that one sentence, she felt she had an ally. Over there across the world, there was someone else who had not lived up to her mother's expectations and it gave her a sense of belonging. She wanted to meet him again. She had to.

'Reading,' Mr Greenwood began dramatically, 'is as critical to your education as maths or breathing. This year, along with revising for A levels, there will be several modern classics I'd like to offer as supplementary to your studies.'

In front of her, Angie, a skittish, bolshie girl with thick long braids and a ring through her nose, turned to whisper, 'Is it true, did Frankie leave school?'

Haruna nodded and pulled a sad face.

'Dude, that sucks for you. What are you going to do without her? Oh my God, what's *she* going to do?'

Haruna shrugged. 'Dunno, she wants to work on our band. Music. Might do a course at college. I really don't know. You know Frankie.'

Angie raised her eyes. 'Sounds like ... um ... a plan?' she joked. 'Doesn't surprise me. She always had a foot out the door. She never came to one History class this year. Not one!'

Haruna shrugged again. She needed to come up with a one-liner for the *what's Frankie doing* question. Something that made it look like Frankie had made a brave, considered decision and had a solid plan so they'd stop asking.

Everyone at school always thought Frankie was a bit

reckless, a storyteller, and a bit of a show-off, but her full-on energy and infectious laugh meant she was pretty popular regardless. But having all that light shining on you meant people really noticed when you went away. Haruna would never have that problem. She wasn't meek or shy, but she kept out of social stuff at school because it was easier that way. No need to explain the freakish home life.

Aimee, Frankie and Haruna stuck pretty tight from the rest, never outcasts, just differently entertained.

Angie wasn't finished. 'Is it true you're dating Cheq? He's, like, what, twenty?'

'Yeah,' Haruna said. Everyone knew Cheq. Not only did he used to go to the same school, he was becoming something of an underground celebrity thanks to one of his songs being used on a commercial for New Balance trainers.

'Really?' Angie said, surprised. 'Where did you meet?'

'Brick Lane,' Haruna replied.

'Brick Lane,' Angie repeated. 'Like, just in the middle of Brick Lane, or what? Standing in the road, dodgin' taxis or at a bar or something?'

Haruna smiled patiently, and then replied, 'Outside Rough Trade. It was Record Store Day.'

'You're lucky. He's hot.' Angie shot her half a smile, and turned back to the front of the class, before turning back for a third time. *Oh, for the love of God, please go away.*

'How did it happen?' she pestered.

'Just, like, I dunno, we got talking.' Haruna could see the

look in Angie's eyes. *Why on earth would he go out with you? You're a moody, quiet, dull thing. What could a guy like Cheq ever see in you?*

'He was sitting with some friends, and Aimee and I were sitting on the table across and we got talking,' she replied plainly.

'You got talking?' Angie rested her chin on the back of her desk, like she was expecting a story. There really wasn't a story, though. That was it.

'He asked me why I'd bought The Raincoats LP,' she said, unable to hide the lilt of irritation in her tone, not that Angie noticed. She was like a goddamn bulldozer. No wonder she didn't like Frankie. Frankie couldn't be bulldozed.

'The what?' she asked.

'They're a band.'

'Oh. And he just asked you out or what? Was he dating at the time, or . . . ? He just, well, I imagine he's in quite a cool scene . . . ' Angie's voice trailed off. She wasn't even trying to hide her dubious thoughts in their odd coupling.

Haruna had had enough. She took a deep breath. 'Look, he's very different when you get to know him. Quite chilled. I know it might seem totally incredible – but we have a number of things in common – *especially* music,' she said, feeling irritated. 'He also got an A in English, you know.' She felt compelled to add this, since Angie, like everyone, had judged him almost immediately on first sight, and one thing she knew for sure about Cheq was that there was much more to him than a punk-ass grime artist.

'Well, he writes sweet music, that's for sure.' Angie nodded, impressed. 'Does he have his own flat?'

'Sure.' Haruna glared at Angie. She was riled now, and couldn't stop. 'He's smart, talented and really kind and thoughtful. And he tells me he loves me and I love him. He's perfect.'

'Angela and Haruna, would you like to share your discussion with the class, or are you finished?'

'Sorry, sir,' said Angie, turning back round.

Haruna dropped her head, and for a moment fantasised about what living with Cheq would be like. Cheq and her, waking up together, bingeing TV, living in his rambling, filthy four-storey flat with three other boys. Last time she visited the toilet was blocked. Blocked for several days. *Maybe not.*

That morning, Haruna had been getting ready for school when her mother caught up with her in the hallway by the bathroom.

She was weirdly forced-smiling and carrying the laundry basket piled with linen towards the stairs. Her eyes were pink, her skin blotchy, as if she'd been crying, her face paler than usual. *Was this about last night?* she wondered.

'Please be a good girl,' she said briskly, looking back over her shoulder to the bedroom door. She slightly winced as she turned her head back to Haruna, and shifted her shoulders around, slowly straightening back up. *Was she in pain?* Haruna had heard the muffled sounds of an argument the night before, but not the content of it. When Greg was angry it was menacingly quiet. He delivered his rage in steady, slow monologues. But it had been a few months since the last time he was *really* angry at her.

For a brief moment she wanted to ask if her mother was okay, but didn't. She knew the answer, anyway. She couldn't be okay.

'I do have music class afterwards, though,' Haruna said quickly, ensuring she would make band practice. 'Is that still okay?'

'If it's education, you can do it,' her mother said sharply.

'Yes, Mum,' Haruna replied as they were both startled by the sound of glass shattering from the bedroom. Her mother's eyes widened. 'Off you go now,' she ordered.

Haruna hesitated for a moment, put her hand on the rail, half turning, half looking back – unable to stop the pleading look in her eyes.

'It's fine. Just an old tumbler. Go,' she said sharply as the door to the bedroom creaked open.

Haruna didn't look back.

Haruna sat waiting in the common room for Aimee who came breezing in at a hundred miles an hour, arms full of books, black spectacles on, hair piled on her head. Like everyone, her look had to be totally toned down for school.

'It's so weird, isn't it?' Aimee said, dropping down next to her.

'So weird.'

'Everyone keeps asking me why she left, and I'm like, *Why does Frankie do anything? She's a goddamn mystery is what she bloody is!* Catrina Black just asked me if she was pregnant. I mean, seriously.' Aimee shook her head before checking quickly, 'She's not, is she?'

Haruna laughed. 'I'm glad you're here at least. Do *you* think she made the right decision?'

'Oh, Greer and I were talking about it last night. Frankie's been bored here since we were, like, fourteen. She's was only really at school to socialise. I think after Doc, you know, she started hanging with people who don't go to school and—'

'More exciting than Mr Greenwood and sporty boys and, I dunno, doing some work?' Haruna interjected.

'Exactly,' Aimee said. 'Though she bloody does work when she wants. Look at the band. It's become totally serious. She's been practising, you know. She does it at the dance studio reception. Hours and hours of it a day. And I can tell, she's getting good now.'

'Yeah, I know,' Haruna said, grinning.

'You and Cheq coming to the party?' Aimee asked. 'Greer said the parties there are notorious – I mean, really really full on. And full of drugs.'

'Yeah, I'll be there. Aimee, can I ask you a question?' Haruna said, turning over the hem of her dress to inspect it. 'You know I'm super private about things, and although I trust Frankie, she's not exactly good with advice of this kind.'

'What kind?' Aimee asked, pulling out her lunchbox and

tucking into some hand-cut carrot sticks. Her mother still made her a packed lunch every day like she was eleven.

'How do you know you can trust someone? Your partner, I mean. How do you know they're always going to be good to you?'

'Always?'

'Yeah, like they won't change.'

'Are you asking if you can trust Cheq?' Aimee gasped. 'Oh, he adores you. You've been together, what, six months or so now?'

'Yeah, near enough,' Haruna said. 'Met him right before Doc dumped Frankie, which in hindsight was probably not great timing.' She wondered a moment whether to tell Aimee about the stalking incidents, but thought better of it.

'Like, I don't want to do it on the one hand. I hate the idea of "giving myself" to someone like that. It's so damn, I dunno . . . I'm not sure I want to *give* that to him.'

'But you're both giving and taking,' Aimee replied. 'And what do you mean, are you talking about sleeping with him?'

'No. I mean, yes, maybe, but I'm more interested in the trust thing.'

'He's doesn't seem dodgy or like a cheater or something,' Aimee said. 'Though I'm no expert on dudes.'

'But how do you know for sure?'

'You have to trust, I guess,' Aimee said gently. 'Haruna, you've been super quiet lately. Is there something on your mind, like more than this? Are you okay generally? Things at home?'

'Yeah. Sure. I just wondered about it, that's all,' Haruna replied. She shifted in her seat, feeling uncomfortable. 'Sorry, I think I over-think things sometimes. I don't know what's normal.'

Chapter 11

Call Me

Blondie blasted on the stereo in her room; around her a fan of discarded outfits lay alongside a plate with the remnants of dinner, two empty mugs, a tea towel, her bath towel and her mother's prized professional make-up box, which she wasn't supposed to touch, but never *really* got in trouble for it.

Frankie stood in front of the mirror in her underwear, a black lace bra she'd got from H&M and a pair of plain black cotton knickers. She put her hands to her belly and gave it a good wobble and then turned side-on, pushing it out as far as she could.

'I mean, it's remarkable, my belly. Look at it,' she marvelled. 'Mum! I ate way too much birthday cake. Come and look at my belly! I look completely pregnant.'

'Good God, no you don't!' her mother said, pushing the door open and shaking her head at Frankie. 'What's wrong with you?'

'I'm definitely getting flabby round the middle again.' Frankie assessed her stomach and then her butt. 'Oh God, my arse. It's kind of flat and saggy.'

'Franks, you're eighteen now. You look just perfect, pet. Now, enough with that nonsense. Can you put my make-up away before you go out, darling? You always leave it in such a mess.'

'Can you pass me that pile of clothes over there, Mum?' Frankie said, ignoring her instructions completely.

She unfolded a vintage white T-shirt with black sleeves and a pair of skinny black jeans ripped at the knees, thighs and butt and laid it on her bed. She pulled on a pair of black fishnets then wrapped a leather cuff around her wrist and squeezed into the jeans and tee and her pair of big, heavy combat boots over her new fluffy Christmas cashmere socks.

'They're for wearing in the house!' her mother protested.

'I know, but it makes these bricks just so much more wearable,' Frankie explained.

'When I was your age, it was high heels making our feet hurt,' her mother said as she passed Frankie her hairbrush. 'I know the teased thing is a *look* but a little brush wouldn't hurt.'

'No. Don't touch,' Frankie said, pushing the brush away.

'You've had more cuts and colours this month than the queen – but now apparently brushes are no longer in vogue?'

'I don't want to touch it. It's good. I'm so happy with it.' Frankie looked in the mirror, admiring the fresh platinum-blonde teased bob and fringe she'd had done that morning.

'Don't you love the colour? Well, you must, it's basically your colour now, Mum!'

'You look like a young Debbie Harry.'

Frankie flinched, then beamed with delight and clasped her hands together. 'Oh my Gawd, Mum, that's exactly what I was going for. How do you know Debbie Harry?'

'My era, darling,' she replied with that puffed-up, excited look she got when there was a chance Frankie thought she was cool. 'Well, the later stuff, at least.'

'Oh, I only like the early stuff,' Frankie said, teasing, suppressing a grin. 'Now, what time is it? I have to meet Haruna at the end of her street, and I'm not hanging around in the cold longer than I have to.'

'Why the end of the street?'

'I'm banned.'

'Banned?'

'Yes, banned. It seems, Mother, I'm trash. A bad influence.' Frankie pulled her leather jacket on, and scoffed, 'I mean, she doesn't even know her daughter! No one in the whole world could influence Haruna. On anything. Ever. She's impenetrable. Impenetrable! Even for poor old Cheq.'

'Frankie!'

'Well, it's true. Anyway, she'll be out of there soon. How do I look?'

'Well, it's certainly *a* look, my darling, I'll give you that,' her mum said, kissing her on the cheek. 'Don't you need something warmer on? It's so wet and cold out.'

'It won't go.' Frankie turned around and looked once more in the mirror. 'And I look too perfect to spoil it with anything as dull as practicality.'

By the time she'd picked up Haruna and they were on their way to Wick Rooms by bus she was absolutely freezing. Her fingers were numb, her butt was numb; in fact, the only things that still had feeling were her toes.

'Happy birthday, sorry I didn't get you anything' Haruna said, kissing her on the cheek, 'aren't you frozen?'

'I should have brought a scarf at least.'

'You want mine?' Haruna asked, unwrapping her big black shrug, which she wore with a simple get-up of black jeans, white chucks and a men's white T-shirt under her camouflage parka.

'No,' Frankie replied stubbornly.

'Okay, well, no more complaining about being cold then,' Haruna said firmly, refixing the scarf. She'd been salty since Frankie picked her up – even more so than usual. Frankie was trying to keep the mood light with chitchat about the upcoming gig, and her plans for recording a demo – once they'd written some songs, of course – and a musical showcase she'd heard of in Austin, Texas, called South by Southwest which she thought the band should apply for later in the year. All exciting stuff, which Haruna from last week would have buzzed out over. But Haruna from tonight wasn't warming.

'Are Aimee and Greer meeting us there, then?'

'Yes, I already said that,' Haruna said sharply. 'You're a bag of nervous energy tonight. It's just a party. We won't even know that many people.'

'And you're a being a bit mean and a total grump,' Frankie said, pointing her finger angrily at Haruna.

'Sorry,' Haruna replied quickly, 'I am.' She looked down, pulled at the laces on her shoes, then sat back in her seat and stared out of the window.

Frankie felt the sting of sadness she had felt for her friend so many times over the last few years. 'So, how's Cheq, then?' she asked, desperate to get Haruna talking about something she liked, despite it being just about her least favourite subject.

'Well, I've been thinking and I've decided I'm going to sleep with him. It's time.' Haruna nodded, looking straight ahead. 'I can't wait any longer. I can't stop thinking about it.'

'Haruna, whoa there. Back the sexy truck up.' Frankie laughed. 'Are you sure? Now? Like, is this *really* the right time?'

'Oh, piss off,' Haruna said, scoffing, 'you had sex when you were, like, sixteen with that loser from South London. I think I can make a decision to sleep with my boyfriend who I know really well – you didn't even *know* him, at all. Or since!'

'Okay, thanks for the reminder.' Frankie grimaced. 'It was on a *train* if I remember, which I barely do. Nick. He had a tattoo of a sun around his nipple, and asked me to put my finger up his bum . . . '

'You were drunk.'

'Of course,' Frankie said. 'I've never had sober sex, except for ... Doc. Oh my God, Sorry! I mentioned him!' She covered her hands with her face.

Haruna's face finally broke into a small smile. 'It's okay, you've done so well. I haven't heard of him since just before Christmas. You're making progress, my little Padawan.'

Frankie shrank back into her seat feeling utterly ashamed. *Is this a good time to tell her? Or shall I let it happen organically. He might not even be here tonight so there's no need to potentially upset Haruna at this point. Oh God,* please *let him be at this party tonight!*

'Are we going to talk about the other night?' Frankie asked, taking the opportunity to bring it up while Haruna's guard was down. 'With your mum? I mean, I know I'm banned, but maybe she's had a change of heart?'

'Sorry about that. She's just so scared of Greg, I think. Anyway, I've decided what I'm going to do. How to handle it all,' Haruna said carefully. 'I'm going to sit tight, get through the next few months, and then I'm going to turn eighteen, go to whichever university will take me, take out a loan to study, and I'll get a job in a pub, working nights, and it will be fine.'

'You should leave, like now.'

'That's what my mum says all the time,' Haruna said bitterly.

Frankie put her hand on Haruna's knee and squeezed gently. They sat in silence for the last few minutes of the journey, and Frankie knew better than to push her any further. As they neared Hackney Wick station she rang the bell and jumped up.

'M' lady,' Frankie said, holding out an outstretched arm, 'your carriage ride is over, and the ball awaits, but remember: you *must* be home at midnight.'

'Before ten!' reminded Haruna with a finger in the air. 'Before ten – or I'm out.'

They jumped off the bus and headed towards Wick Rooms. They stank, those back streets of Hackney Wick. They had that dank city smell of lorries and bins and car parks and waste water. As they neared the building they could hear the music booming, and the chatter of voices coming from the large doors on the street, and as they turned the corner, they saw the crowd.

'Holy hell!' Frankie said, her stomach dropping. 'This is going to be awesome.'

Outside, about two dozen people milled around smoking cigarettes and weed, huddled up in big overcoats, except for one short, stocky guy with a thick Manchester accent who was inexplicably topless and shouting 'cock-waddle' at the top of his voice.

'Haruna!' Aimee came rushing forward, arms outstretched. 'Frankie, do you have a drink?'

'I totally need one,' Frankie replied, giving Aimee half a hug, her eyes scanning the crowd for Doc. 'Many people inside?'

'Heaps,' Aimee said, offering her a bottle of beer. 'Greer has a small stash we can drink. Frankie, did you bring her ten quid to chip in? But honestly there's heaps inside. You should see our practice room, it's the dance floor!'

'This'll do nicely,' Frankie said, struggling with the bottle top.

'I can help with that,' said a voice next to her. A boyish, big-lipped indie-type with long floppy hair pulled out his lighter and after two attempts flipped the top off her bottle, and as he handed it back, his fingers brushed hers a moment longer than needed as he tried to hold her gaze.

'Took you long enough,' said Frankie with a wickedly flirtatious grin, before turning quickly away, but relishing the attention.

She took a huge swig of the beer and prepared herself. Frankie's self-esteem oscillated between a withering zero and bulletproof, irrepressible bravado; tonight she was most definitely *on form*.

She knew she looked a million miles from the girl *he* met in those grubby bar toilets nearly a year ago but she was nervous. She bit the side of her thumb nail and tore off a small strip of skin, causing a slight sting. *Oh God let him be here*, she thought.

As they pushed in the front door, she noted with irritation that all but one of their gig posters had been removed from the front pinboard. *Stupid rules.* There were obviously a couple of sound systems on the go; some kind of retro house was being played in their practice room. As they walked past, Frankie peered in, relieved to see Haruna's huge painted canvas backdrop still stuck to the wall. *More evidence of the early success of Seven*, she thought.

Haruna was following close behind her. 'Can you see

Cheq?' she shouted above the booming noise, looking down at her phone at a message from him. 'I mean, he says he's here!'

Frankie turned to her and shook her head, rolling her eyes. 'I'll let you know, Rooney. Where do you go, do you think? There's just a bunch of rooms.'

'I guess we just find somewhere to hang,' Haruna said. 'But since I've only got a couple of hours, I'm going to find Cheq.'

'Sure, whatever.' Frankie pushed ahead to the concrete stairwell at the back of the building. The little kitchenette was taking quite a battering, absolutely bursting with bodies. A short, stocky guy in a check shirt with an epic beard walked out with a tray of shots.

'Don't mind if I do,' Frankie said, grabbing the largest one in reach. She knocked it back in one, placing the plastic cup back on the tray. She wiped the remnants from her lips. 'Eww. Tequila.'

The music switched: 'Blue Monday', New Order. A pulsing, sexy beat.

A girl in a plunging, fire-engine-red jumpsuit and clashing pink coat leaned against the wall between the entrance and the stairwell, giving Frankie a long lingering look as she moved towards the stairs. To her left, a sour-looking boy, hunched and moody, tried to grab the girl's hand, which she immediately ripped away.

'Fuck off, Roger,' she said, folding her arms and turning back to watch Frankie as she moved passed.

Frankie giggled. 'Who on earth is called Roger under the

age of fifty?' She turned to Haruna, but her friend was long gone, so she made her way up the stairway alone. She passed two posh boys with almost identical cropped hair, and dark expensive-looking winter coats, one with his hand casually in his pocket, the other waving his hand about, his voice audible only between moments in the song. 'I just . . . date a girl like that. She's so . . . loud and . . . fuck . . . obnoxious.' Up and around them she climbed on to the second floor where the queue to the toilets was long and lively. A fashionable couple – both tall, he was broad, long straight hair, blue oversized vintage suit; she was in a leather skirt, white tee – were nose to nose, deep in some lovers' tête-à-tête on the landing, blocking her way.

'Excuse me,' Frankie said, and they pulled themselves apart just far enough to let her squeeze through. The guy looked her up and down as their bodies touched, and Frankie bit her lip, shooting him her most flirtatious eyes.

The music switched: Joy Division, 'Transmission'. A pulsing, dizzying, driving beat. Dirtier. Frankie needed another drink.

Down the hall she scanned for Doc, swigging the last of her beer. She walked past a plastic barrel filled with ice, and plunged her hand in, quickly and confidently, and pulled out a second bottle. Twist top.

To her right, two girls – blunt fringes, chambray and denim posh-cool, fixed expressions, playing the wallflower. To her left, an older punk woman – tattooed, skinny, nineteen-forties vibe – nodded at her as she lifted a lighter to her pipe.

Round the corner into the next room, some white fairy lights were hung round the window and a thick cloud of weed came billowing into the hall. Doc had to be in there. She was ready to accidentally bump into him. *Oh, what are you doing here?* She practised the surprised tone in her head. *Doc, my God. How are you?*

'Hey, Frankie,' said Jules, appearing in front of her from nowhere, knocking her right out of her Doc-focus. He was wearing a gold velvet sweatshirt and black suit pants with a white stripe down the side that was mildly interesting, if a bit eccentric. Unfortunately, he was also blocking her way. She offered him the world's fastest smile and motioned to move past, but he was distracted by a dude who looked like Jon Snow tapping him on the shoulder to say *hey*. She watched him smile back. Everyone knew Jules, and everyone liked him.

He was somehow sobering to look at. Frankie felt compelled to be real with him because he was really real with her. It made her all jittery.

'You're practising here now, in room three, Cheq says?' he said, turning back to her.

Frankie tried to peer over his shoulder to the sofas on the far wall, but her view was obscured and Jules wasn't moving. She took a swig of her beer. Better to quickly engage.

'That's right,' she said, holding her free hand out for a shake.

'Left-handed shake?' he said, grinning. 'I'll take it. How've you been?'

'Good.' she said, then thinking she needed to be a bit polite at the very least, she replied, 'You guys practice here too?'

'Yeah, for about a year now. Doesn't everyone?' He laughed. 'So, Cheq tells me you've got a gig coming up? Punked-up rock 'n' roll at a bingo hall?'

He was being supportive but it made Frankie blush. She knew it wasn't cool, but they had to start somewhere – and since she really couldn't bare the idea it *wasn't cool*, she obviously had no choice but to make up a big backstory.

'Yeah, It's a gig for my grandfather. He's a war veteran and we offered to play for free to raise money for the cause. Normally we wouldn't do free gigs 'n' shit, but since it's family.' She took another large sip of her beer.

'That's cool of you,' he said, nodding his head, a knowing grin on his face. He didn't believe the story, that much was obvious. And damn it, of course he would know it was their first proper gig after the Christmas Market. *Bloody Cheq. Bloody Haruna.* He probably knew everything about the band.

'I remember one of our first gigs was at a bingo hall. Singer got wasted and puked on the big bingo-ball dispenser. We got kicked out before we'd even played a song.'

Frankie looked at him for a moment, a bit taken aback, and laughed. 'Well, I'll have to make sure we top that, then.'

'I'm sure you will,' he said. 'I might come, if that's cool?'

She looked back over his shoulder, craning her neck a bit. 'Sure,' she nodded, losing attention for a bit . . .

'Am I holding you up?' he asked, glancing over his shoulder

to see what she was looking at. 'I'll let you get on. Where'd you get that beer?'

'Over there.' Frankie waved at the plastic barrel down the hall. 'Hurry, though, there weren't many left.'

'I can take a hint.' He grinned, stepping out of her way and heading off down the hall. 'Maybe see you later?'

For a moment Frankie watched him go, stopping briefly to hug a guy and exchange some kind of warm gag. Then, as if sensing her staring, he looked back at her and gave her what was unmistakably *the eyes.* She drew a sharp breath. *Ignore, ignore, ignore.* Then she pointed to the plastic barrel behind him, as if she was waiting to make sure he got his beer.

Thanks, he mouthed, holding her gaze for a beat, and then he was gone.

Frankie shook herself out of the moment, just as the main hall lights switched off so everything fell into virtual darkness, except for the intermittent flashing of the fairy lights.

The music switched: The Cure, 'Lullaby'. Soft, sensual, ominous.

The track was trance-like as she neared her destination, and she felt the warm waves of tipsiness giving her that confident swagger. She took a step in, the music even louder in the room, and squinted towards the couch, just as a hand tapped her on the shoulder.

'Frankie?' Doc smiled, taking a suck back on his joint. There he stood. His eyes trailing the length of her body. He rocked slightly, uneasily, and smiled at her. 'I wondered if you'd be here. I'm glad. Come get a drink with me.' He held out his joint, and Frankie smiled, taking it from his hand without and word and sucking back on the slightly damp end, letting the smoke trail slowly out into a billow in front of her face, until she blew it away.

Chapter 12

Cherry Bomb

She ran a hand down his face and kissed him again. He had his arm round her waist and his hand rested in the small of her back, inching down ever slowly. It was loud and chaotic in the hallway, and Haruna was enjoying people-watching from their corner of the hall. So many beautiful, edgy girls and boys, so chic and stylish. Haruna tugged at her own outfit, feeling that stab of anger that she couldn't really, fully dress and express herself. *Yet.* The hallway once again snapped to dark. Haruna fished around for some money in her pocket to feed the meter.

'Don't … It's better in the dark,' Cheq said, pulling her even closer.

Haruna rolled her eyes and nodded at Greer and Aimee who were making their way, arm in arm, into the adjacent practice room, holding a half-empty bottle of vodka. Aimee was so happy with Greer. That happiness was a long time coming, for her friend had struggled with her queerness for years.

'Really not a fan of this music,' Cheq complained. 'New Wave. It's fucking Old Wave. Old-as-fuck Wave. Don't you guitar band people ever diversify?'

'There's plenty of synth,' Haruna said, smiling.

'Hey, did I tell you I finally got a manager?' Cheq said. 'I didn't want to, but it was starting to get so busy and Tim said he wanted to do it, so I said, cool, and now he's my manager. Sure as shit he's never managed anything in his life, but he's my bro, so.'

'That's cool. What will he do, then? Book gigs and that kind of thing?' Haruna asked. 'Frankie mentioned getting a manager the other day.'

Cheq laughed. 'Of course she did.' Today he wore thick, black-rimmed glasses, a white and fluoro-green baseball cap and a chunky silver necklace. Haruna reached up and slipped the glasses off his head. 'Now I can see you better,' she said.

'I can't really see you, though. No contacts,' he whispered into her ear, kissing her neck. Then he gave her a warm squeeze. 'How are you doing, Ru? How are things at home?'

'Awful,' she said, feeling the unexpected sting of tears in her eyes. She breathed slowly out. 'But it's okay.'

'Well, it's not,' he said firmly.

'I know,' Haruna replied, looking into his eyes. 'I'm ready.'

Cheq closed his eyes and rested his forehead against hers. 'Baby, don't.'

'I'm ready,' she said again. 'I've thought heaps, and I am ready.'

He pulled back and looked at her again, a wicked twinkle in his eyes. 'Let's go. We can stay in my brother's flat – he's in New York for work. It's totally free, he lives alone.'

Haruna laughed. 'I can't now. I have to be home in, like, an hour and a half.'

'It'll only take a minute,' Cheq joked.

'Jesus, what a way to get a girl excited,' Haruna replied, frowning. 'I expect you to tell me it will take as long as *I* need.'

Cheq laughed and pulled her in close, giving her a gentle kiss on the forehead. 'I love you, Ru.'

'Don't do that.' She pulled back, shaking her head. 'That kiss-on-the-forehead thing. It makes me feel like you think I'm some little girl.'

'Whoa,' Cheq said, 'sorry, Ru.'

'Look. If we do this, Cheq, I expect utter equality. It's not some gift to you, you got it? I'm a willing participant.'

'Well, I'd hope so,' he said, trying to suppress a smile. 'I wouldn't have it any other way.'

'What's so funny?'

'You are. No one in the world found out their girlfriend wants to shag them in this way. It's all you, Ru.' He shrugged. 'You're a rare girl and I'm here for it.'

'I can only be myself,' she said, folding her arms, 'but thank you.'

She looked around, craning her neck for a sign of Frankie. 'D'ya mind if I go and see if Frankie's okay?'

'Frankie's always okay,' Cheq said, his tone hardening. 'If anyone is okay in a building full of booze and boys, it's Frankie. I'd go as far as to ask if everyone else is okay around Frankie.'

'You don't know her as well as you think you do,' Haruna replied simply, kissing him on the cheek before pulling away. She looked around, squinting a bit in the dark. 'Gimme ten. I just want to make sure she's cool.'

Five minutes later and Haruna had scoured the bottom floor and made her way up the stairs. As she passed the queue for the toilets she spied Frankie at the end of the second-floor hallway, right by the window.

Talking to Doc.

She stopped short.

Oh no.

Haruna took a couple of steps forward, when she noticed his hand was half on hers. It was an unmistakably intimate, flirtatious scene. Frankie was glowing, her face lit up, gesticulating, excitement and flirtation bubbling from every surface. *What was Doc doing here?* She wondered if Frankie had known he would be at the party. Should she interrupt? See if Frankie was okay? On the one hand it seemed weird to worry, but on the other, Haruna had seen the notebook. No, she had to interrupt.

She marched to the end of the corridor and found Frankie mid-sentence, a flicker of shock on her face when Haruna approached. She turned away from Doc immediately, pulling her arm away from his grasp.

'Ru. You remember Doc?'

'Hi,' Haruna said, nodding at Doc with a blank expression before turning to Frankie. 'Can I speak to you for a moment?'

'Doc and I are just catching up,' Frankie said, nodding, her eyes wide as if imploring Haruna to bugger off.

No fucking chance, thought Haruna. 'Oh yeah?' she said, turning her face back to Doc. She folded her arms. 'And what's your news?'

'Oh, not much. You know me,' he said, shrugging, 'working a bit and practising.'

'Yes, and how's the band?' she asked, tilting her head to the side. He looked the same except perhaps a little skinnier and a little more drawn in the face. His hair had been bleached and dyed green, but was well faded. He looked so pasty and ill compared to Cheq, Haruna really didn't get the attraction.

'Well, we're doing okay. No gigs right now, as I've been a bit creatively worn out, you know. You guys are doing great, though? So much happening, so quickly.'

Haruna looked confused for a moment, and then glanced at Frankie who was pulling that 'play along' face. 'Oh yeah. Things are going great,' she replied sarcastically. 'What part of our amazing news are you talking about, though?'

'That you got accepted to showcase at South by Southwest. I mean, it's amazing. Most bands need to have a pretty experienced background for that kind of gig. It's really cool.'

'Oh, the showcase to play at South by Southwest.' Haruna raised her brows and looked at Frankie, nodding. 'Yes, that's very interesting news.'

'Well, we've had all that interest from those record labels,' said Frankie, 'and with the invitation to go and record a demo, I mean, I guess we're a bit of a rare thing, an all-girl punk band.'

Haruna died a little. 'Frankie, can we talk?'

'Yeah, sure, Rooney,' Frankie said casually. 'Guess I'll see you soon?' she said to Doc as Haruna grabbed her arm and jerked her away.

'Sure. Be great. Are you going to be around . . . or give me a bell sometime?'

Haruna died completely. 'Frankie, what the hell are you doing?' she snapped as they were out of earshot, though Haruna could feel Doc's eyes on them. She tried to smile. 'What's going on?'

'Nothing. Just making out things are going great,' she said, biting her lip, swaying slightly as she spoke. Haruna could see in her eyes she knew she'd been absolutely sprung. 'You know, trying to make an ex feel like you're doing super great without them? It's normal. It's what you do.'

'It's psycho,' Haruna said. 'What the hell did you tell him? South by Southwest? Good luck keeping that lie going. And we're recording a demo now? Of what? Elvis Presley covers?'

'Don't shout at me,' Frankie said, swaying a little more as the hall lights snapped back on and Haruna got a good look at her smudged make-up and dopey eyes.

'Oh and you're wasted. Again.' Haruna shook her head, just as Aimee bounced over to them, a wide slightly-sloshed smile on her face.

'Guys! Isn't it just the best? You were right, Frankie, it was a really good idea to get a room here,' she enthused, offering Frankie another beer, which she took with a glare in Haruna's direction. 'Greer's relaxing about it all now. She says there're so many free rooms at the moment we're probably fine for a while. Oh, and bonus points, she thinks I look hot with a bass.'

Haruna, feeling she'd wasted enough time on bloody Frankie, pulled out her phone to check the time and saw a message from her mother.

> MUM: Lots of work here so we won't drive back tonight. See you early tomorrow. Mum.

She put the phone back in her pocket and stared at Frankie, stewing.

'I was so annoyed with you when you first asked me,' Aimee continued, 'and Greer thought you were just trying to get closer to Dick, but it's been perfect. It's just so great.'

'Closer to Dick?' Haruna shot back.

'You know who I mean – Doc. Greer and I call him Dick, because, let's face it, he really is,' Aimee said, before giggling.

'I mean, even if I was a straight, I'd still struggle to see the attraction. Sorry, Franks.'

'Shhh . . . ' Frankie said. 'He's just down there.'

'He won't hear over the noise, Jesus. And what do you mean, Aimee? I'm confused,' Haruna probed. There was some kind of Frankie-style muck afoot here.

'Well, you know, cos Blood Soup Rabbit, or whatever, practise here too,' Aimee leaned in, 'so Greer thought that was the reason, but now we know it's because you really want to give this band everything you've got. Hug time!' Aimee tried to jolly the girls up.

Frankie was suppressing a drunken smile, a smile so smug and antagonistic it made Haruna seethe. 'Sprung, I guess,' Frankie said, shrugging.

'Don't go back there, Frankie. Don't do it. I'm begging you,' Haruna said, attempting one final time to shake some sense into her.

'It's not like that. We're just friends now. You know, we're both in bands and that's cool. I think we can do this. You don't need to worry about me.'

'Okay,' Haruna snapped, looking back at her phone to check the time. 'I am going to stop worrying about you, and I'm going to go and find Cheq. Because, you're now on your own.'

'What's going on, you guys?' Aimee said, confused. 'You must've known Doc was here. You know Frankie, Haruna? There's always a double deal going on. Oh, please don't fight, it's so upsetting.'

Haruna stormed off without looking back, down the stairs and straight over to Cheq. She grabbed him by the hand and jerked him away from the conversation he was in with Jules.

'I don't know why I care, Jules, but would you keep an eye on Frankie?' she said over her shoulder as she dragged Cheq towards the door.

'Of course, is she in some kind of trouble?'

Haruna paused for a moment, and then relented. 'No. Probably not.'

'Okay,' Jules said, swigging his beer, then looking around for Frankie. He would be worried now because that was Jules: kind and considerate. And, right now, too good for Frankie.

'Forget her,' Haruna said to him, touching his arm. Then she turned to Cheq. 'Let's go.'

'Where?' he said, grabbing his parka and almost stumbling from the force of her grasp.

'Your brother's place? Let's go do this. Don't ask any more questions or I might change my mind.'

Chapter 13

I Want to Grow Up

Frankie woke up, head thumping, still in her same outfit from the night before, luckily *sans* boots. Her mouth felt rougher and dryer than the floor of a parrot's cage. She rolled out of bed, moaning, and headed to the bathroom.

'Morning, Frankles,' shouted Hamish as she tripped over a pile of her washing by the front door.

'Jesus, what's all this shit doing here? I nearly broke my neck.'

'Oh morning, darling. I thought if I put your washing here you might remember to do it,' her mum said, rather too brightly. 'You need to be at the studio in two hours, darling.'

'Can I wake up first, damn it?' she said, slamming the bathroom door behind her as she leaned over the sink and spat out twice, before reaching for her toothbrush and forcing herself to clean her teeth and her tongue. She turned the shower on, but the water would not run warm.

'Oh man, what's happened to all the bloody hot water?' she shouted, before deciding to brave a thirty-second ice-cold dip, just long enough to wash off a bit of the sticky stench of alcohol sweat, cigarette smoke and spilled beer.

She crawled out of the shower and into the hallway, where she was greeted by her brother's amused face. 'You were really drunk last night.'

'Okay, great. Thanks for letting me know. I'll be sure to come back here when you're seventeen and return the favour.' She pushed past him and into the bedroom, pulling on her favourite PJs and jumping back into bed.

'Mum! Can you please bring me some water?'

The bedroom door opened an inch and her mum leaned in, shaking her head at her.

'Please don't make me feel any worse than I already do,' Frankie said, pulling a pillow over her head.

'Let me go get you a bacon sarnie, and a tea,' she said, smiling, 'then I'll run you to the studio if you like?'

'Please, Mum. Thank you, you are my lifesaver and I am forever in your debt.'

'Speaking of debt,' her mother said, as Frankie peered out from behind her pillow. 'your father wants to speak to you.'

'Aghhh, what now?' Frankie moaned. 'Can't a girl just shake off a nightmarish hangover in peace?'

'Hey, twinkle toes.' Frankie's dad popped his head in as her mum scurried off.

'Hello, Gross-Farter,' she replied. 'What on earth could be so important that Mother needed to introduce you?'

'Just wanted to talk to you about two things, really,' he said, sitting on the edge of her bed. His face was lined, but the lines were happy, breezy and bright. He looked like a kind of pink, shiny, hairless Santa Claus.

'Okay, this whole sitting-on-the-edge-of-the-bed father–daughter chat is making me feel nauseous.'

'No, that'll be the booze. You smell flammable. Did you actually shower?'

'There's no cold water,' Frankie complained. 'I mean HOT, there's no hot water. Oh God, I need a glass of water.'

Her father picked up last night's half-full pint glass of tepid water, which had a film of dust settled across it.

'Ugh,' she recoiled, shaking her head.

'Frankie, we need to talk about your plans. Your mum and I are proud of you, whatever you decide to do, as long as you earn a living and pay your way.'

'Oh God, really? We have to do this now?'

'We've noticed that you've left school, and there's been no indication of you actually applying for music school.'

'You mean radio school?'

'Yes, have you applied?'

'No.'

'As I thought.'

'I mean, I was going to, but God, the *forms*, Dad. So *many* forms. And to be honest, with the studio and the band, I've got tons going on now.'

'The band?'

'Yes, Seven. The punk band. Remember – you bought me a guitar?' She was beginning to feel a bit irritated.

'Oh yes, the band. Is that gonna stick?'

'What do you mean?'

'Let me see, Franks: piano, ballet, judo,' he said, counting on his fingers, 'pottery (I knew that one was a short-term gig), photography.' He nodded to her discarded camera in the corner of the room. 'What else? Oh yes, theatre, then musical theatre. That winter you wanted to ski. Wasn't that because of a boy called Rupert?' he said in a really bad posh accent.

In truth, the photography was because of a boy too. The judo because of the cool girl from South Africa who came to school for that one term. Honestly? There was inspiration from other people behind all of her passions. *But how else do people find things to do they like?* she thought grumpily.

'Okay, okay, I haven't fully decided what I want to do with my life, but the band feels different. There's something that happens with me and the girls ...' Her mind wandered to Haruna and she cringed when she recalled the conversation from the night before.

'Look, love, I'm not going to rain on your parade. You've always jumped from one thing to the next. It's who you are. I was like it too, but I took a job, started saving for my future, and took some responsibility. And you need to do the same.'

'It's only been two months. And I'm working at the studio!'

'Yes, but I imagine a dance studio receptionist is not going to satisfy you for long.'

'Dad, can't you just let me do the band for a bit, see if it takes off?'

With that he gave her a pitying look, and Frankie felt her heart sink.

'If you love the band, you'll find time for it. And if it's meant to be, it will be,' he said unconvincingly. He was brushing her off. 'You know, I was in a band once—'

'Oh God, here we go.'

'We were a Beatles covers band.'

'Shock of the day.'

'I'm just saying that I did that alongside learning The Knowledge so I could be a black cab driver. The band didn't take off, but my career as a cabbie was there as my safety net. I know it's different today for you kids, but you do need to think about a safety net, Frankie.'

'I know about how life works, Dad,' she said, feeling sad about her dad's story, although he had surely meant it to be inspiring. 'I know the deal.'

'The deal was that you pay rent here. But we've thought about it, and I'd like to see you take the next step as an adult – you're eighteen now – and move out on your own.'

'You're throwing me out?' Frankie sat up, horrified.

'No, drama queen, can you please listen?' he laughed. 'I've found a place for you. Uncle Ben has a—'

'I don't have an Uncle Ben. Come on,' Frankie said dubiously.

'Well, he's a great-uncle, really. Anyway, his granddaughter has a flat in South London – Peckham, please don't laugh – and you're welcome to a room at a very competitive rate for central London.'

'Peckham!' she yelped. 'South of the river?'

'It will be good for you, Frankie – getting out, paying your way. Think of it like training wheels. At least you won't have to pay rent to one of those nasty landlords I read about in the *Mail*. Fourteen to a room!'

'But Peckham!' she moaned, shooting her father the very best puppy eyes she could, before the reality began to dawn on her and she marvelled at the prospect. 'I guess it's not that far. And it would really be a place of my own . . . '

'Well, a flat share,' he said, 'but yes, it will be very much your place too.'

'Okay, fine, I'll do it,' Frankie said quickly, suddenly feeling a thrill course through her. *Her own place! This was it! Freedom! Adulthood! Parties! Friends over WHENEVER. No more sharing a room with her brother! It was—*

'Hang on,' Frankie said, sitting bolt upright again, reaching for a couple of ibuprofen from her bedside table, and in desperation taking a swig from the glass of stale water by her bed. 'I can be down with Peckham, but am I paying the rent *really*, because I don't make a lot at the dance studio. I'd have to get a proper job.'

'Yes, Frankie,' her father said, a huge grin, teeming with satisfaction, crawling across his face, 'and that's part of being an adult. Now you know how I bloody feel.'

'Ugh. How am I supposed to have a band that takes over the world if I have to work at bloody Starbucks?'

'Nothing wrong with working at a Starbucks.'

Frankie pulled a face.

'We've all had to fund our dreams. Anyway, you're not alone. We're always here if you need a leg-up. You know that.'

Fund our dreams, Frankie scoffed inside. Her parents weren't like her. They didn't dream of being *someone*.

She felt mixed emotions as her father left the room and the smell of frying bacon wafted through the doorway. A place of her own; but also a whopping big rent bill each month. She would be the first of her friends to have their own place, but there'd be no more breakfasts in bed. Through the open bedroom door she could see the pile of washing her mother had left for her. *It was time.*

She fished her phone out of her coat pocket.

Eight missed calls from Haruna.

Three texts.

Frankie – where are you?

PICK UP, MOFO

HELLLLLLLP. Are you there? You better not be screwing Doc while I'm here, dying.

Her heart began to race; she hit dial right away.

Come on, pick up. Frankie thought, racking her brain to try to remember if she'd seen or spoken to Haruna later last night. Haruna was angry that she was talking to Doc, and angrier still that she'd not been clear about her full motivation for getting a room at Wick, but this was Haruna. She was never mad with Frankie for long.

On the third attempt, Haruna picked up. 'Frankie,' she whispered.

'What's happened?'

'Oh nothing. Well, I lost my fucking house keys and I wanted to see if you had them for some reason. It was very late. It's okay, though, I broke a window. I'm going to have to pretend some kid did it but I think it's okay. It felt kind of good, actually. Maybe I need to break more windows,' she said playfully.

'Oh Jesus. How did your night end up?' she asked with trepidation. 'I was looking for you . . . at one point at least.'

'Were you?' Haruna said, the lingering resentment apparent,

and then after a huge sigh she volunteered, 'We should probably talk about what happened.'

'With what?' Frankie chirped, hoping she'd cooled somewhat.

'Wick Rooms. Doc. Your never-ending obsession with someone who, actually, by the way, looks like a junkie.'

Frankie laughed. 'No he doesn't. Look, I know it seems like some kind of cunning plan to be around him.'

'Yes, that's what it looks like,' Haruna said, 'because *that's what it is.*'

'I'm committed to the band! You don't think it's all made up or some shit, do you?' Frankie protested. 'I spend every minute on it that I can, coming up with ideas. I even put a down payment on your drum kit; why do you think we've still got it?'

'And I'm hugely grateful and I will do what I can to pay you back at some point.'

'And I've been practising. And you know how much I hate learning shit. But see, why would I do that if it was to impress some dude?'

Frankie had to admit she was starting to enjoy playing. She was getting steadily better, and with each small improvement came a real sense of satisfaction. And the better she got, the less she focused on why she'd started the band in the first place, and the more she just craved the fun. No. This band wasn't *really* about Doc any more.

'Oh Franks, I don't know how much of this is about Doc. I know it's not all about him, but it's just frustrating because now it's all dirty. It was our thing, the three of us girls, and now it's dirty.'

'I'm sorry,' Frankie said, genuinely. 'Honestly, I've never felt as awesome as when we're practising together. And I am literally buzzing about our gig.'

'We're not ready,' Haruna said flatly.

'I know, but who cares? No one's going to be there. Do you know how hard it is to get a gig? We've got no music to send, no official photos; the website, I will now admit, is rubbish. We need something called a 'press pack', which I keep trying to do. I posted three things on Instagram and only got one like, so screw that for a joke. If I can pull a few family strings and get a gig, I may as well, right?'

'Well, yeah. It's great you did it, but I'd rather play when we're ready,' Haruna muttered, the conversation falling silent for a moment. 'Oh my God.'

Frankie cringed for a moment, knowing what was coming, before Haruna exposed her completely. 'The posters were for Doc's benefit?'

Frankie giggled nervously. 'At first, maybe.'

'Oh God, you are something else,' Haruna said. 'I was too distracted by the art direction to question the point of them.'

'Haruna, I'm really sorry I wasn't straight with you about Doc. But you know me. I'm normally straight as an arrow. With you at least. Mostly. I was . . . ashamed, maybe?' Frankie said, bathing in a moment of arresting honesty.

'Hmm,' Haruna said, 'well, please don't lie any more. You lie all the time and it's annoying.'

'I don't lie,' Frankie lied, wounded by this bullet of truth. She knew she embellished, told the odd fib, but being called a liar really hurt. 'I don't *lie* lie. I just . . . I, like, spin things, you know?'

'Yeah, okay. Well, no more spinning in my direction, please.'

'Anyway, enough about boring boys, I have some news,' Frankie said, keen to move the conversation on.

'What?'

'My parents have found me a flat.'

Haruna gasped. 'They're kicking you out?'

'No, no, not really. They just found me affordable accommodation that isn't with them,' she said, laughing. 'I mean, they want me to be an *adult*, and if that means my own flat in Peckham, then I'm in!'

'Peckham?'

'I know. South of the river, but I can do it. Peckham's actually quite cool.'

'I can't believe they're kicking you out!'

'Haruna, listen to the news. I have a flat! That's the headline!'

At that moment her mother crept in with a bacon sandwich and a cup of sweet tea and gave her a little pat on the head, creeping quietly back out so as not to interrupt. Frankie watched her slowly close the door with a wink, and felt a pang of sadness about leaving home.

And then she was immediately distracted by the memory of Haruna's revelation before the party.

'Oh my God, I almost forgot to ask. Did you shag Cheq?'

'Don't say it like that,' Haruna said, the whine in her voice giving away her embarrassment.

'OH MY GOD, YOU DID. TELL ME EVERYTHING NOW.'

Chapter 14

Trying

Frankie and Aimee sat on the stairs – the only dry spot – in the alleyway beside the bingo hall by the back door as instructed, clutching their instruments and awaiting Haruna.

'She's going to come, right? You guys made up?' Aimee asked, tugging at the suit jacket which was never going to pull round her waist. 'Who in hell was this small? Vintage people were tiny little things.'

'You look cool,' Frankie said, full of jealousy. Aimee's hair was piled on her head and pulled forward into a quiff, and her suit jacket, faded black rolled-up jeans and loafers were all pure Teddy boy punk deliciousness. 'Did Greer dress you?'

'No,' Aimee said, pausing for a moment. 'Well, she helped me roll and pin the hair. And this is her jacket. Lord knows how *she* does it up.'

The grimy alley was far too clearly visible in the daylight

and the musty whiff of recycling bin and the putrid stench of drunk man wee and God knows what else wafted across the way. Frankie spotted something lurking behind a discarded car tyre which may or not have been—

'Is that a human poo?' Aimee asked, covering her eyes and shaking her head.

'Must be, I don't know any other animals that use napkins to wipe their butts.'

'Ewww,' they both said in unison.

Frankie put her arm around Aimee and pulled her in for a side hug.

'What's that for?' Aimee asked. 'I mean, it's nice to get a hug from you.'

'What do you mean? You sound like I never give you no affection, man.'

Aimee laughed. 'You're just focused on other things, I guess. How did things end up with Doc, by the way? Haruna said you guys kinda hooked up again.' There was no judgement in her voice, and Frankie smiled at Aimee, feeling a swelling of love and appreciation for their enduring friendship.

'He disappeared after Haruna left. I couldn't find him so I just ended up hanging about trying and failing to avoid Cheq's flatmate Jules. We danced for ages. It was quite fun, actually. A lot of laughing. He looks different. Do you think he looks different? *Almost* attractive.'

'He's completely cute,' Aimee laughed, 'and talented and cool. We've been telling you this for the last year.'

'There's like this barrier,' Frankie said, wondering herself why she didn't want to at least have one date with Jules. 'I don't know. Why I am turned off?'

Aimee shrugged. 'Dunno. You like the bad boys?'

'Christ. Do I have self-esteem problems?' Frankie laughed. 'Anyway, I know you all hate Doc, but look! Yesterday I got this.' She pulled out her phone and held up the text from Doc.

Lets hook up for a drink sometime. Dx

'I don't even know what that means? Am I supposed to call him?' Frankie said. 'He's interested again, right? I mean, it's an invitation, but why isn't it specific? He doesn't say whether I should call, or he's going to call, or what? Why are people not straight up?'

Aimee shifted uncomfortably 'Um, I dunno, Franks. I think you need to be careful. You were kind of a hot mess back then.'

But I'm not now, thought Frankie. She was wearing a floor-length coat to cover up, because her outfit was . . . well, skimpy, to say the least. She'd fashioned it out of stuff from her mum's old dance costumes, much to her mother's irritation.

'You just claim ownership of everything in this house!' she'd complained.

'Stewardship more like. Anyway, *you're* never wearing this

again,' Frankie had said, holding up a pair of tiny, shiny, high-waisted black dancing knickers with a matching belt, which she was now wearing with a white vest and a black bra.

From nowhere, the door behind them swung open, and Frankie, caught off-guard, fell backwards into the hallway and looked straight up to see the manager, a bossy little man, at least fifty, with a red puffy nose and a face lined from chronic frustration.

'You're the band?' he asked, his voice high and nasally.

'Two-thirds of it. Waiting on our drummer. She'll need this door to unload the kit.'

'No problem, just keep it closed. You can soundcheck until three forty-five, then you have to be gone. We're screening the game between four and six and need to pull the screen down over the stage.'

'You got it, captain,' Frankie said, knowingly *un*endearing herself to him, but she didn't like grumpy old people, unless they were family. She pulled herself up and they walked down the small corridor into the hall. The floor was big, clearly carpeted in the mid-eighties, and had a slightly damp texture as they crossed it. The room was set out with dusty, orange velour chairs and long picnic-style tables, with a bar wrapping the front wall by the entrance. Frankie turned to look at the stage which was big, with an impressive lighting rig and plenty of room for a three-piece band, although it was currently occupied by a huge bingo ball cage thingy and podium.

'You can work around all that stuff, I hope,' Mr Manager ordered rather than asked. 'I'll get my guy to move it later.'

'Cool,' Frankie said, and unsure what to do, she announced confidently, 'We'll go get sorted then.'

She turned to Aimee and grinned in excitement.

'Oh my God, it's pretty cool,' Aimee enthused. 'So, what do we do?'

They walked up to the stage and climbed the carpeted stairs. The sturdy rail suggested it was used by elderly bingo winners who had to come up and have their cards checked and their wins verified. Frankie poked around a bit, looking for the power cables and something that resembled their set-up back at Wick Rooms, but suddenly realised that she didn't really have any idea what they were doing in this new space. It was far more complex than she'd anticipated. Everything was alien. There was no Greer to show them the ropes. There was no school music teacher to set up with them before practice.

'I think *this* is the PA,' Aimee said, looking for an on switch for a moment before resorting to just staring at it blankly and poking her finger at random knobs.

'I think I found the power?' Frankie said, squeezing down under a table to inspect the far wall.

'Umm, do we know where this goes?' Aimee asked, holding a small mixing desk which was sat on a high stool – completely unplugged.

'Oh God, it's the Christmas Market all over again,' said Frankie as she pulled herself out from under the table, unable to manoeuvre around much in her big coat, but too shy to remove it just yet. 'Only this time we were *almost* prepared. Two months of practice. I could cry.'

'We'll sort it out. Shall I ask the manager guy?'

'No. You can't; we should know what we're doing,' Frankie said, annoyed. 'We need Greer. She knows how all this works. Where is she? Is she busy?'

Aimee looked at Frankie, paused then sighed. 'I'll call her, okay? But no promises and you can't freak out if she says no.'

'Of course not. I'll go see if I can spot Haruna,' she said, checking her phone. 'No word.'

Frankie jumped off the stage and headed for the back door, before pulling out her phone and calling Haruna. It went straight to answer phone.

'Rooney? Where you at?' she said, agitated. She slipped the phone in her pocket and decided to check the main street. But as she pushed open the back door, Haruna was there, standing at the back of Cheq's car, unloading the kit on to the road. Frankie was about to call out to her but she stopped herself, realising there was something wrong.

She is crying. Haruna never cries.

Then, slipping out of the driver's seat, Cheq came round to help Haruna unload, catching Frankie staring down at them.

'Hey, Frank,' Cheq said with a nod, before Haruna turned around, tears evident on her reddened cheeks. She wasn't dressed for the gig. She'd promised to get her look together. She had on a plain pair of jeans and a roll-neck, and her hair was tied back in a grip. She looked shaken, but focused on unloading the car.

Frankie took a step forward, unsure what to do. 'Haruna, what's happened?'

'Just the usual,' Haruna said, her voice wavering slightly. She put down the snare drum with a thud and a delayed rattle then headed past Frankie to the door, her eyes to the floor. 'I need to go to the bathroom. Can you help Cheq get this inside?'

'Of course I can,' Frankie said, turning to Cheq for an explanation once Haruna was out of earshot. 'What the hell?'

'It's nothing I did, so save the outrage,' Cheq replied, lifting the bass drum out of the boot and carrying it over to the bottom of the stairs.

'I didn't think that,' Frankie replied, moving down to the car to help. 'Is it something at home? Is it her mother? Greg?'

'Of course it's *Greg*,' he replied, 'he burned all her stuff, or something.'

'What stuff? Why?'

'Dunno,' Cheq said, shrugging, 'she won't say.'

'She won't say? Why?'

'I don't know, dude,' Cheq grumbled, shrugging his shoulders in an exaggerated manner. 'She doesn't tell me every goddamn thing, you know. Ask her yourself.'

'How do you know it was Greg?' Frankie asked, pushing him. 'You must know more.'

'Because I saw him pacing about when I picked her up.

Short motherfucker, too. Could totally take him out.' Cheq clenched his jaw and a muscle in his neck flexed for a moment, and then he relaxed and returned to unloading the drum kit.

'What was he doing there?' Frankie probed. 'And he let you drive off with her?'

'Oh, he didn't see Cheq; that would have sent him into orbit,' Haruna said with half a smile, having arrived back from the bathroom. 'He's probably burning the rest of my things right now. The old pizza oven is getting a real workout.' She raised her eyes at Frankie, reminding her of the notebook. Her face had been splashed with cold water and her hair now fell down around her shoulders. 'It was all very sudden, hence the very un-punk-rock outfit.' She shrugged.

'Haruna, I'm fucking stressing here; what are you going to do?' Frankie said. 'Do you want to play? We don't have to. We can totally cancel if you want to sort things out. Or talk. Anything. Did he really burn your stuff?'

'Yes, I want to play. I can't think of anything I'd rather do right now. I wanna play, and I wanna play really fucking loud. I don't care if we're not ready. I don't care if I just bash out incoherent noise for short three-minute bursts. I'm here for it.' She turned to Cheq. 'You gonna come and watch, right? Oh God, I've never felt so much like bashing a drum kit.'

Just then Aimee burst out through the back door. 'Greer said no,' she said, panicked. 'So we're screwed. And I'm sorry, Frankie, but I just asked the manager dude what bands usually do to set up, to see if he could help, and he wasn't impressed.

We look unprofessional, he said. Well, he literally said, "What kind of shit show are you girls running here?"'

For a moment Frankie felt dizzy with stress and panic. 'I need a drink.' But then, the light bulb went off and she turned to Cheq, plastering on her most charming smile. 'You wouldn't give us a hand, would you?'

Everyone stood with baited breath while Cheq looked across at Haruna with such love that Frankie felt a sudden stab of jealousy. 'Of course I'll help you,' he said, speaking directly to Haruna, the subtext undeniable. 'Whatever you need, anytime. Just ask.'

After they loaded everything inside, Cheq quickly went to work arranging the set-up. They all worked in virtual silence, until Frankie headed to the bar and bought a round of beers for everyone.

Within moments Haruna was behind the kit, tapping out the snare, as Cheq adjusted the sound on the desk. He was completely at ease.

'Cheq, you're a lifesaver,' Frankie said, handing him a beer, before gulping down some of her own. She was feeling the nerves. *Okay, this is it.*

'Gimme one,' Haruna said, reaching out for a pint and raising it to the sky. 'To Seven, may we conquer the world.'

'To Seven,' Aimee and Frankie replied. Frankie looked at her friend with a grim smile, trying to get her to connect, but she looked away immediately, tapping out runs on the kit.

'Cheq, one two. Cheq, one two,' Frankie said into the mic, grinning at Cheq.

'Yeah, like I've not heard that gag before,' he said, smiling back at her. It was their first, ever, natural exchange that didn't make Frankie want to barf. But then, he was helping her, so . . .

'Okay, shall we start with "Hound Dog"?' Frankie asked.

'Let's do it!' said Aimee, dragging her finger down the length of the neck on her bass.

Chapter 15

Yuk Foo

Haruna sat on the edge of the booth as Frankie ordered their food from one of her hundreds of uncles. This one, Uncle Dave, owned a greasy spoon off Bethnal Green Road, which was only a short walk from the venue. The walls were cluttered with framed photos of local people shaking her uncle's hand next to plates of food (mostly steak and chips), and two prized shots, one of Phil Mitchell from *EastEnders* and one of Idris Elba.

'If only he was a bit younger,' Haruna said dreamily.

'I know,' Frankie agreed, sliding into the seat opposite her. 'He's so old, though. I mean, he must be at least thirty-five.'

'We should be getting back,' Haruna said. 'We're on in an hour. I can't believe I just said that. *We're on in an hour.*'

'I know, it's so fucking cool,' Frankie said, bursting with excitement. 'Haruna,' she went on, pulling her hand suddenly across the table, 'I know you don't like to talk about things, but what happened at home? Tell me. What did he burn?'

Haruna stared blankly back at her, before looking down at their hands clasped together. She unhooked her fingers from Frankie's and placed her hands in her lap. 'The story is that Greg found my box of keepsakes, and of course there was a sexy card from Cheq there and so he tossed them into the fire.'

'What was in there?'

'Um, letters, a few photos of Dad, some stuff from gigs I've been to and shit like that.' As she said it, she looked up at Frankie and pursed her lips together.

'Oh shit.'

'I didn't write down my dad's address or anything, did I?' she said sourly.

'You've got his email.'

'But the awful thing is, Frankie, Mum knew about that stuff; she knows I have some things tucked away,' Haruna started cautiously, 'so I don't understand why she told Greg. Unless he's been through my room. But that feels unlikely. I can't help but think they had a fight, or maybe something to do with the money, and he got angry? Anyway, it's war now.'

'You have to leave, Haruna,' Frankie said. 'You could speak to the court. I bet you could get a benefit. Haruna, he's abusing you.'

'I fished this out of the ashes,' she said, holding up her left hand to show Frankie a little ring, 'my parents' engagement ring. It didn't burn.'

'Oh, it's really sweet,' Frankie said, reaching up to turn it round, admiring the small blue stone, despite its charred appearance. 'Haruna, did you hear me? He's abusive.'

'Not really. Well, once. The second time he didn't hit me, as such.'

'But all of this is abuse. It's emotional. A court would definitely hear you. I know because my cousin's friend Ash—'

'No.' Haruna interrupted, shaking her head, 'that's never going to happen. I don't want to go through it. What a joke.'

Frankie sat back in her seat, frustrated. Haruna was all for sticking it to the man, until it was the one man she should be sticking it to, and Frankie didn't understand why.

'Shall we head back?' Frankie asked, standing up. 'Have a couple of shots at the bar like a real band, and then hit the stage.'

'Yes. I can't think of anything I want more.'

An hour and a half and several shots later, three very drunk girls sat at a table near the front of the stage while a crowd of about twenty-eight mostly men sat glued to the game, which had gone well into extra time.

'I don't think I can play any more,' Aimee said, holding out her hand and inspecting it for signs of shaking. 'But on the upside, look, I'm not trembling any more! Whoop whoop! Stage fright slayed by two-pound shots.'

'Every cloud . . . ' mused Frankie, chin resting in her hands. 'I can't look back. Did anyone turn up to watch us?'

'Not really,' Aimee said.

'Phew,' said Frankie.

'Cheq's here,' Haruna said, waving at him, 'and looks like he brought Jules.' She glanced at Frankie and then squinted back out at the empty hall. 'Other than that, it looks like a bunch of pensioners.'

'Oh God, Jules is here,' said Frankie, sighing. 'He's like herpes. Never goes away.'

'We get it,' Haruna said. 'You don't like Jules.'

'She thinks he's cute, actually,' Aimee said, teasing Frankie. Aimee was very clearly drunk now. 'You won't date Jules, Frankie, because you want the drama of guys like Doc. No, the chase. You like the chase. Did you reply to him, by the way?'

'What?' Haruna scoffed. 'Oh God, he's in touch now, is he?'

'Shut up, Aimee,' Frankie said, peering over at Jules who was deep in conversation with Cheq. He *did* look good. He looked like he smelled good too, unlike Doc, who had developed some kind of epic armpit stench over the last few months.

'She's right,' Haruna said, shrugging at Frankie.

'You guys suck,' Frankie said, rolling her eyes. She looked back at Jules and wondered if what Aimee said was true. Was she into the drama of Doc? Why did she want him so much, when clearly, on paper, someone like Jules was way better?

'Oh, by the way,' Aimee announced proudly, 'I think I wrote a song. I mean, only on the bass, but Greer thinks it's got potential.'

'Wow,' Frankie said, shaking herself out of her daydream,

and not to be outdone she added, 'So have I. I've finished a couple, too. Was holding them back until we didn't have to practise "Twist and Shout" any more.'

'Praise the lord, the fucking game is over,' Haruna said, standing. 'Let's go do this.'

'Wooo hoooooo!' Aimee squealed, fist in the air, her chair falling back as she stood.

Frankie was waiting for the manager to leave so she could reveal her outfit, but he was hovering by the side of the stage. He was like a helicopter mum, trying to interfere with every little thing as they got ready. Cheq had hurried forward to double check their instruments and he gave Frankie a supportive nod.

'Is this it?' she asked him. 'I mean, no one is forward or anything. Will they come forward?'

'Probably not.' Cheq shrugged. 'But that's first gigs, man. You just gotta get through the set, then you've done one, and the next will be better and it just builds.'

'Okay,' she said gratefully, reaching into her handbag. She pulled out a Canon camera and handed it to Cheq. 'It's just point and shoot. We don't have any pics for the website.'

Cheq took the camera. 'No sweat.'

'None of the crowd, obviously. Or the venue. Just us.'

'Oh – there's Greer!' Aimee waved across the stage to Greer who had just arrived and was heading straight to the bar.

'I just thought people might at least come forward,' Frankie said.

'Don't stress. A few might. Remember where you are – a bingo hall – most people are not here to listen to punk rock.' He laughed – a weird, sweet kind of high-pitched laugh. 'Lord knows how a grime set would go down. Oh – there is *someone* here to see you, though.'

'Is there? Who?' Frankie said, panic stricken, racking her brains to think who she'd told about the gig.

'Yeah, he's a really awesome guitarist and singer, and his band's just been signed, and he's okay-looking if you like that kind of thing, *and* he's single.' Cheq grinned like there was some secret she wasn't in on, except it was totally obvious he meant Jules.

Frankie blushed.

'Don't look so embarrassed, Frankie, maybe he saw one of your posters?' Haruna teased.

'God,' Frankie muttered, 'I wish you guys would stop with this already. I'm not interested in Jules. And I really wish he wasn't here.'

'Sure you're not,' Cheq said. 'I mean, that's why you hung out with him all night at the party.'

'Ugh, did he tell you about that?' Frankie groaned.

'He likes you,' Aimee chimed in, with the puppy-dog eyes.

But Cheq had already walked over to Haruna and knelt down next to her, whispering something and putting his hand on her knee. Checking she was okay. Always checking on her.

Frankie felt suddenly nervous. She didn't want to play in front of Jules with his bloody penetrating stare, thinking things she couldn't guess. And she definitely didn't want to take off her coat. But she couldn't play in it. She took a deep breath and disrobed, quickly pulling her guitar on to cover her skimpy outfit.

'Howt,' Haruna said from behind her, and when Frankie turned to face her she let out a little wolf whistle. Frankie sighed and rolled her eyes.

'All right, ladies, you're on,' manager dude said tediously, lifting the last of the bingo equipment out of the way. 'Try not to scare the customers into an early grave.'

He jumped down from the stage and walked the few steps to the side of the room to watch. As he turned and leaned back against the wall with his arms crossed, his face filled with trepidation.

They had to just go for it.

Frankie looked out at the mostly empty, open hall and saw Greer smiling, looking up at them, then the back of Jules, at the bar ordering, and without blinking she turned back to Haruna and nodded.

Haruna tapped her sticks, *one, two, three, four.*

'You ain't nothing but a HOUND DOAAAAWG,' Frankie screamed into the mic, as Haruna bashed out the beat and Aimee danced next to her on the bass. It was exhilarating. Cheq had doubled the volume since the soundcheck so it was loud *as fuck*, and over before Frankie could hear the manager shouting.

'Cut that appalling noise out now!' He took a few steps

forward, before clapping eyes on Cheq who stood between them, like a bodyguard. Thinking better of it, he shouted, 'Six songs! Then it's over! SIX.'

As the last screech of the guitar rang out around the bingo hall, Frankie came to – looking out to the room full of pensioners. Several had their hands over their ears. A few were politely clapping. Frankie didn't dare look at Jules.

'You won't be paid! Get out of my building!' the manager was shouting at Frankie. 'Tell your father I'll be in touch. Bloody Taylors – you're all the bloody same!'

'That was awesome,' said Aimee breathlessly.

'Job *damn well* done,' Frankie said into the mic, nodding at Cheq, who gave them a very proud thumbs-up.

She turned to Haruna who was sweating and panting behind her kit, smile as wide as the ocean. This was it. She wanted to feel this way, and have Haruna feel this way for ever.

Chapter 16

Typical Girls

It was the hotly anticipated girl band audition day, and Frankie, now a fully fledged gigging punk rocker, was waiting to open the doors to the huge queue that had formed outside. In the reception area, two young assistants were being loudly briefed, aka vaguely shouted at, by a stout, angry-looking man with yellowing teeth.

Frankie pulled off her large headphones and turned off Siouxsie and the Banshees so she could properly eavesdrop.

'So, no one under sixteen. No one over twenty-one,' he said, 'and even then . . . ' His voice trailed off. 'But the girl on reception can help you vet for age.'

'Yes, Geoff,' the girls replied in unison.

'Let's not turn this into some all-day saga, either; efficiency on the in and out, please. They can sing ninety seconds of their song. We'll do first-round call-backs on the spot, then take them through into studio two to learn the routine. Then we'll do second round this evening, with next-round call-backs by phone tonight. No special treatment. If they miss the call, they miss the call-back.'

'Wow, lots of rules,' Frankie interjected with all available sass, looking down at her phone, staring at the message from Doc, still unsure whether to reply.

Frankie had deliberately dressed to shock today, her thick black eye make-up smudged, her hair, with its dark roots coming through, teased and sprayed. She'd rolled up the sleeves of the dance studio T-shirt and wore it with a black leather vest, a short red and green kilt and ripped black tights.

Geoff turned to Frankie, double taking briefly as he took her in.

'You know what you need to do? Have you been briefed?'

Frankie nodded at him, plastering on her most bored and unimpressed face, to which he returned a smidgeon of a smile – just enough that Frankie felt a slight connection which piqued her interest. And then he spotted her guitar sticking out from behind the desk.

'Do you have a name, or . . . ?' he asked.

'Yes. Frankie,' she replied.

'You sing?'

'Yes, in a band. A *real* band,' she said, smirking.

He returned her smirk with one of his own. But his said, *You know nothing, little girl.* Frankie squirmed a bit.

'Okay, I'm going in. James will be along in half an hour, so he'll miss the first couple, but do bring him in as soon as he gets here,' Geoff said to the girls, before turning back to Frankie. 'James is the label head, Can you bring him a coffee or whatever he wants when he arrives? He likes to feel pampered. He's a bit precious.'

She nodded, looking back at the message she'd drafted.

> Doc! Nice to hear from you, yep, let's def catch up sometime.

Too vague, no action required. But if she requested a specific meet-up – what if he didn't reply? Could she take it? What if he did reply but didn't want to meet? What if he did reply and did want to and then what? Was it a date? She wasn't sure catching up as a 'friend' was really a great idea.

> Hey, sure. What you up to later? Got time today after work.

She deleted the smiley face.

Then deleted the part about work. It needed more allure . . .

'Hi,' said a pretty girl in grey sweats with mid-length

straight brown hair pulled back in a ponytail. She was the perfect canvas waiting to be girl-banded.

The doors were open, and the queue was titanic. This was going to be a long day with a lot of sunken dreams.

Frankie handed the girl a form to fill out, nodded for her to take a pencil and take a seat in the large waiting area. Next up, a tall, lean, black girl in a charcoal cotton dress and sneakers. *Kinda cool*, Frankie thought, handing her the form. Next, a girl much like the first, grey sweats – *was it actually the first one again?* She looked over to the waiting area to see first girl filling out the form whilst stretching her leg on the practice bar. No, this was a new girl. *Uncanny*. Then she looked down the queue. *Christ, they're all almost the same. What is this record company looking for? It's like they had the whole menu and only ordered the fucking chicken.*

After about an hour, with no sign of the crowd thinning, a man in a suit appeared through the automatic doors. He was handsome in an older dude kind of way. The kind of guy who works out. Who drinks smoothies. Definitely cycles in some middle-aged man group on the weekends. *Probably has some woman somewhere who whips him for 200 quid an hour*, thought Frankie smugly.

'Hi there. James Falls,' he announced with a broad grin in a thick New York accent. 'Where do I have to go?'

Frankie's eyes peered sulkily up through her lashes; she felt compelled to lay her opinion of this whole nightmare on thick. 'Hi James,' she said – familiar, brazen – 'you need to be down the hall, studio one. Oh, and your friend said that, apparently, you like to feel pampered. So, can I get you a coffee, because I don't do massages?'

James flinched a moment, before laughing. 'Damn Geoff,' he muttered. 'Yeah, I'd love a coffee. Black, please . . . And your name if I might ask?'

'Frankie Rose Taylor.'

'Well, nice to meet you, Frankie,' he replied, amused. 'So, down the hall, studio one. Not auditioning today, then?'

'I'm actually busy for the rest of my life,' she said playfully, pretending to arrange the audition forms.

He nodded at her, tapping on the counter with a grin, and then headed off down the hall, the auditionees craning their necks and whispering among themselves. There he went – the man who held their futures in his hand.

There was a part of her that was enjoying watching the inner goings-on of the pop industry in action. Here was an audition for one of the biggest record labels in the world, happening in her studio, and in attendance a couple of the industry's biggest talent scouts, with the ability to change a life with the tick of pen . . . *Hang on.*

Frankie sat back in her seat. This was a goddamn gift. How could she have been so daft? She sat for a minute letting the weight of the situation dawn on her. She was at her mum's work, she couldn't cause any chaos or do anything silly, her mum was way too excited about this to do anything to embarrass her. *But then.* Nope. She had to do something.

She quickly stood up, putting a *back in five minutes* sign on the reception desk, much to the irritation of typical girl no. 107 who was next in line. She went to the kitchen to make Mr James Falls a coffee, and while she waited for the machine to warm up, she pulled out her phone, deleting her draft message to Doc, and googled James Falls.

Owner, Falls Records. Image after image of him with a huge array of artists – mainly pop, but lots of surprisingly interesting-looking bands, particularly from when he was younger. There was even a picture of him with Kathleen Hanna of Bikini Kill.

Okay, now I'm impressed.

Frankie quickly poured three coffees, put them on a tray and walked by one of the ushers, whispering, 'You'll have to take over on reception for a minute, I'm needed in the studio.'

She sashayed confidently down the hall, waiting outside the doors until the next hopeful emerged, nervous, jittery, excited. Frankie threw a pitying look her way, just to mess with her, and pushed her way in.

She marched confidently down to the table where James sat with Geoff and another younger man who smiled as she approached. *Three men in suits.* Just as she'd predicted to her mother all those weeks ago. She put the tray down on the table and audaciously pulled up a chair to join them, plonking down right next to James, who glanced over at her, surprised, but didn't stop her. What could he say, really? She was just taking a look.

‘Mind if I watch?’ Frankie asked.

‘Knock yourself out, kid,’ James replied, a smirk on his face. ‘Just don’t say anything,’ he added, before looking at her again with a kind of fatherly eye roll, ‘or do anything.’

In front, sheets of paper, head shots, scribbles, a pack of cigarettes, a zippo and a box of tissues (for the ones who get overly emotional). Next to them, a guy with a camera was loading a new drive, and adjusting the tripod height.

‘How’s it going?’ Frankie asked brazenly.

Geoff looked across at her, amused, before sighing. ‘It’s going,’ he replied, then turned to the usher by the door, ‘Send the next one in.’

They like me. They fucking like me. Because they know I’m real, Frankie thought, stretching her neck and settling into her seat.

In came seventeen-year-old Samantha Miller from Chiswick: ballet, tap, modern, grade four piano. She introduced herself, cleared her throat, and belted out ‘I Kissed a Girl’ by Katy Perry. *Good Christ on Earth.* Frankie was embarrassed for Samantha, for music, for feminism.

‘What do you think?’ she whispered to Geoff out of the side of her mouth.

‘Shhh,’ he said, side-eyeing her. After a brief pause, he turned to her and whispered back, ‘What do you think?’

‘I’m not sure what you’re aiming for,’ she said. ‘Is it for girls, women, men? Help me out here with the target audience, because right now, it looks like, I dunno, Christian virgins from Richmond with a side of cut-price Kylie from Grimsby.’

'How did you get to be so fucking gobby?' Geoff asked, unable to hide his grin.

Emboldened by this unusually endearing description of herself, Frankie went for it. 'If you want a real girl band, I mean, I could show you what one's like.'

'You could, could you?' he replied dubiously, as Samantha finished her song, and stood breathlessly, staring at James, then the young A&R guy and then Geoff, the anticipation palpable.

'Thanks, Samantha!' Frankie said.

'I wasn't sure if that song would be too edgy,' Samantha said, unaware Frankie was an imposter.

'Thank you very much, Samantha,' James jumped in, glaring at Frankie. 'I think,' he went on, looking towards Geoff and the other dude, trying to gauge their feelings, 'yes, I think we'd like you to report through to studio two for the next round.'

Samantha closed her eyes. 'Thank you so very much,' she said, letting out a huge breath and clasping her hands together as if in prayer.

'I thought so,' Frankie said to Geoff, whose eyes narrowed on her.

'Frankie, isn't it?' James said curtly. 'What you're doing. It's not cute.'

Frankie was taken aback. 'Oh, I'm not trying to be cute,' she said, rattled, 'I just thought, you know, *you* –' she looked to Geoff, '– would have better taste than this.'

James looked over to Geoff, and sent a *get this girl out of here* look his way. Frankie had pushed it too far. But Geoff was intrigued and nodded to Jeff as if to say *give me a minute, here.*

'What's so amusing to you?' he probed.

'Nothing,' she replied.

'You think you can do better?' he asked.

All or nothing.

'No, I think *you* can,' she replied.

'Which is what, your band?'

'Yes.'

'And who is your band?'

'We're Seven. We're awesome. We're a real girl band. We all play. We write our own songs. And no man was involved in the making of us,' Frankie declared, pushing out the image of Doc that involuntarily appeared in her head. *Okay, maybe he was the initial inspiration, but that was it.*

Geoff raised his eyebrows at James and then looked back to Frankie. 'All right, well, I'll do you a deal. You get in front of us today and sing a song and I'll come see your band - what are they called?'

'Seven.'

'Seven.'

'Sing you a song?' Frankie's lip curled.

'Yeah, choose a song from our song sheet and sing us a song.'

'I only sing punk rock,' she said defiantly.

'Well, that's my offer.'

'This is dumb. Why don't you just come and see my band

sometime?' Frankie said, standing up, pulling on her skirt, feeling suddenly self-conscious. 'Give me the bloody song sheet. I'll see if there's anything tolerable on there.'

She caught James glaring at Geoff, who was trying to placate him. 'Just, let's see,' he whispered to James. 'Be great to have someone a bit lippy in the line-up.'

'I heard that. I'm not going to be in your girl band,' she said, huffing. 'This is blackmail, but I'll do it.'

'Show me how you perform now. Then maybe I'll listen to your demo, check out your tracks, all that shit – and then, if I like it, and if I've finished watching reruns of *The West Wing*, I'll come and see you play. Deal?'

'Deal,' replied Frankie, before she could stop herself.

CHAPTER 17

Baggage

'Oh my God, what did you do?' Haruna asked, securing the buttons on her parka, and pulling her scarf tight around her neck.

They were sitting outside Wick Rooms, waiting. Frankie was pirouetting down the length of the brick wall that ran along the pavement by the front of the building, her voice rowdy with excitement. Haruna sat perched on the stairs directly in front of the door. Cheq had been kindly dropping her home from practice when he was free, but tonight he was a little late.

Practice had been draining that day. Frankie had come in all boisterous because of what had happened at the dance studio, and of course, if Frankie was excited, everyone had to be. Even if it was the last thing Haruna felt like being today. She was struggling. Frankie had arrived armed with song sheets and some vague thing that might have been the start of a couple of original songs. The rehearsal had been a shambles, Frankie jumping from one idea to another, and Aimee was stressing about school work.

All that, and the band seemed to have no direction. It was frustrating Haruna.

'I said to the dude that I would audition, but that he had to come see our band.'

This was pure Frankie. Anyone else would have shown some shadow of fear or nervousness, or even just known their fucking place in this situation.

'Hang on.' Haruna's eyes widened. 'You did what?'

'Well, mostly I think I misfired, and was a little, um, arrogant,' Frankie said with a vague hint of self-awareness, 'but if you'd seen the girls auditioning, and seen the depressed and very bored faces of the dudes on the panel thing, you'd have intervened for the good of women, and music, everywhere.'

'The more feminist thing to do would be to support your fucking sisters,' Haruna remarked. 'They're just trying to do something, just like us. Just a different something.'

Frankie was all for women coming first when she was an underdog, but as soon as she got a leg up, she forgot about the injustices against which she'd railed the day before. It drove Haruna mad.

'I know, I know,' Frankie said. 'I've had to be around that pretty, sparkly, girlie shit all my life so you know me, I can't stand it.'

'*I know, I know*,' Haruna mimicked her. 'But cool, so you auditioned. What did you have to do?'

'Oh my God, it was hilarious. I had to choose from a song sheet and I only knew the words to two of the songs.'

'No.'

'Yes. I mean, do *you* know all the words to Katy Perry or Demi Lovato, or bloody anything by Ariana Grande, cos I sure as shit don't.'

'What did you sing?'

'Belinda Carlisle,' Frankie said, shamefaced. 'Heaven is a fucking place on fucking earth. I'm not proud. Dad has the record, so I know it off by heart. And, get this, do you remember that dance routine we learned to that Justin Timberwank track "Rock Your Body" back, like, a hundred years ago? I did that.'

Frankie jumped down off the wall with a thud and started performing the very passé dance moves they'd learned together all those years back. 'Remember? You were in front and I had to sashay round? Do you remember? Then we went down for the floor bit?'

Haruna threw back her head and burst into laughter. 'Oh hell, no,' she cried, 'that is hilarious. I wish it was taped.'

'It was.'

'Oh my God.'

'What the hell they did say?'

'No comment on the dance routine, which was, of course, totally on point. They said my voice suited the song. Husky, they said. That it was clear I'd had no training,' Frankie said, pouting her lips with faux pride, 'which I'm not sure was exactly a compliment, but I think we all know I can't sing, so—'

'You *can* sing,' Haruna said. Frankie had never had training, that much was true, but she was easily the better singer of the three of them and without question the most confident performer.

'So he's coming, this Geoff guy then, to our next gig?'

'Yep,' Frankie said proudly. 'Well, he wants to hear a demo first. So, you know, we're going to have to figure that bit out. Anyway, he's not just some dickhead record label dude: he once nearly managed The Smiths.'

'No way.'

'Way. He told me. He didn't seem that into the girl band he was putting together; I think he might just like us,' Frankie went on, nodding. 'And the other guy, James, said I reminded him of his daughter. I don't think he liked me, honestly, but still. I was totally in charge.'

'That's great, Frankie,' Haruna said, her laughter running off, feeling the sink in her heart that had been coming in waves lately.

'So, I guess we need a "next gig",' Frankie said with mischief. 'And that demo. Basically, we've got a lot to do in the next couple of months.'

'Couple of months?'

'Yes. You see, I need this band to take off so Aimee doesn't go to med school and you don't run off to Japan. Or Bristol. Or both.'

'You really think we can take this band somewhere?' Haruna said, frowning. 'I put a lot into it, Frankie. I lie to my mum. I sneak around. I practise hard. I don't want to do all that if you're just trying to hook up with a dude.'

'No no. I'm not doing the Doc thing any more,' Frankie said, unconvincingly.

Just at that moment Cheq pulled up. The car was new; he'd made a bit of money in the last few months gigging. Things were starting to get serious for his music, and although he'd been busy, there was always enough time to pick Haruna up and drop her home after practice.

Haruna hadn't learned to drive yet – her mother refused to pay for lessons and Greg's strange offer to teach her made her ... uncomfortable. Frankie, on the other hand, had refused to learn. 'I can't trust myself behind a wheel, it's too much pressure. I'd definitely kill someone,' was her standard response. *Driving lessons*, Haruna thought. It was another thing to tackle when she finally got out.

Haruna leapt up, a shot of relief coursing through her at seeing Cheq's face. He waved at her through the windscreen.

There was something that had changed since *that* night. Haruna had floated home ten feet off the ground, drunk on intimacy and sweet vulnerability. But now, memories of the awkward gentleness of their night together – when she had finally slept with him – were no longer intoxicating. As that delicious haze lifted, she could remember everything clearly and now she felt weirdly exposed.

'I have a few ideas for a gig, anyway,' Frankie was saying, while Haruna stood uneasily on the kerb, wondering if Cheq would get out and give her a hug. Instead, he leaned across the seat and pushed open the passenger door.

'Get in! We gotta get going,' he said sharply, reaching out to help her in, and then pulling her across the front seat for a kiss.

'I said we'd drop Frankie home. Last time, I promise. She's moving to Peckham.'

'Ahh ... Okay, no worries,' he said, nodding to Frankie. 'Jump in. I'm going to have to drive fast.'

'Is it okay?' Haruna said uneasily. 'I don't want to be a pain.'

'It's fine,' Cheq replied, shaking his head, then leaning over to rub her leg. 'It's okay, babe. Sorry, I'm just running late.'

Haruna relaxed a little at his touch, and they pulled out, down the back streets of Hackney Wick, and over Lea Bridge Road into Hackney proper.

Outside, winter showed no signs of shaking. Victoria Park looked grim, baron, leafless, damp, muddy and empty save for a few brave joggers and dog walkers. Haruna found the gloom weirdly comforting, as though the segue from outside to her home was less dramatic. Gloom to doom, stark to dark, cold to ... lonely.

'Moving to Peckham, huh?' Cheq said to Frankie.

'Yup. Can't wait,' she replied. 'I'm just so excited to have actual *freedom* at last.'

Haruna swung her head and glared over her shoulder at Frankie. 'Yeah, cos you're so oppressed.'

Frankie frowned at Haruna, before leaning forward and offering a pitying hand on her shoulder and a light squeeze. Haruna shrugged her hand off gently, turning back to look out of the window.

'What you doing later?' Cheq said, looking into the rear-view mirror. 'Wanna come see some grime?'

Since the gig at the bingo hall, Cheq and Frankie had gone from aloof, distant frenemies united only in their cool dislike for each other to this new, polite and cheerful kind of *friendship*. It was really starting to irk Haruna who, as it turned out, preferred the solid predictability of their cold war.

'Where are you playing?' Frankie asked, an irritating lift in her voice.

'The Box. Brixton. I can put you on the door?' Cheq replied.

'That would be awesome. And I'm actually not working tomorrow either. Yeah, why not? I'll come. Will I know anyone?'

'Maybe,' he said, turning the corner into Frankie's street a little fast, causing them all to swing in their seats.

'Whoa there,' Frankie joked.

Haruna continued to stare out of the window, as the afternoon slipped away into evening, although it was barely 5 p.m. She had plenty to do the next day. She had a History essay due on the War of the Roses. She had to finish a tedious English assignment – to write a poem that explored themes of pain and loss – *thanks a lot, Keats*. And she also definitely needed an early night, because she was inexplicably exhausted. But she couldn't shake the fear of missing out.

'I could come?' she said.

'Haruna, you can't come. How? It's a week night,' Frankie said.

'Don't be mad, love. You can come another time,' Cheq said, with a firm tone. 'It's not worth it.'

'No, I'm going to come,' Haruna said decidedly. 'I'll sneak out. I've done it before.'

'Haruna – I don't think that's wise,' Frankie said, gently this time.

'Really?' Haruna said with a healthy dose of attitude. 'And why's that?'

Frankie was silent for a moment. 'Um ... because, you've got school and also ... Greg, your mum ... ?'

'Oh, yeah. Sorry, I forgot for a moment,' Haruna replied sharply.

Cheq leaned over and rubbed her leg again, and this time it didn't feel comforting.

'Don't do that,' she snapped at him, 'don't try to shut me down.'

'Shut you down?' Cheq said, with half a laugh. 'What's going on?'

'I'm going to come, okay? I want my name on the door,' she said, knowing it sounded childish. 'Shall we go together, Frankie? I can be out by nine, I reckon.'

'Ru ... ' Cheq protested, as he pulled up outside Frankie's estate.

Frankie didn't move. 'Haruna, are you okay?'

'Yeah, I'm fine. Shall we meet at the tube?'

'Sure,' Frankie said, shrugging. 'As you like, Rooney.'

It was a fleeting glance as Cheq's eyes lifted and met Frankie's in the rear-view mirror. A brief but meaningful look, which made Haruna feel even more alone.

'Let's go,' she said as the car door closed and Frankie walked off through the gates of her building, glancing back over her shoulder briefly.

'Haruna, *are* you okay?' Cheq turned to her, concerned.

'Fine,' she said, staring out of the window.

'Since the other night ...' Cheq's voice ran off for a moment, and Haruna knew where he was heading. 'Do you wish we didn't? Do you regret it or something?'

'No,' Haruna said quietly. Flashbacks of their night together still filled her with intense pleasure, her quiet, untouchable secret that she lay with in the isolation of her room, reliving over and over, warming her inside. 'It's not that. It's just this whole thing at home. It grinds me down sometimes ...' She nodded towards her house.

'You're nearly there,' he said. 'And if it's too much – you could live with me. I'd love it.'

'Live with you?' she said, confused by the suggestion.

'Yeah, wouldn't you like that?'

'Ah, um ...' Haruna searched her feelings. 'I don't think that's an option.'

'Well, it is, actually,' he said, shrugging.

'Look, I'm fine,' Haruna said sharply. One part of her understood that Cheq was being practical, but the idea made her feel panicky. Shouldn't she want this? Isn't this what she's supposed to want? *Why, since the night that I slept with him, do I feel like he's suddenly not doing anything right? He is exactly the same. What do I actually want here? From him?*

'I'm not going to hassle you any more,' he said, 'so if you're really fine then—'

'Good,' she interrupted, before adding as brightly as she could, 'I really am fine.'

Cheq pulled up at the end of her street and sat quietly while Haruna got her things together. She was moving slowly, waiting for him to say something, but she didn't know what she wanted to hear. He sat there with a puzzled look, his brow furrowed, hands fixed firmly on the gear stick and steering wheel. He didn't speak.

Haruna looked at him once more. 'See you later on, then?'

He pursed his lips for a moment, opened his mouth to speak before he let out a huge sigh. 'Yes,' he said, shaking his head, 'yeah, okay, I'll see you later.'

'You don't want me to come?' Haruna said, her voice tight and ridged.

'Of course I do,' he said with a stiff smile. 'Text me when you're on your way and I'll meet you outside. I just don't want you to get into shit with your mum or something. You're nearly there, you'll be free soon.'

'Okay,' she said, stepping out on to the street, a flash of

anger shooting through her at those words, *you'll be free.* 'See you later, Cheq.'

She didn't look back as she turned towards her house, a feeling of bubbling anger coursing through her. A few steps later, when she was sure he'd driven away, she swung her school bag hard against the fence. A loud, satisfying *thwack* rang out.

It felt good. She was exhausted from the quiet, oppressed rage inside her longing to be free. *Free.*

She came to her house, Greg's car sitting just outside, and reached into her pocket for her keys. She pulled them out and selected the long, thick front-door key, fixing it between her thumb and forefinger. Then she walked over to Greg's car and held the key hard against the red paint.

The satisfaction of gouging a deep line round the circumference of his car was overwhelming. She stood for a moment, looking at the result. A silvery-white wavy line caught the light of the street lamp above. She smiled and turned towards the front door, blowing off the flecks of red paint on her key, her heart pounding in her chest.

CHAPTER 18

Bad Girl

Frankie stood under the light of the Bethnal Green tube sign. It was 8:55 p.m. and blowing a gale. She hugged herself as the wind whipped up, sending some papers into a whirlwind in front of her. They trailed off into the sky, catching the light of the street lamps before blowing down towards the church on the corner. Frankie leaned down and picked one up. *Let Jesus be Your Guide*, it read, with a cartoon Jesus standing in a dark alley lighting up the way ahead with his halo.

'Jesus looks creepy,' she said under her breath.

Moments later, Haruna came running up the street, breathless, her cheeks red and her hair wet and flowing out behind her. She was coming fast and heavy; her bag was secured on her shoulder by one hand but was flapping awkwardly behind her, her arms were stiff, she was slightly on her toes, and just ahead of Frankie she stumbled, fell to the footpath, landing on her palms. The fall looked hard, but Haruna was up in an instant.

'Quick,' she said, 'let's go!'

'You run like a broken robot,' Frankie remarked, as Haruna brushed the dirt and tiny grey stones from her palms, and yanked Frankie towards the tube entrance.

When they were inside, Haruna reached into her bag and pulled out four tiny, one-serve bottles of Baileys, eyes darting left and right nervously.

'What the hell?'

'I just grabbed the first thing I saw.'

'From where?'

'The shop,' Haruna said, pulling Frankie down the second set of stairs into the ticket area. 'Let's go.'

'You nicked it?' Frankie said, a thrill coursing through her. She looked at her friend, pink-cheeked, breathless, and was just a little impressed. 'Haruna, what's going on with you?'

'Shhh. Let's go,' she said again.

'How did you get out of the house?'

'I snuck out. A bit precarious really as they're up late tonight.'

'Oh shit.'

'I don't care. If I get caught, who gives a toss?'

Frankie sighed. 'Okay, Ru.' She placed her oyster card on the reader and walked through the gates, before stopping suddenly to look back at her friend.

'Ru, do you have any money?'

'Yep,' she replied firmly, before adding, 'We'll never be able to do this again, you know.'

'Do what?' Frankie said, in a panic.

'Meet at the tube and go out.'

'Why?'

'Cos you'll be in Peckham.'

'Oh.' Frankie sighed. 'Are you feeling abandoned?'

'What?' Haruna shook her head. 'No. I'm just saying, you'll be in Peckham and we won't be able to go places together any more because . . . you'll be in Peckham.'

'Okay, but it's not the moon. I'm just south of the river. All my friends are still in Hackney.'

'Yeah, I guess.' Haruna shrugged.

Frankie tried to keep her cool as she watched Haruna fish two crumpled twenty-pound notes from her coat pocket and fumble with the ticket machine. There was something really amiss here. *She's stealing?* Haruna joined her through the barriers and they headed down the escalator. Frankie bit her lip, and decided now was not the time to confront her. She needed somehow to distract Haruna from whatever was going on. And she knew the perfect deflection.

'So, Doc texted me.'

'What?' The old Haruna, with her comforting yet disapproving glare, appeared almost instantly. 'You did what?'

'I didn't do anything – he texted me!'

'Oh man. When?'

'After the party.'

'What did it say?'

'Let's have a drink some time, signed *Doc* with a little kiss,' Frankie said with all the composure she could muster.

Haruna's eyes widened, unscrewing the top off one of the mini Baileys. 'That idiot. What are you gonna do? Did you reply?'

'Not yet. Dunno what I'm going to do,' Frankie said coolly, downing her sickly, sweet drink in one go. 'Christ, that's bloody sweet.'

'Frankie, I'm impressed you didn't reply yet. Did you *really* not reply? Hmm, maybe a bit sickly, yes,' she said, licking the Baileys off her lips.

'*Really*. I'm a picture of self-restraint, as my mother would say.' Frankie grinned. 'I have to say, I'm kind of enjoying stringing him along a bit. There's a certain power in not replying, isn't there? Holding something back. I have this vision of him sitting at home staring at his phone wondering if I've read the message, eating ice cream, watching *Riverdale*, stressing over if should he send another text, that kind of thing.'

Haruna laughed. 'Well, I'm proud of you.'

Frankie was amazed how easy the lying came. I mean, it wasn't all a lie, she hadn't replied ... *as such*.

Earlier that day, she'd in fact bumped into Doc outside Wick Rooms. It was their first spontaneous encounter since Seven started practising there.

He was carrying his guitar into the building just as she arrived with her own. He was looking even more thin and stooped than usual. His hair was freshly dyed black and spiked up like Robert Smith, a smear of black eyeliner making his skin appear sallow and drawn. Frankie momentarily fantasised about taking him for a sausage sandwich and a cup of sweet tea.

'Doc,' she called out, just as he was about to disappear into the front door.

'Hey, Frankie,' he said with a touch of frost. He flicked the tail end of what was likely a joint into the gutter. 'I wasn't sure if you got my text?'

'Oh. Yeah. I totally forgot you messaged me. I'm such an ass. Sorry I didn't reply,' Frankie said quickly, the usual verbal cascade of lies and bravado tumbling out of her mouth unabated. 'Things have been super busy, getting ready for recording. You know. Trying to focus. Write a great single. That kind of thing. So busy. No time for anything right now. So much to do.'

'Recording? Where?'

'Not sure yet,' she said airily.

'Really. Wow. Who's paying?'

'Oh, we are. But it's just a demo,' she said, tripping up slightly before correcting herself. 'We've been asked for a demo.'

'Yeah?'

'Yeah,' she said, trying not to smile too much, 'do you know Falls Records?'

'Falls Records? Of course I do. Everyone knows them,' he

said, somewhat wearily. Frankie sensed a touch of disbelief in his voice.

'Of course, sorry, I'm just so new to all this,' she said coyly, trying to pull back. But she couldn't help herself. 'They're coming to our next gig.'

Doc rested his guitar down on the edge of the stairs, holding it by the neck. 'Falls Records are coming to your next gig? Like, to see you?'

'Yep,' Frankie replied, flicking her fringe out of her eyes, fixed eyes, defiant.

'Which is where?'

'The Roundhouse.'

'You're playing at the Roundhouse?'

Frankie shrugged. 'We're supporting another band, can't remember the name.'

'Well, that's cool,' he said, his eyes narrowing. 'Making waves, Frankie. Always knew you would.'

There was a moment. His eyes lingered on hers. She felt a tingle down her spine. He looked *interested.* Like, properly, though. That was the undeniable look of a guy who was into a girl.

He glanced up at the door of the building, contemplating something for a moment. 'I have to get going. The band are waiting for me. You gonna go for that drink or what?'

'Sure. Text me,' she said teasingly, before tapping his arm. 'I promise to reply this time.'

By the time she got into the practice room she felt sick with excitement. Maybe he really was interested again. She skipped through the door towards room 3.

But it was the band that was mostly on her mind. She was, in truth, starting to live for Tuesdays and Thursdays, and practising was starting to be . . . rewarding? She smiled to herself. *Who are you and what have you done with Frankie?*

Now Frankie toyed with the edge of her black leather skirt. She'd found it at a charity shop off Brick Lane for 50p and had cut it very short and a bit crooked. As they disembarked at Brixton she tried to pull it down as much as possible over her wild-rose patterned tights. Sometimes she felt a little self-conscious next to Haruna, who was wearing her usual conservative boots and jeans, with a long green parka, but as they neared the venue – she unzipped the parka and slipped it off. Underneath Haruna was wearing a massive, oversized black singlet as a dress, with a dark red lace bra completely visible under her arms.

'Oooh, you look a bit racy,' Frankie observed; it was yet another slightly out-of-character step for her friend.

'Best I could do at home. This is Greg's.' She giggled, holding on to the strap of the singlet. 'Classic black wife beater's.'

Frankie didn't laugh.

As they neared the club, they spotted Cheq standing by the door with a couple of his friends. Frankie nodded her head his way, noticing the loving but concerned look on his face when he saw Haruna shivering in her skimpy get-up. As they approached, she realised one of the friends he was talking to was . . . Jules.

'You made it.' Jules smiled, and for a moment Frankie thought he was referring to Haruna, who was already wrapped around Cheq. *Still gross*, she thought, despite the fact her cold dislike of Cheq had warmed to more of a tepid appreciation.

Nope. Jules meant *her*.

'Cheq said you might come,' he explained. 'Good to see you.'

'Hi, Jules. *Strange*. I didn't know *you* were going to be here,' Frankie said, shooting Cheq a furious look.

'Oh,' Jules replied, momentarily confused. 'Shit. Sorry. This wasn't a thing. I didn't ask Cheq . . . '

For a fleeting moment, Frankie was disappointed it wasn't his idea. He pulled a grim face, shaking his head and staring at the ground.

'No worries. It's really cool to see you again.' She punched him on the shoulder, a gesture meant to be a relaxed and casual but which turned out to be a bit rough. Now it was Frankie's turn to cringe.

'So, the Wick Rooms soirée was fun.' She wasn't entirely sure how their adventure at the party ended. 'I hope I behaved?' She seemed to recall a joint? Perhaps he walked her to a taxi? It was fuzzy.

'Mostly,' he said with a grin. 'You were fun.'

'Shall we go in and grab a drink?' he asked. He looked different today, in a deep navy hoodie, and a cap pulled down over his slightly wavy hair. Older, maybe.

Frankie drew in a breath. She was going to have to endure this or leave. She looked over at Cheq, who raised both his eyebrows and smiled. *Wanker.*

Haruna, on the other hand, buzzing on stolen Baileys, was already heading inside the tiny venue to get another drink. Cheq followed her in and they resumed their nauseating, loved-up position against the bar. Thank God he would be playing soon and Haruna could at least hang with her.

'Fancy one?' Jules asked, pulling his wallet out of his back pocket. Frankie was annoyed, but not so annoyed she couldn't accept a free drink. She was burning through the money this month again. A few morning shifts at the dance studio weren't going to buy her independence any time soon.

'Vodka tonic?'

'Sure.' He turned to the bar and while he was distracted she scanned the room for anything more interesting, but they were pinned up against the bar, and visibility was at a minimum. The room was already crammed with people and someone was working overtime with the smoke machines.

'So, tell me properly about your band, then,' Frankie said dutifully as Jules handed her a drink. 'Haruna says you're quite good. What are you called?'

'Giants of Earth ...' He paused for a moment, looking, perhaps, for a hint of recognition in her eyes. She gave him nothing. 'Anyway, we've been together since school, so a couple of years now. Three years, really.'

'Oh yeah?' Frankie said, glancing at Haruna who seemed

to be having a slightly heated discussion with Cheq. 'What kind of music?'

'*Pitchfork* called us Psychopop,' he said, shrugging. 'It's guitar music, at any rate.'

'*Pitchfork*?' Frankie said, momentarily impressed. 'You're getting proper reviews?'

'Yeah,' he laughed, a bit embarrassed, 'it's starting to take off a bit, I suppose.'

'Will you record an album or something?'

'Yeah, we're just about to do an EP, actually. We signed to a great indie label in June, so that's pretty much our focus now. They're arranging it, so we're just knuckling down writing songs and getting ready for that. It's pretty exciting, really. Our manager, Tony, he arranged it.'

'How did you get a manager?'

'Oh, he approached us. After a gig.'

'Right,' Frankie replied, frustrated, but not to be outdone, 'we're speaking to some potential managers at the moment too.'

'Really?' said Jules, surprised. 'That's great. And *fast*. I loved the punk bingo gig, by the way.'

'You did?' she replied, dubious.

'Yeah, so fun. So much energy. You're a great front person. Covers or not.'

'Thanks,' Frankie said, feeling flattered and then in turn feeling irritated that he could make her blush so easily. 'Yeah, it was fun.'

'I think you're really great.'

'Yeah, I know we're good,' she said with all the bravado she could muster, 'we've already been told that by Falls Records.'

'Really?' Jules said with a half-smile. 'Well, that's impressive. Are you guys going to record a demo yourselves or something soon? I take it you've got originals? It's not all just punk Chuck Berry?'

'Yes, we have originals,' she lied, remembering Geoff's request for a demo. She decided to do a little digging. 'Of course we do. We're recording at some point soon; it's just all about timing, you know. It's so busy right now.'

'Sure, I get it,' he replied, nodding his head again and biting his lip as if to suppress a laugh. She downed the vodka tonic, trying to swallow her embarrassment at the little lies that kept coming. Especially since he could clearly tell she was just making shit up.

'So where are *you* guys recording?' she asked. 'And who's paying for it?'

'The label,' he said. 'It's going to be at a small studio in Hackney, actually.'

'Do you know how much it costs?'

'What, recording a few tracks?'

'Yeah. Like, is it super expensive?'

'No idea. The label takes care of it all. I mean, I probably should know since we have to pay it back eventually.'

'Huh.' She nodded, her mind starting to buzz. 'What's the studio called?'

'People call it The Church,' he said. 'What about you guys – got your next gig booked? I'd love to come see you again.'

'Oh, we're looking to book some soon,' she said.

'Well, if you need any help, like a support slot with us or something – I know how hard it is to get off the ground – just give me a shout.'

Jules had clearly first-hand information on the band from Haruna and Cheq. She hated that he knew *exactly* where they were at. It was bad enough that Cheq knew, but how could she create the appearance of a band on the rise when some people knew they weren't.

'Um, we're cool. Just sifting through offers,' she lied. Jules continued to nod his head at her, seeming to suppress a slight smile or something. She knew her exaggerations were pointless and silly but she couldn't stop them coming. She looked over at him again, and couldn't help but break into a smile of her own, and before long they were both laughing.

'We're really hot right now,' she said, giggling, 'haven't you heard of us?'

'Well, if you don't talk yourself up, no one else will,' he said, echoing her dad.

'That's what I keep saying!' said Frankie.

'Another drink?' Jules asked.

'Um, maybe,' she said, suddenly remembering the whole night was a set-up and returning to feeling annoyed again. Although, maybe a little less so. 'Yeah, okay why not.'

A few moments later, Cheq stepped on stage and there was

a huge surge of people to the front of the room. The lights went down and the venue plunged into darkness.

'What town you from?' said Cheq, over the mic.

'BRIXTON!' shouted the crowd.

'What town you from?'

'BRIXTON!'

The venue was tight, and purpose built for watching the performers. The stage was pretty tiny, but Cheq didn't need much – just his decks and a mic. As the lights flashed back on, the beat kicked in, and a drunken Haruna slipped in next to Frankie.

'He's amazing,' shouted Frankie over the noise.

'He's controlling,' Haruna replied, swaying backwards, she'd got drunk so quickly.

'What? What's he done?' Frankie shot back.

'He tries to control everything. Don't go out. Pick me up. Take me here. Drop me there. Have me. It's suffocating.'

'What?' Frankie said, confused. 'What are you on about? He didn't want you to come in case you got in trouble.' Truly, something was up with this girl.

'I should go in thirty, okay?' Haruna said, suddenly appearing drawn and tired.

'Are you okay?' Frankie asked as Jules considerately stepped out of earshot.

'Fine. Just . . . ' Haruna shrugged. She looked defeated. 'How's it going with Jules, then? He's so much better than Doc. Frankie, you so gotta give him a chance. Just because he likes you doesn't mean there's something wrong with him.'

'Oh, shut up,' Frankie said.

'Are you coming with me? Or Staying,' Haruna continued, holding on to Frankie's arm to help steady herself.

Frankie looked over at Jules who was bobbing his head to the music. He looked back at her and they locked eyes for a fleeting moment and he smiled at her. She found herself involuntarily smiling back and feeling an undeniable connection before she looked away. Something had definitely shifted, but there was still something holding her back. She longed for the brooding, moody, enigmatic mystery of Doc. She needed to scratch that itch.

And one thing was undeniable: she hated being predictable, and being told what to do, and dating Jules was literally doing what she was being told to do. By everyone.

She pulled herself away from his gaze, feeling her own resistance for a moment as he smiled once more at her. *Jesus, does he do anything but smile?* She turned back to Haruna. 'Yep, no worries. I'll come with you.'

Chapter 19

Kool Thing

'Hi, my name's Frankie. I'm calling on behalf of my . . . self?' Frankie boomed confidently down the phone.

Damn, I should have thought this through.

She panicked when, earlier that day, Geoff from Falls Records had called to say he was leaving town in a few weeks and was waiting to hear from her. Frankie had lied, of course. She'd told him they'd been caught up recording at The Church, and she'd send across the demos next week. Of course, that meant, she now had to actually record at The Church. Her lies all had to become concrete plans, which was intensely motivating, if nothing else.

'You shouldn't be here!' whispered Aimee, pulling her school books towards her and hastily packing away her stuff. 'We'll get in trouble too.'

Frankie was pacing the length of the library study area as

Haruna and Aimee watched on, her big boots thumping on the floor, occasionally stopping to kick the broken radiator at the end by the photocopier. She'd got in by confidently striding past the librarian and despite the crazy get-up of jeans torn to near oblivion, the librarian could only spy the relatively normal black coat and beanie from behind the desk.

Frankie nodded seriously and apologetically at Aimee, mouthing *trust me* before returning to her call at the same volume as before. 'I had a question, not sure if you can help?'

Without a demo, the Falls Records team wouldn't come and see the band, and if this recording studio was good enough for Jules's band, it was good enough for her. And she'd already told Doc there was a demo, so, frankly, it had to happen.

'I'll try,' said a girl's voice. She sounded young, maybe even Frankie's age. 'What were you after?'

'Can you tell me ... I was wondering ... ' She pulled a face across at Haruna who gave her an encouraging nod. 'I was wondering how much is it to come and record a song?'

'How much? Well, there's a few different prices, really. It depends what you're after. What label are you with?'

'No label.'

'Then a demo? It depends. Da—' She stopped for a moment. 'I mean, Mike is quite particular about who he works with and so the prices can vary quite a bit depending on that.'

'But can you give me a vague idea? Is it, like, a million dollars to record a song or closer to a hundred? Like, we're a punk band, so it doesn't need to sound like Ariana Grande or some shit.'

After a brief pause, the girl on the end of the phone laughed. 'Cool. Well, for an afternoon recording it might be, like, around a grand – but that is very rough. As I said, the price can vary as Mike sets the costs depending on the artists.'

'A thousand quid.' Frankie's heart sank and she looked over to the girls, shaking her head. 'Jeez, how can anyone afford that? Most of the bands in my building can't even afford a carton of milk.'

'Ahh, yeah, I know, it's a bit pricey when you're starting out. Have you tried doing the demo yourself? That's what I did. In fact, I still do sometimes. Some of the kit you can get, or at least borrow, can give a near polished finish.'

'I don't have a clue how to do that. Also, it's kinda urgent. This label wants a demo.'

'Ah, congratulations. That's great. Do you want to come and speak to Mike? He's around on Friday afternoon? You never know, he might be able to do you a deal.'

'Uh, like, it would need to be a really good deal,' Frankie said, defeated. She paused for a moment before adding, 'I better see if I can find someone at the practice rooms who can help. Thank you, though.'

'There's another possibility,' the girl said quickly and slightly uneasily, 'if you wanted, like. I'm one of the assistants here, although I *can* run the desk. In downtime we could maybe . . . '

'Record with you? You can do that? You know what you're doing?' Frankie was already in.

'Yes, I'm slow, but it should only take a few evenings.'

'Oh my God, that would be fucking awesome. YES!'

'Well, hang on, I'd need to ask my dad. Mike. Mike who owns the studio is my dad. But I know what I'm doing, and I can get some help from the junior engineer here, but yeah, I'd be up for it. It's practice.'

'What's your name?' Frankie asked.

'Amelie,' she replied, 'and I do kind of know what I'm doing. And I'd love to record some punk.'

'Well, fuck yes!' Frankie bellowed, laughing.

'Shhhhh,' one of the monitors came rushing over with a finger over his lips. 'This is study time, you need to be quiet.'

Frankie put her hand over the phone. 'Chillax. I'm nearly done. Important business call here. One minute, I promise.'

The monitor folded his arms and glared at Frankie. *Stupid nerd*, Frankie thought. *God, I'm glad to be out of this crap hole.*

'Well, why don't you come down tomorrow? I finish school at three and there's no one in the studio. I'll speak to my dad in the meantime. Give me your number and I'll call to confirm.'

'School?'

'Final year.'

'My band is still at school. Where are you at?'

'Hackney College.'

'Ah, they're at City.'

'No judgement.' Amelie giggled. 'Now, your number, please?'

When the call was over Frankie put her phone down on the edge of the table, and looked from Haruna to Aimee and back again, grinning. 'Who wants to record a demo?'

'HOLY shhhhh— Oh my God!' Haruna said, leaping up.

'What?' Aimee's eyes were dancing and Frankie revelled in the excitement.

'We're in!' Frankie said. 'Can you believe it?'

Aimee and Haruna both came around to her side of the table, threw their arms around her, and they all jumped up and down and squealed.

'Final warning!' the monitor barked. 'Or I'll have to tell Miss Judd.'

Haruna quickly stuffed her school books into her bag. 'This is so amazing. But you guys, we need some songs.'

'I mean it! I'll tell Miss Judd, Haruna.'

'We're off, no need to tell Miss Judd,' Frankie mocked him. He balked for a moment, humiliated, before his eyes narrowed on Frankie.

'You're Francesca Taylor. Didn't you leave?'

'Yep. Just leaving,' she smirked, slipping her phone into her back pocket.

'You're not supposed to be in here!' he called after her as they hastily made their way out of the library, pushing through the glass doors and outside.

'We'd better get you out of here,' Haruna said. 'Why did you come to school, you nutter?'

'I thought I'd walk you both to practice,' Frankie said.

As they came out through the school gates, a group of boys huddled around a car that had pulled up by the bus stop. The girls walked past, silent. *Here we go*, thought Frankie.

'A dyke, a freak and a bitch walked into a bar . . . ' Kyle Sunderland said loudly, the other boys snickering along. An empty drink bottle flew over Aimee's head and landed next to the bin beside her.

'Sorry!' one of them called out, clearly not at all sorry, but the girls didn't look back.

'Well, I'm definitely the dyke,' Aimee said, threading her arm through Frankie's.

'Dudes are dicks,' Haruna remarked.

'Do you think I'm the freak?' Frankie asked the others. 'Because I'm very happy with this assessment.'

'Well, I know I'm the bitch,' Haruna said with a moan. 'That loser Kyle is just pissed because I refused to kiss him, like a year ago, and he's been calling me a bitch ever since. What is it with guys? Like, can't I decide who I want to kiss?'

'It's much easier with girls, you guys.'

'Must be, no penises,' Haruna said.

'Well, not real ones, anyway,' Aimee giggled.

'Anyway, forget them. On to more important things. Did you move out yet?'

'Hell yes!' Frankie enthused. 'Dad moved me in on Sunday morning.'

'Oh God, tell us about it,' Aimee said. 'Must be so weird being south of the river.'

'They still speak English,' Frankie joked. 'But seriously, you guys, I have a smallish room on the second floor. The flat isn't just part of a house, it's the whole house – four floors.'

'Wow. So you have a garden?'

'A garden front and back. The kitchen is in the lower-ground then a lounge and bathroom on the second floor. My flatmates are Jesse, he's nineteen and works in construction or something. He leaves at like five thirty every morning. Nira is pretty quiet. He's a chef at a restaurant, but I can't remember where. He's training. It's super posh, I think. Carla says he makes the most amazing test dinners at home so there's that to look forward to.'

'Wow.'

'And Carla is my cousin, or second cousin. Her dad is maybe my great-uncle? Or her granddad. I dunno. Anyway, the place belongs to the family so basically Carla and I are in charge.'

'Do you chip in for food and shit?' Haruna asked.

'No, we all have to buy our own.'

'What about milk?'

'We kind of share that.'

'And bills?'

'They're included, thank God.'

'It sounds great. Man, I can't wait to get out,' Haruna said grimly.

A silence fell between them, as they walked quickly towards the practice studio. The days were getting longer, but no warmer, and Frankie for one was absolutely hanging for summer. A brave cyclist pulled up beside them at the traffic lights, gloves on and hat pulled all the way down over his ears. As the lights changed, a taxi took the sharp corner just in front of them, splashing gutter wash up on Aimee.

'Gross,' Aimee said, breaking the silence. 'Guys, I keep thinking. The main issue we've got is that none of us really know how to write songs.'

'I like the one Frankie wrote. What was it called – "Mother King"?' Haruna said.

'It's okay,' Frankie shrugged, 'but Aimee's right. We need to commit to writing some songs. We need, like, a dozen if we're going to properly gig one day.'

'Well, it's only one song we need, right? For the demo,' Haruna countered.

'Maybe. I don't know. What actually goes on a demo?' Frankie wondered aloud.

'No one is as professional as us,' Aimee laughed, the three of them bursting into fits of giggles.

'Can we ask someone?' Frankie wondered, as they arrived at Wick Rooms and made their way into their practice room, which was ... *a mess.* Their gear was still set up, which was just so much easier. They'd become lazy about putting their stuff back in the storeroom, not to mention food scraps, rubbish, empty bottles – even Aimee had relaxed to the point that she had installed a mini fridge for milk.

'Why don't you call Jules?' Haruna said, unzipping her

school bag and pulling out her sticks. 'He must have had a demo before they got signed. He'll know.'

'Can't you or Cheq ask him?' Frankie whined.

'I probably won't see him this week.' Haruna shrugged.

'Ugh, well, I *can* ask Jules,' Frankie said, sliding her guitar out of its soft case, 'but to be honest, I'm worried about giving him any reason to think I'm interested.'

Haruna coughed, and Aimee giggled, and Frankie looked at them both and shot a double finger. 'You two suck.'

'We see you, that's all,' Aimee said, blowing her a kiss. She picked up her bass and practised a run with the volume down. 'You know, I'm really starting to love playing this. And also, I was watching some amazing bass players – Kim Deal, Kim Gordon – and did you know David Bowie had a woman bass player?'

'I'm literally going to marry this drum kit,' Haruna said, shooting Frankie a loving look. 'Which reminds me . . . '

She leaned into her school bag and pulled out a fifty-pound note. 'Here is my first down payment! Thank you so much.'

'Hey, you didn't need to,' Frankie said, accepting the cash with silent relief. She really needed a proper job. 'Where did you get the money? Cheq?'

'No, no.' Haruna shook her head and gave Frankie a look, before tapping on the toms ominously, *thud, thud, thud, thud.*

'You're stealing off Greg?'

'And Mum. Both. Screw 'em. I found where he keeps his money, the loser. I'm just taking back what I'm owed,' she said, shrugging. 'Anyway, call Jules, ask about the demo! Stop being silly.'

'Okay, okay,' Frankie said.

Haruna shook her head, tapping her sticks on the edge of the tom. 'He's a decent guy, you know. I mean, I know he's not Doc and he might actually treat you like a human being, but . . .'

'I know. He's great,' Frankie said, pouting, 'satisfied?'

'Took you long enough.'

'He's great, but I just can't.' Frankie curled her lip up. 'I don't need to explain myself.'

'Sounds like a Doc-shaped excuse,' Haruna said under her breath, but loud enough for Frankie to hear.

'Christ – can we do this?' Frankie said, turning up her amp to drown out the sound of Haruna's deafening logic.

Chapter 20

Army of Me

Greg sat at the head of the table, as he always did. He cut at his chicken with a heavy hand, the intermittent scrape of his knife cutting through the silence like nails down a blackboard. Her mother sat to his right, opposite Haruna, quietly sipping on water while her eyes remained focused at her plate.

Greg looked a bit like Martin Freeman's Watson. Small, greying and gentle faced. The kind of man who looked like he would take his kids out badger watching or searching for hedgehogs. Except that wasn't Greg.

Between the scraping and the silence in the room was her mother's chesty cough, which was juddering.

Haruna felt nauseous. She wasn't sure if it was the stench of the boiled meat or the fear of being caught that was driving this churning knot in her stomach, but she was struggling to keep from retching. She raised a hand to her forehead and wiped the dampness with the back of her sleeve.

'Those neighbourhood kids set fire to the bin last night,' Greg said, without looking up. His accent was thick, Irish, with a slight American twang from his ten years living in Nevada. Haruna dropped her fork, which crashed to the floor.

'Excuse me,' she said quietly.

'No problem, Haruna,' Greg said, with his strange, broad, pantomime smile. The one he saved especially for her. A smile thick with pretention and condensation and warning. A smile that at ten years old she believed to be open and kind and warm until she discovered it wasn't.

She looked back down at her chicken, the flesh pulling back from the bone, the fatty, limp skin hanging off the edge of the thigh. She had to swallow hard, her saliva glands working hard to wash away the taste.

'I feel a little sick,' she said quietly. 'May I be excused?'

'Haruna, the food,' her mother said quickly, 'we shouldn't waste it, should we, Greg?'

'Yes, Haruna, you should be grateful for your dinner, and eat what has been placed in front of you.'

Haruna nodded at Greg, the nausea starting to overwhelm her, and a strange dizziness disorientating her. She set her fork down calmly, and felt waves of anger start to pulse through her. She looked at her fork, and then to her knife, momentarily fantasising about ramming it through his eye. Inside she was screaming, but as she spoke she matched Greg's cold, slow tone with the same unwavering chill. For the first time, she looked him right in the eyes.

'Greg, I need to leave the table. I feel ill, and I need to lie down.'

'Haruna, you look fine,' her Mum insisted.

She stood up and placed her napkin on the table. 'Shall I clear up my plate, Mum, or can I just go?'

'Haruna!' her mother squeaked, placing her fork down, her eyes darting to Greg.

Greg calmly put his knife and fork down and wiped his mouth with his napkin.

'Stay where you are, and finish your dinner,' he said quietly.

'No,' she said sharply.

'Excuse me?' he said, without looking up.

She felt the bubbling in her stomach, her mouth start to water and a then came a sharp cramp under her ribs. She grabbed her side and ran to the downstairs toilet just in time. The first retch was chicken, potato, orange juice. The second ran clear, like chicken soup. The last, nothing came up.

She sat on the cold tiles of the toilet floor, reeling from dizziness and their short, unprecedented interaction. Reeling also from the thrill of setting the bin on fire the night before. She was on the edge, and she didn't care. And yet, her stomach seemed to tell a different story.

It was untenable. She couldn't do it any more. She thought about her plan to go to university. The plan she had worked towards her whole life, diligently. Every day believing in this one thing – this pot of money – this symbol of belief in her. Her money, put aside by *her* father, had been, for the last lonely years, a lifeline waiting for her at the end of school. But now it was gone – did she even want to go to university? And if not, what could she do?

Her mind wandered to Frankie. Frankie was just out there, facing it all with the confidence and optimism of someone who'd always had back-up. Even her bloody flat was a cut-price deal her dad had arranged for her.

Then she thought about Seven. The band practices had become a new kind of lifeline for her. Drumming. Who knew it could get so deep into her veins? The precision and wildness of it all at once. It reminded her of dancing, but deeper, more primal. Aggressive. Could she throw everything in for the band?

There was a knock at the door.

'Haruna, are you okay?' Her mother.

'Yes, Mum, sorry, it must be something I ate.'

'Well, get yourself cleaned up. Greg wants to talk to you.'

'I don't want to talk to him,' Haruna said pitifully.

'Haruna, please.'

'What does he want?'

'I think he would like to speak to you.'

Nah. Enough, she thought, the fatigue and sickness making her feel exhausted, unable to play the game any more.

She was done.

'It's not going to happen, Mum.' Haruna pulled herself

up, stood on the other side of the door and put both palms on the wood.

She was done.

'You guys want to kick me out? Is that where we are?'

'Haruna, please,' her mother begged. Haruna could hear the sound of Greg's footfall in the background, he was pacing. Waiting for the rabbit to get let out of the cage.

I'm no fucking rabbit.

She was done.

Her hands started to tremble. She dug her nails into the wood finish of the toilet door, scratching at the glossy varnish. There was such anger seething through her she didn't know what to do. She didn't want to come out, but she couldn't stay in here for ever.

'You'll have to come out at some point, Haruna. Don't make Greg wait. Please.'

Cheq. She reached for her phone and dialled the number.

'Haruna?' Her mother knocked, louder, more frantically now.

He picked up within less than three rings. 'Babe?'

'Can you come get me?'

'What's happened?' He sounded stiff and worried – *good* – she needed him to act.

'Come now. I need to get out.'

'I'm on my way, stay on the phone.'

Haruna glanced around the toilet. On the far side, under the stairs, was the coat rack, and her trusty parka was right there. And so was Greg's coat. She crept over, unzipping his inside breast pocket where he kept his wallet. She pulled it out, her trembling fingers fumbling with the flaps inside. Twenty-pound notes, eight of them. That would do.

What else do I need? All her most special things had been burned. Her school bag was by the door. *I don't have the passport*, she thought bitterly. She put on her coat, fishing her headphones out of the pocket. With trembling hands she put the jack into her phone, and put the earpiece in her ear and slipped her phone into her pocket.

'I'm here. I've left my phone on. I can hear you,' she said to Cheq.

'Five minutes,' Cheq said, just pulling on to Mare Street.

'Mum, I'm leaving,' Haruna said loudly through the door. 'Greg and you don't get to kick me out – got it? I'm leaving. I hate this house, and I hate you both.'

The smell of sick was strong. She sniffed her hands. Turning in the small room she pulled back the sleeves of her parka, lathered her hands with soap and washed them vigorously. Then she washed her face with the same soap, the pungent perfume stinging her eyes for a moment.

A loud knock this time, and then some kind of commotion.

'Haruna.' It was Greg's voice. 'It was you, wasn't it? The bin, the car? You need to face the consequences of your behaviour. Get out here now, or so help me God I will break down this door and drag you out by your hair.'

She stayed silent, fear rising in her. She felt it was safer not to engage.

'Babe, talk to me, are you there?' Cheq said, his voice high and tight.

'I'm here.'

'I'm one minute away, do you want to wait by the gate?'

'I can't. I'm inside. The downstairs toilet under the stairs. I don't want to come out—' Her voice cracked, and the tears began to sting her eyes.

'Haruna, this is your final warning.' Greg's voice was louder now. She heard her mother yelp, muffled, as if she was being restrained.

'Mum?'

Nothing. She had been silenced. She'd failed to keep her freak of a daughter under control. *What was the price?* Haruna wondered. Haruna's heart began to ache. She knew, deep down she knew, that her mother still loved her, but here we were. She couldn't think about what might happen. It wasn't fair, that burden.

'Stand back,' Greg commanded. There followed a booming THWACK as his boot hit the door. The wood strained under the weight of his foot. A small crack appeared in the white paint. Haruna's heart thumped in her chest, her breathing was hard, fast.

'Jesus Christ!' Haruna shouted. 'Get the hell away from me. I'm calling the police.'

'What the hell was that?' Cheq yelled in her ear. 'I'm pulling in.'

'Hurry,' Haruna cried, as another loud THWACK forced the door to fully crack down the panelling.

'Hey, Greg?' Haruna said, her voice steady and loud. 'You're going straight to hell, you fucking loser.'

The door bell chimed, the light, jingling bells providing a jolting juxtaposition to the weight of the situation. Then the banging began in earnest. 'Haruna!' she could hear Cheq in her ear and sounding through the front door.

More commotion. Shouting. A loud bang. Something wood hitting something wood. Cheq was in.

'Get the hell back,' he shouted. 'Haruna!'

'I'm here!' she shouted through the door, her heart thumping.

'Haruna!' Frankie was here. Her heart swelled. *Frankie.*

Haruna grabbed her moment. She unlocked the door and stepped out into the hall, making a beeline for Frankie who was holding the front door open. Cheq had a cricket bat in his left hand, and was shaking out his right fist.

Greg was on the ground with a bleeding nose. He looked stunned, and maybe even scared.

Her mother was cowering on the stairs.

Haruna stood by the door with Frankie at her side. 'Bye, Mum. I forgive you.'

She turned to Greg. 'You piece of shit,' she said before her eyes narrowed.

She sucked her cheeks, and with disgust and fury, spat at the floor by his feet.

She was done.

Chapter 21

Edge of Seventeen

'I think what we all need is a drink,' Frankie said, sitting on the edge of her new bed as Cheq paced the room and Haruna sat quietly on the floor, crouched between Frankie's dressing table and the bedroom door.

'I don't want a drink,' Haruna said quietly.

Frankie's bedroom was small but sweet, with a large sash window overlooking the garden. Living over four floors felt absolutely enormous compared to the small flat she had lived in her whole life with her parents, and despite having four people here, there were some days she barely saw her housemates. It would be great to have Haruna around for a bit.

'I can't believe you punched him in the face, Cheq,' Haruna said, looking up through red, blotchy eyes. Frankie wanted to touch her, but she'd shrugged off half a dozen attempts so it felt best to give her some space. 'I can't believe you did that.'

'I wanted to do much worse,' he said grimly, looking at Haruna before returning to pacing around. 'I panicked when I heard the banging. And then when I saw his face, when I saw what he was going to do . . . '

'Christ, don't be sorry,' Frankie said, eyes wide, 'if my dad was there he would have smashed his kneecaps or something.'

'Why were you together?' Haruna asked, rubbing her temples.

'I dropped by to speak to Jules about the demo,' Frankie replied, 'like I was literally on the door step when you called Cheq.'

'Oh. What am I going to do?' Haruna said. 'I have nothing. No clothes. No money. No family. Nothing.'

'Well, you can live with me,' Cheq said.

'We've been over that,' Haruna said.

'Just move in with me, Haruna,' he snapped, before stopping in his tracks. 'Sorry, I'm all worked up. I'm sorry.'

'Stay here,' said Frankie quietly.

Cheq looked at Frankie, grateful and relieved. 'And when you're sick of Frankie, you can stay with me.'

'You've only got two or three months of school left, we can get you through that,' Frankie went on, 'and as for the clothes – let's face it, you aren't going to miss that lot.'

'I'm not going back to school.'

'Oh yes you are,' Frankie said, 'you can't let them take that away from you.'

'Should've just shut him down when I had the chance,

ignorant motherfucking . . . ' Cheq muttered under his breath, and then banged his fist against the back of the door. The sound made Haruna jump, and then her eyes filled with tears again.

'Cheq, I'm sorry but can you please go?' she said meekly. 'I just want to be with Frankie.'

There was a time, only a few months ago, that Frankie wanted to hear these words from her best friend. In the midst of her break-up with Doc, Haruna was in the throes of new love with Cheq and she was just not available for Frankie. But now, that resentment had lifted, and in Cheq she saw a decent person, who truly cared about – no, *loved* – her friend. She looked over, pleading at him with her eyes, shaking her head, clasping her hands to her mouth. *Please don't feel hurt*, she begged.

He nodded at her.

He got it.

'No problem, Ru.' He kneeled down next to her and put a hand on her knee. 'I'm here. Call me any time. I'm sorry I hit him. I don't know why. I've never done that kind of thing before.'

'It's okay. I know you were trying to protect me,' she said, her voice shaky. 'I just want to be with Frankie for a bit. Is that okay?'

'It's okay. I understand.' He leaned in for a moment, looking like he might kiss her, then pulled back. 'Call me.'

When he was gone, Frankie made two cups of tea, and

ordered Haruna into her favourite pyjamas and into the bed.

'I'm just so tired, Frankie. But I also feel, like, full of energy. Jumpy. Like Greg might walk in. Or the police. I might get arrested for setting the bin on fire.'

'You did what?'

'Frankie, I've been on some kind of trip. I don't know why, but I just started doing these things. I keyed his car. I weed in his aftershave.'

Frankie said nothing, but her eyes were on stilts. She suppressed a nervous laugh.

'It was just a bit. But enough to make me smile every time he wore it. I've been stealing money. I set the bin on fire last night. And I loved it. It felt amazing. I loved watching Greg get up out of bed in a panic. I loved seeing him all afraid. What the fuck has happened to me, Frankie? I'm losing my mind. I'm so fucking tired all the time.'

'Why don't you put your head down? Tomorrow we'll come up with a plan.'

'I don't think I can sleep.'

'Oooh, I think I have a Valium somewhere. Mum gave me one when we went to Tenerife. Do drugs go off? Let me find it.'

As Frankie pulled out the box in her room marked 'toiletries and other gross stuff', Haruna continued to talk.

'Mum can't really love him, can she? I don't understand. How could she choose him over me? And give him all my fucking money. *My Money.* Oh man, and the Church. Do you think they know what he's really like? Are they all like that? Is it like the Catholic Church has paedos and this church has abusive needle-dick assholes.'

'Well, not the *whole* Catholic Church—' Frankie began.

'I know, I know, I don't even know what I'm saying any more,' Haruna interrupted. 'I googled it once, you know. The church they go to. It seemed ordinary enough.'

'*Really?*' Frankie said, pulling out a small pill box with two yellow pills inside. She handed them over with the mug of tea. 'Valium.'

'What does it do?'

'Relaxes you, I think. Well, my mum takes them all the time and you know how chilled she is.'

Haruna didn't ask twice. She swallowed both pills and settled back into the pillow. 'Sometimes I think maybe they just go dogging.'

'What do you mean?'

'You know, like they drive to the country every weekend to hang out at picnic areas and shag strangers.'

'Jesus literally wept.' Frankie burst out laughing at the thought of those two doing anything even remotely sexual. 'That's totally gross. Church as a cover for swinging.'

Haruna shrugged. 'Why not?'

'But you don't mean that really. I've seen the folders with the paperwork – we went through it that Saturday a year back, remember? It was all pretty dull, kind of self-helpy, with a splash of God?'

'I don't care, anyway,' Haruna said, yawning. 'They're not going to heaven, that's for sure. If there even is a heaven. Apparently, my dad was an atheist. That sounds so nice.'

Frankie came back and sat next to Haruna and stroked her hair, and this time, Haruna didn't push her away.

'I've never hung out with him as an adult, Frankie. I don't know where a whole part of me is from. Do you think my dad would like to hear from me?'

'Shhh,' Frankie said, looking at the time. It was only ten thirty, but it felt much much later. 'Get some sleep.'

CHAPTER 22

(Ooh Yeah) Cool in the Cool

Frankie was a good half-hour early after a surprisingly fast bus ride from Peckham, aka the other side of the goddamn world. Travelling between work at the dance studio and Hackney Wick was becoming a massive drag, but the independence was totally worth it.

She pulled her large headphones on and hit play on Patti Smith's 'Because the Night'. She'd been given a new playlist by Haruna who wanted her to think more broadly about songs they could write, and she was diligently listening to it when she could. Haruna's taste was more pure punk than Frankie's, who preferred the post-punk early-goth sounds of Joy Division and Siouxsie and the Banshees.

In expectation of a night of drinking she bought a couple of cans of cider and sat outside the church on Mare Street waiting for Doc. It was strangely warm for March; spring was definitely in the air. Winter coats had been traded for thick jumpers and raincoats, and the days were ending later at last.

Frankie wasn't thrilled with her outfit, but she couldn't spend too long getting ready or she would have aroused Haruna's suspicion, and with her nerves already frail, she couldn't throw *oh I'm going on a date with Doc* into the mix. She had jeans rolled up, loafers without socks, a vintage Marmite T-shirt and her leather jacket. Her blonde hair was piled on her head, and now after weeks of regrowth had about an inch of dark striking contrast at the roots.

Doc was late, but that wasn't unusual for him. During their five months together he'd been late all the time, and on occasion simply didn't turn up. *But not this time*, she thought, tingling with anticipation.

Frankie sat on a length of brick wall, right next to a fruit seller with those chrome bowls full of fruit for one pound each, and opened her drink. From her back pocket she pulled out a pouch of tobacco and some papers and attempted to roll a cigarette.

'Hey, baby.' A couple of dudes swaggered past. It was easy to lip-read misogyny, it wasn't the most complex of languages. One had rather optimistically removed his T-shirt and had his pasty white chest on display. She blanked them both.

'Give us a kiss,' he tried, making kissing motions at her. It was laughable, but not at all funny.

'Go fuck yourself,' she retorted.

'Bitch dyke,' he replied.

Doc arrived just as she had managed a slightly droopy-looking roll-up and was fumbling with the lighter. She slipped the headphones off her head.

'Hey there. You started smoking?' he said, annoyingly. Frankie was getting tired of everyone noticing the *new her*, like it was some kind of novelty act.

'Yeah, for a while,' she said, jumping up. 'How's you?'

'Good. Good,' he said, roughing up his hair, which was sticky with spray and standing straight up in a black mass. 'What do you fancy? There's a rooftop bar just back there,' he said, motioning towards London Fields, 'has outside heaters?'

'Sounds great.'

'You're eighteen now, right? Did you bring ID?'

'Yes,' Frankie replied, annoyed again. It was lucky he looked so sexy and effortlessly cool, like he'd just woken up or something. Her eyes narrowed as she spotted a crease on his cheek. *Had he just woken up?*

'What you been up to?' she asked casually.

'Oh, been rewatching *Eraserhead*.'

'Oh, cool.'

'You've seen it?' he said, looking over at her as he motioned towards a walkway between two new-build apartments.

'Sure,' she lied. 'Who hasn't?'

'I just love early Lynch,' he said wistfully.

They took some nondescript stairs up through a building next to the park, and just as Frankie was about to check that they were in the right place, they burst out on to a terrace covered in mismatched deckchairs and picnic tables, and decorated with string lights and bunting. It was jolly.

'Cute,' she remarked, hiding her cider from the bartender as they took a secluded seat in the corner. 'I'm just going to finish my cider. Don't want to waste it.'

'Got any more?' he asked.

'Sure. Here, I've got one in my bag, but maybe we should order at least one drink or they'll get suspicious.'

'Nah, don't worry. There's enough people here,' he replied, opening the can of cider with zero concern.

For a moment they sat in silence, looking out over the park. Despite the sunny afternoon, the damp of winter had not abated, and pools of dirty, muddy water sat above the drains. Joyously dotted around the walkways were thousands of bright daffodils heralding spring like a vast orchestra of tiny golden trumpets. A strong, broad, young jogger effortlessly dodged a weeing dog, a speeding cyclist and then a pram as he weaved his way around the track.

'Consequence is a preference for the habitual voyeur of—'

'Confidence,' he interrupted.

'What?'

'The lyrics. It's confidence not consequence.'

'Oh, right. Yeah,' Frankie said. 'I've finished my cider, Imma go get a drink?'

'Can you get me one too?' he asked, downing the last of his cider.

'Whoa, that was quick,' she noted.

'Yeah, catching up with you,' he replied.

After about an hour and two trips to the bar, Frankie was feeling a bit tipsy, and pretty broke. It was definitely Doc's turn to buy a round, but the sound of him talking about how actually seminal *Andy Warhol's Dracula* was, probably, was too brooding and important to interrupt.

'... but enough about that,' Doc said, 'do you want some MDMA?'

'MDMA?' Frankie said, caught off guard. She had to think quickly. 'Umm ... maybe. What are we gonna do?'

'Well, I thought we could go to see a band. Do you know Giants of Earth? They're playing somewhere, I can't remember where. But whatever, we can drink, get high. Hang out.' He looked over at her and leaned across the picnic table and kissed her on the mouth. Hard. Frankie jumped at the surprise, and returned the kiss, awkwardly, not that she felt like she had much choice in the matter.

'Mmm, I remember those lips,' Doc said, slowly opening his eyes and offering an overfamiliar smile.

Christ, Frankie thought, pulling back a bit. Has he always been this much of a dick?

'Gimme all the drugs,' she said quickly. 'I want all the good feels.'

He pulled a little wrap out of his jacket and carefully unfolded it, holding it out to her so as not to spill the fine white powder. Frankie didn't know what to do.

'Just dab your finger and put it on your tongue.'

'Like this?' she said, as the chemical taste spread through her mouth. She quickly washed it down with her cider.

'Yeah, okay, but maybe not so much next time,' he said, laughing. 'You never took drugs before, when we were seeing each other.'

'Yeah, well, people don't always stay the same for ever, you know,' she said sharply.

She was still feeling weird about that kiss. She could feel the memory of his heavy, wet lips and pungent cigarette breath on her, and his weird expectation that she wanted it. Even though she mostly did, it was a strange kind of ownership and it made her uneasy. She looked at him again, and watched the way he sucked back on the wet end of his filterless roll-up, stopping to pluck tobacco strands from between his lips. It was like a weird haze was lifting from in front of her, and the person sitting opposite wasn't this lustrous, brooding demigod, but rather a dull, weedy dude with far too much of a sense of entitlement over her.

'Can you feel it yet?' He grinned. 'Feel all warm and loved up?'

'No,' she said coolly, 'I'll need a lot more than that.'

Doc laughed, and reached into his pocket again, this time pulling out a bag of small pink tablets. 'I mean, we could just do a pill—'

'Christ, we should call you Dr Feelgood.'

'I know, my dealer had a ... deal? Anyway, I don't usually do uppers.'

'Well, I'll try one.' Frankie nodded, finishing off her drink, before standing to get a third round. 'I better get more drinks in then, if you're providing the drugs.'

'Get some water too,' he said earnestly.

Frankie didn't feel any different. Just brighter. She headed to the bar and ordered a couple of beers, two shots of tequila and two pints of water. When she sat back down, Doc was fiddling with another roll-up cigarette. She noticed his fingers. His nails were dirty, and his hands dry and flaky like her dad's used to get when he'd been outside working.

'You look good,' he said, momentarily coughing into his hand. 'I think I might have said that already like a million times.'

Frankie smiled. 'Thanks.'

'I'm sorry, by the way. About breaking up with you. It was probably a mistake. I just was drinking a lot at the time, and there was this girl . . . '

'Yeah, the redhead.' Frankie said. 'I saw you together.'

'Oh, yeah, Jess . . . Well, I kind of got together with her when we were together and I couldn't face you to tell you. But I was really wasted, and I dunno, going through this rough patch.'

'It doesn't matter,' she replied, feeling a surge of something – *pity?* – for him. It was nearly dark and the rooftop bar was starting to empty as people headed off to find warmer places to sit. 'Shall we go find a pub somewhere?'

As she stood she suddenly felt a fluttering in her stomach,

like butterflies, and then a wave of nausea. The floor started to feel like it was moving in waves, like an earthquake, slow and disorientating.

'Drink water,' Doc said, standing up next to her. She took a big gulp, and the nausea abated, but the fluttering was stronger. 'Not too much, just have sips.'

As they walked towards the exit she felt the rush, definitely a chemical rush, but warm and engulfing. *Everything* felt warm and bright. Her hand, which Doc was holding, felt amazing curled up inside the heat of his. Her limbs felt heavy but like they were floating at the same time. The rush was overwhelming her and she had to stop and steady herself.

'You're just coming up, it will pass,' Doc was saying.

'Oh man, it's overwhelming,' she said, flopping into Doc so he put his arm around her and guided her out of the building and on to the darkness of the street. The rush was intense now, from her toes to the tip of her head, where she could feel the warm buzzing the strongest. She tried to focus on the lights on the street ahead, then for a moment she seemed to have clarity, and then it started again. And then followed a euphoria that was both physical and emotional; she floated with Doc down towards the lights, feeling a surge of love and happiness unlike anything she could quantify or explain.

She snuggled into him, 'I love this,' she murmured. 'Oh man, I feel amazing.'

Doc laughed. 'We better go somewhere where we don't stand out as two completely wasted people.'

Frankie looked up at Doc and felt a rush of compassion and love for him. She reached up and touched his cheeks and then suddenly the heat of his body became too much, another wave took over her and she pulled away.

'I want to be free . . . ' she said, wandering alone towards the street, stumbling, smiling, feeling warm and cool all at once.

'Ah, Frankie, you need to stay with me, you're wasted.'

'Take me somewhere; I need to hear some music.'

Doc looked at his watch. 'We could go see Giants of Earth?'

'Let's see that fucking band. I wanna see them now. NOW. I need some music.' She was aware of his hands on her shoulders, steadying her, and felt disorientated. 'Where is Mare Street?'

'Over there,' he said, pointing to some lights ahead that blurred into and out of focus. She turned back around. 'And where is the water?'

'The water?'

'Didn't we have water?'

'Back at the bar. Babe, you're really rushing. I think we should sit for a moment.'

'I need music.' She pulled out her headphones and fumbled with her phone, pushing in the jack and trying to make Spotify come up. 'I can't make it work. I need The Cure. The Cure please. Only The Cure will do. But not "Disintegration". Something fun, like "Why Can't I Be You?". Oh no, my playlist . . . Haruna's playlist . . . Where's Mare Street?'

Everything blacked out for a moment and when she came

to she was sitting on the footpath – right in the centre of the footpath, with people walking past – on the ground next to Doc listening to Joy Division.

She pulled off her headphones. 'Doc, I'm totally wasted.'

'I know,' he laughed. 'It will calm down in a sec. Are you ready to walk? I think a gig would be good for you. Some dancing, maybe? Loud music? Sound good?'

She nodded and Doc took her hand and led her through the bright lights of Hackney to the Moth Club.

An hour later, she had settled into a kind of warm bliss, unable to let go of Doc's hand, wanting to chain smoke, wanting to dance, wanting to talk. 'Let's go smoke,' she whispered to him.

'Again? Okay.'

Then they were outside and the rush continued and Frankie felt this surge of excitement and pride. She was here with Doc. She was his date. Just as she'd always wanted. A couple of girls, kind of sporty, stared at her, one whispering to the other. Sport chic, really. Baggy trackies, trainers, blunt fringes. Tall. Thin. Frankie stared from one to the other. Why did friends always dress the same?

'Baby, you're a star,' Doc whispered into her ear, and she felt a thrilling burst of warmth course through her.

'I feel amazing.'

'Enjoy,' he said, kissing her ear.

'I want to dance. When are the band on? I know this band, I think. I know the name . . . '

'I think,' he looked at his phone, 'now-ish?'

Frankie was up like a shot, cigarette still in her mouth pushing back into the bar area. It was packed. And hot. And as if just for her entrance, the band kicked in. The music was loud. REALLY LOUD. She felt it reverberating through her, bouncing off her bones and through the floor. She pushed her way through the crowd of mostly men and took a place right up the front.

A guy pulled the cigarette out of her mouth, took a drag and then crushed it on the floor. Frankie hugged him.

'Thank you,' she said, falling back into the guy behind her.

'I love you all!' she said, throwing her hands in the air. Somewhere, somehow, she knew she was wasted, and had acute awareness of how she was behaving, but for reasons she couldn't explain, she was doing it anyway.

'I'm like Frankie on *crack*,' she said to a girl next to her who looked at her like she was a total freak. 'I like your hair. I'm not on crack. I'm really not.'

The girl moved swiftly away.

'I'm a dick!' she shouted, to no one, as the band started their next song. 'Jules! Oh my God, this is his band. JULES! He's in this band,' she explained to a dude with floppy blond hair who had wrapped his arms around her waist.

'Don't touch me,' she said, unhooking his arms and pushing him back, momentarily losing orientation. *Where is the fucking stage?* She pushed further forward and looked up, trying to focus on the stage. And there he was. There was

Jules, standing at the front with his black Strat slung round his neck. He was watching her while he sang. *How long has he been watching me?*

She liked the feeling of his eyes on her. She looked back, but she couldn't focus; in the sway of the crowd she kept losing the stage.

Jules is a goooood singer. She realised she had never really imagined him in a band. She knew he was, but she didn't really even picture it. And here he was. She liked seeing his face. *Such a nice face*, she thought before her head rolled back and the warmth took over her again, and she was swallowed by the small crowd.

The stage was about waist height, so it was hard to brace herself against the shoving from behind. Twice she was pinned to it, feeling an almighty crush in her stomach, and had to push back to free herself. She tried to dance, but kept falling into people with the waves of the small crowd who were moshing violently. The music was driving, thumping guitar music – aggressive and bold. She tried to focus but the music was too penetrating, too brilliant, too overwhelming; she could only close her eyes and dance.

Her eyelids were stuck together. She blinked again and felt the gluey crust pull apart. She could only see white ceiling. Her jaw ached. She tried to move it but it was stuck. She put her hand up and forced her jaw back, and with a hard click, it loosened and she could open her mouth.

She blinked again, swiping her eye with her middle finger to remove the crust, and rubbing. Her head thumped. This was a new kind of hangover: deep, chemical, aching and brutal. Her limbs ached, but mostly her neck, as if she'd been stuck asleep in a car for a hundred years with her chin on her chest. But, like, worse, or something.

'Aghhh . . . ' she said, rolling over, before the smell hit her.

Sweat. And possibly sex. She ran her hand down her body to her legs, realising she was naked underneath her T-shirt. Was it even her T-shirt? She blinked again and lifted the purple floral sheet up to inspect. It wasn't. She was wearing his Dead Kennedys T-shirt, and no knickers. And why did her legs hurt? She had a flash of pushing Doc on the bed, and kissing him. A memory of her pulling his pants down.

'Ughh . . . ' She groaned again.

'Doc,' she whispered, touching him lightly on the shoulder. 'Doc.'

She reached her hand across to him and shook him, and he stirred briefly before settling back to sleep, this time with a deep, rumbling snore. *I remember that snore.*

She pulled herself out of bed, squinting across the room to see if she could make out her clothes. Her knickers were dangling off the wooden chair in the corner as if hastily tossed to land where they may.

Where's my fucking T-shirt?

She took a few steps to the bedroom door to head to the bathroom. All she could think of was a shower. A shower and water. All the water. She walked down the hallway, and pushed on the bathroom door but it was shut and the shower was running. She pushed again.

Her head thumped. She headed back to Doc and crept up to the edge of the bed.

'Doc,' she tried again, pushing him harder, 'wake up.'

'Huh?' He sat bolt upright, hair flat on one side, a trail of drool down his right cheek. No T-shirt, his myriad tattoos on full display. 'What? What the fuck?'

'I need an aspirin.'

'Jesus, you gave me a fright,' he said, settling back into his bed, and falling almost instantly back to sleep.

'Doc,' she said again, 'wake up! I need, like, sweet tea, water, and bacon and prescription drugs and all that shit. I think I'm literally dying.'

'Jesus, Frankie, can't I sleep? You know where everything is.'

Frankie sat for a moment, unsure what to do. 'But I don't want to just help myself.'

'Oh Christ.' He rolled back over to face her. 'I forgot about Frankie needing her hand held all the time.'

'What the hell?'

'I'm kidding.' He sighed, rubbing his temples. 'Come back to bed, baby.'

'I can't. My mouth feels like the floor of a parrot's cage, and I need Nurofen. Like, now!'

'Christ.'

Doc pulled himself up and rested on his elbow. 'Over there

in my top drawer. There should be something. And there's bottled water in the bottom of the wardrobe if you really can't walk the five metres to the kitchen.'

'Bottled water,' she said with a posh twang, 'fancy.'

She walked over and pulled out the drawer in his wobbly, cheap-ass, falling-apart Ikea drawers, and inside was a shoebox filled with over-the-counter painkillers. And next to it a wooden box which she instinctively lifted the lid off. A pipe. Weed in a plastic bag. An empty wrap and a dirty glass pipe.

'Jeez, you really are Dr Feelgood,' Frankie said, fishing through the legal drug box and settling for two codeine-based ibuprofens. 'What's this pipe for? The glass one?'

'Smoking. Put it back.'

'Like what?'

'Frankie, get out of my drawer. You got the painkillers, right?'

'Are you smoking crack or something?'

'Heroin.'

Frankie blinked twice, dropping the little glass pipe straight into the box and gently putting the lid back on.

'Heroin?' Frankie said. 'What's it like?'

'Hurry up. Come back to bed,' he said, pulling back the sheet and patting the spot next to him. The spot with a very uninviting stain. Her head thumped again. He smiled at her, but it wasn't a warm smile, it was an attempt to stop her from doing whatever it was she was doing at that moment.

Flashes of the night before came back. Flashes of dancing.

Of Jules smiling at her, with his Strat slung low on his hips. Of peeling paint and plaster crumbling from the ceilings. Of swaying and falling into Doc. Of being in a taxi. Of begging Doc to sleep with her. She felt nauseous. Her memory was so patchy – but pulling Doc's clothes off and pushing him on to the bed was cruelly clear.

'Uhh, I have to go,' she said, suddenly feeling weird. She pulled out the bottled water and unscrewed the top. She downed the two pills, and for a moment wanted to crawl back into the bed just to be simply horizontal until they kicked in. 'Where's my T-shirt?'

'I don't fucking know,' he said, lying back down and rolling over so his back was to her once again.

She stood for a moment, just looking at the back of his head. Then around his room. Under the window his guitar was perched against the wall, next to a stack of magazines and books that were spilling across the floor. An orange towel sat next to a cardboard box full of laundry. There were greasy wrappers from takeaway food. Half-empty coke bottles. Beer cans. An ashtray overflowed on to the carpet beside his bed. The fitted sheet was off at the bottom corner of his bed, revealing an old coffee-coloured, stained mattress. The floor under the bed nearly made her retch. Inches of dust. Mouldy coffee mugs. A condom wrapper.

'I'm going to split,' Frankie said abruptly.

'Okay,' he said, without turning around.

'I feel like shit.'

'Yeah, so do I. You're coming down,' he said impatiently. 'We both are. Just get back into bed and sleep it off. Then we can get up and go to a greasy spoon or something.'

'Um. Nah. I gotta get back to my own flat. Haruna is waiting for me.'

Haruna. Where the hell is my phone?

She found her jacket at the foot of the bed, and her T-shirt crumpled up next to it. She quickly dressed and fished in her pockets for her mobile. She found it: nothing from Haruna. She pulled open her wallet and checked for money. Nothing. Not a penny.

'Doc, have you got any money? I need bus fare.'

'I don't, sorry.'

She fished through all her pockets and looked around on the floor. 'I had money on me, where is it all?'

'You spent it,' he said flatly, pulling the pillow over his head.

You spent it, she thought, remembering he hadn't paid for a single round. Did she even pay for the taxi home?

'Okay, I'm off,' she said. 'See you round?'

'Yep, sure,' he mumbled, half asleep.

When she got out on to the street, the chilly air refreshed her. She looked over to the spot by the trees she would often come to, back when she was still infatuated, and stare up at his room, longing for him to see her and fall for her all over again. She thought of the countless times she'd tried to bump into him 'accidentally' by walking routes around Hackney that he *might* have been. And then she pictured him upstairs, half naked in bed in his stinking room, with a heroin pipe in his drawer. A dude who was cool with having sex with a girl who was *that* wasted, and couldn't be arsed making her a tea.

She zipped up her jacket and braced herself for the long walk back to Peckham.

Chapter 23

Volcano Girls

Haruna had planned to sneak back into the house to pick up some of her things, but her key didn't work – Greg had already changed the locks. Cheq helped her scale the gate at the side of the house on the off chance that the back door was open, but of course it wasn't. She peered through the window, craning her neck to see if she could make out anything inside, but everything was quiet.

She could just see the downstairs toilet from that angle and could see the door had been removed from its hinges ready for fixing or replacement.

'I don't know what I was expecting,' Haruna said out loud. *There's not even a ghost of me here. I'm gone.* She felt the pain swelling in her belly as she looked up to the sky, steadying her breath. *But I was never really here. There was a shadow of me. Someone else lived in my room. A player in a game.*

Something hollow that existed in my place, just to get through. She put her hand up to the glass and felt a tear roll down her cheek.

As she turned to leave, she wiped her eyes and nearly fell over the cardboard box by the back of the pizza oven. She leaned down and flipped open the flap. Some of her things had been carefully folded inside. A few T-shirts, a sweater, her school books, a pair of sneakers, her hairbrush, toothbrush and other basic toiletries.

And an envelope.

She pulled it out with shaking fingers and peered inside. Money. About five hundred pounds and a copy of her birth certificate.

Had her really mum left them for her? Were they to be burned? Not with the money inside. *No, Mum meant them for me.* She wondered whether it was left in kindness. Or was the birth certificate an assurance she would never need to come back?

She shoved everything back in the box and unlocked the side fence, leaving it open to slam in the breeze as she walked back to the car.

The drive to the studio was quiet, but Cheq held her hand the whole way. He awkwardly changed gears with his right hand, steering with his knee, but never letting go of her hand. He was in his geeky black glasses again this afternoon, off to another gig, this one sold out – but he still always found time to help.

It was the first time they'd been together since *the night*. The night he'd punched Greg, Haruna's abusive stepfather, her mother's lover and oppressor, a liar and thief, square in the nose, leaving it bloodied and swollen. Haruna had felt a certain lust for vengeance when she saw the blood, and saw Greg sprawled on the floor, his hand up over his face in defence of any other potential attack. But in the minutes after they had sped off in Cheq's car, she had felt guilt and shame. And Cheq was now forever intertwined in it.

And that complicated the *other* thing that Haruna needed to face. She had missed a period, so long ago now she hadn't noticed. Or perhaps she didn't want to think about it. But soon she *had* to, because the days were passing at speed.

She hadn't really settled at Frankie's flat. It was difficult sharing a bed and a small space and trying to keep out of view of Frankie's flatmates who were probably none-too-pleased at having a new addition to the house.

Frankie was out working most of the time, having extended her hours at the dance studio, and Haruna hadn't been to school since she left home, so she was spending a lot of time alone with nothing to do. . In fact, she was getting a real look at how hard Frankie actually worked. She was always coming up with ideas for the band, and with each week she became more proficient a musician, the more she seemed to get out of practices. Haruna really felt Frankie might be as into Seven as she was.

Frankie was mostly caring and patient and kind, but

Haruna feared it wouldn't last. She needed a plan moving forward that didn't rely on other people. Something permanent and sustainable.

They pulled themselves out of the car and Haruna shoved her box into Cheq's boot. She felt heavy and weary, and unsure how to be excited about today, but she didn't want to let Frankie down.

Amelie Ayres met them at the studio door. She was all fresh faced, with clean hair and dressed in loose jeans and a baggy T-shirt, and despite being the same age, she was incredibly knowledgeable about the business side of music, recording and ... basically everything that Frankie and Haruna were not.

She greeted Haruna and Cheq warmly: 'I couldn't say no to an all-girl punk band. We have to stick together, right? So, come in! Welcome.'

Haruna felt immediately in awe.

They wandered into the foyer where Frankie was sprawled out on the sofa like she owned the place already. Haruna stood transfixed, staring through the huge long window into the studio itself. A drum kit was already set up with a mic for each drum, and a screen blocking her off from the guitar and bass.

'Holy shit,' Haruna said, turning to Amelie, 'this is completely awesome.'

'Thanks,' Amelie said. 'Well, it's my dad's, as you know. But yeah, it's pretty fun playing around in there. I'm kinda lucky.'

'I'll leave you to it,' Cheq said, kissing Haruna on the cheek. 'Call me if you need a lift back. I'm just hanging with Jules about five minutes away, okay?'

'Oh, how is Jules?' Frankie chirped up, bouncing out the couch. 'I saw his band a few nights ago.'

'Yes. He told me,' Cheq said, with a wry smile.

'He did? Oh God. I was wasted.' Frankie shook her head. 'I remember chatting to him after the gig but I can't remember how it ended – he was just suddenly gone.'

'Yeah.' Cheq shrugged. 'Don't know what to tell you, Franks.'

'Oh dear God, did I do something horrible?' Frankie said under her breath. 'Haruna, help me out here.'

'Bye, Cheq,' Haruna said, ushering him to the door, and giving him a little appreciative smile as he made his way out the door. 'Where's Aimee?'

Aimee was already inside plugging in her bass, beaming. She'd just had a fresh undercut and the ends of her hair were dyed magenta, and she had huge cat's-eye eyeliner painted on her upper lids. She looked absolutely stunning, and Haruna reached up to play with her own hair in its dull bun, wondering, with her new-found freedom, if it was time to do something drastic.

She slipped behind the drum kit and picked up the sticks that had been left sitting on one of the toms and did a quick run. 'Extraordinary.' She broke into a wide smile for the first time in days. *Oh yes, I am ready for this.*

After they were all set up, Amelie came in and sat on a stool with a notebook.

'Normally, if we were recording a kind of regular set-up, I would lay down the parts separately, but I wondered if you guys would like to record all at once. It's more in keeping with the style, I think. I looked up some techniques from a few engineers, and punk is often just recorded wild in one take.'

'Did you hear the tracks I sent?' Frankie said. 'Bikini Kill, The Slits?'

'Yep, heard all that. Do you have access to Joan Jett?' Amelie asked, smirking at Frankie.

'Huh?' Frankie said, looking confused.

'Joan Jett does guitar on "Rebel Girl",' Haruna interrupted. 'I read it somewhere. She used to go to their gigs.' Sometimes Frankie could be annoyingly clueless.

'I think we should go for live takes,' Amelie repeated. 'Julian, the other studio assistant, and I spent ages setting up the room so there's plenty of bounce and ambience. And this is a demo so we need to capture your soul as a band.'

'Jeez, you really know your shit,' Haruna said, awe-struck.

'Course she does,' Frankie said, rolling her eyes at Haruna.

Amelie blushed. 'I really geek out at the technical side of all this stuff. I grew up with a dad who did it, so I love it. How many tracks will we do?'

'My friend said we need three or four for a decent demo, right?'

'Yeah, about right,' Amelie agreed. 'Okay, well, we should probably crack on. I was going to suggest we do a track here now so I could listen and adjust while you're playing, but we may as well just go for it and record. I'll use a bunch of tape compression or even dump it across to a Tascam and we can recapture later if we want more trash.'

'I don't know what you just said, but I'm fucking here for it.' Frankie squealed with delight and clasped her hands together. 'Can I have a beer? Get us in the mood.'

'Sure, help yourself.' Aimee motioned to the kitchen through the studio door. 'Just no smoking.'

'Rooney? Aimee?' Frankie nodded at them. 'You guys want one?'

'Sure,' Aimee replied.

'Ugh, no thanks,' Haruna said, recoiling at the idea of beer. 'I'll take water, though.'

An hour later and the mood was considerably less optimistic.

Amelie had asked them to play their opening track, 'Dumpster Dave' six times through already, and after each time she came in to the studio, fiddled with an amp, a mic, twisted another knob, adjusted a drum mic, and asked Frankie less and less politely to try to do it the same way as she'd done it before.

'I *am* doing it the same,' Frankie insisted, 'more or less.'

'Oh God, I'm sorry, I'm losing the plot here,' Amelie said with a huge sigh. 'It's just every time I set it up, you kind of change it and it's hard to get the right sound. The last two songs you didn't go to the chorus at the end, you just ended on that opening riff with Frankie saying … What were you saying?'

'I think I was just shouting "Kick you in your mouth", for some reason.' Frankie shrugged, taking a swig of beer. 'Sorry, I was thinking of this dude I know.'

'We never do it the same way,' Haruna said to Amelie. 'Frankie doesn't even write down lyrics.'

'We only really wrote this particular song last week,' Aimee admitted, then looked over at Haruna with a worried look. 'We're not ready, are we?'

'Yes. Yes, we are,' Frankie insisted. 'Amelie, what do we need to do to make this work? Help us out here. You're supposed to be the producer.'

Amelie flinched a little, and Frankie immediately reined herself in. 'What I mean is, you know *best*. We know nothing. We really love this band but none of us are trained. Aimee and I have only been playing for a year or so. If you can help us, we're asking you. Please help.'

Amelie put her hands up to her face and shook her head. 'I dunno. I mean, I can tell, with respect, that you're not songwriters. It's, like, passionate three-chord punk, but it's not really structured in any way.'

'Can you help us? *Please*,' Frankie said. 'We have this label coming to see us, but only if they like our demo, so we need a demo or they won't come.'

Haruna felt her heart sink as she watched Amelie shaking her head, hands across her face. She was conflicted. She put her hands on her hips and pursed her lips, thinking, and then she said, 'Can you guys wait a moment? I wanna call someone.'

'Sure.'

As Amelie left, Frankie turned to Aimee and Haruna. 'No one gives up, you hear me? We deserve to be here. Our band is the best thing in my life right now. I'm giving it all I've got. I don't believe we can't make these songs work.'

After about thirty minutes, Amelie returned.

'I've called the other engineer, Julian, he knows more than me, and I need some help,' she explained. 'He's going to listen back to the recordings, and while he does that, we're going to work on the songs. Come and sit over here. Frankie, here, you'll need this pen and paper?'

Frankie looked at her, confused, and didn't move, except to push her guitar out of the way so it was hanging behind her. 'What for?'

'We're going to write the songs down and make sure they're structured.'

'Okay, but that doesn't seem very punk to me. Why can't we just do it like we were doing it?' Frankie challenged.

'You!' Haruna said, slipping out from behind the kit, and taking a seat next to Amelie. '*You* put so much work into every aspect of this band but the music. Come on.'

'I find it hard,' Frankie admitted. 'I'm not all talented like you two. I find practising hard. It's like school work. I just want to rock out.'

'I get it. I mean, we're different. For me, it's all about the musicality,' Amelie said, carefully. 'But you need the structure in place first, then, do what you want! Tear it up. But you can't, I dunno, tear up the rules without there being some rules in the first place. Does that make sense?'

'Ugh. You sound like Anya.'

'Who?'

'This Russian dancer at the studio. She gave me the same lecture.'

'It's not a lecture,' Amelie insisted. 'I'm sorry. I'm just trying to help you guys.'

'Yes, you are.' Haruna gave Frankie the eye. 'And we're super grateful, aren't we?'

'We are!' Aimee chimed in.

'Frankie, let's do this,' Haruna urged her.

Frankie sighed and plonked herself down next to Amelie. 'Okay. What do we have to do?'

Amelie set them to work creating first a simplistic structure of intro, verse, chorus, verse, chorus, chorus. Then she made the girls play it through quietly, without the amps. Once they'd agreed it worked, she sent Frankie off to re-jig the lyrics to fit the new structure. Then Amelie printed out the final scribbled sheet. Four copies. One for each of the girls and one for her in the studio.

Haruna looked over at Frankie with excitement. 'So awesome,' she marvelled.

Then Amelie started making some suggestions on arrangement: Aimee comes in first for four bars. Drop the guitar in the second chorus. Basic harmonies to fill out the vocals.

Another hour or so later, a tall, jolly goth called Julian appeared at the studio door.

'How's it going?' he asked Amelie.

'I think we're ready to try again,' she said, smiling at Haruna. Haruna liked this girl completely. She was so unruffled, so organised, so brilliantly cool, and she felt at last like she'd found an ally to help rein Frankie in and focus her at last.

'Thanks so much,' Haruna said, giving her a hug. 'I love this band, but now it feels . . . just so much more . . . amazing.'

Julian slipped his backpack off, and smiled. 'Hi, guys. Don't mind me; I'm just going to do some tweaking in the control room.'

The girls took their places. Frankie plugged in her guitar. Aimee shook out her hands and stretched out her neck. Haruna pulled the snare drum in snuggly between her open knees. She spun the sticks round in her fingers. For the first time, they felt like a real band. She felt a warmth spread through her and then, as Aimee came in with the bass, she tapped her sticks together and let completely loose, losing herself in the music.

As the song finished, Amelie came rushing back through from the control room with Julian at her side, carrying an ambient mic which he proceeded to fix to the ceiling.

'We've just got to make a few little tweaks, but that was amazing,' Amelie said. 'I've never seen such raw energy, and now it's just so brilliantly channelled.'

Julian was nodding.

'It's going to work?' Frankie asked.

'Oh yes,' Amelie beamed.

Chapter 24

Cool Schmool

Frankie stood outside the studio trying to roll another cigarette, but once again it just came out like some ill-shaped floppy hotdog. She tossed it in the dumpster by the end of the drive, then, after ten seconds of solitary contemplation, tossed the entire pouch of tobacco in behind it.

'Stupid habit,' she said, thinking of Doc's spindly tobacco-stained fingers. And then, his tobacco-stained fingers on her. She shuddered. How could she have ever fancied that loser?

'Did you quit?' Amelie said, carrying two full rubbish sacks out of the studio. 'It's bad for the vocals, you know? Well, maybe yours could take it.'

It was the last day. Amelie had given them four evenings, free, at the studio; she'd even played guitar and keys on a couple of the tracks. It had been gruelling, both creatively and emotionally, as they explored their music with Amelie.

What was a bunch of kinda angsty, shouty, tracks were unceremoniously pulled apart, thematically explored, rewritten and re-arranged.

Amelie had the ability to extract the essence of what they were trying to do and mould it into finished, if not polished, songs. Frankie never new that performing could feel so raw and so intense.

Frankie was so grateful to Amelie she wasn't sure she'd ever be able to vocalise it.

'Let me help,' Frankie said, relieving her of one of the bags and tossing it into the dumpster. 'I never really smoked; I took it up as part of a half-baked, half-assed plan to hook a dude. A dude who turned out to be a bit of a dick. Do you have a boyfriend ... or girlfriend or whatever?'

'Kind of. Well, yes, I guess so,' Amelie said, looking sheepish. 'He lives overseas so it's not very practical.'

'Long distance!' Frankie said. 'That must be hard. I mean, I found it hard to live a few streets away from my ex-bore-friend.'

'It's been a journey,' Amelie laughed, 'but so far worth it. He's just a really good person, you know. And we both make the effort. And also he's a musician so we have that in common. We actually did some recording here last year together.'

'So where are you at with your music? It's going well, I see.'

'Yes,' she said, blushing, 'it is. I'm actually on this kind of development thing with a label now, so, um ... '

'You're signed to a label? Which one?' Frankie said, with a stab of jealousy. But of course she was signed to a label, all that natural talent and hard work . . .

'Yeah.' Amelie tossed the rest of the rubbish into the dumpster. 'Falls Records.'

'No shit,' Frankie said.

'No shit,' she said, laughing, 'but like, my dad has worked for them, and we kind of know a few of them, so it's not like I didn't get a leg up. I mean, I was in a super privileged position.'

'Bullshit. You've earned it, I'm sure. I've seen you working,' Frankie said, in awe. 'But this is such a weird coincidence – Falls is the company that said they'd come see us if they liked the demo.'

'Oh man, no way!' Amelie grinned wickedly. 'Who is it? From Falls?'

'This old guy called Geoff.'

Amelie burst out laughing. 'Oh, I know Geoff.'

'You do?'

'Yeah. He's really good friends with my dad.'

'The dude that's putting the girl band together? The loud, ginger dude? Mr Angry?'

'Oh yeah, that's him all right,' Amelie said, giggling. 'He's a big rough round the edges, but he's cool. Superior taste in music, actually.'

'I looked him up. He *did* have good taste, but he's made some weird-ass choices.' Frankie had been surprised to see that among all the fairly interesting indie and rock bands he'd repped over the years, he'd also managed boyband The Keep.

'Yeah, well, I guess with a career that long, you might not like *every* artist you work with,' Amelie said, shrugging. 'I used to be all snobbish about music, but then I realised everyone's just trying to do shit and putting yourself out there in any way at all should be applauded.'

'Yeah, but he worked with The Keep.'

'I bet you secretly liked them once. Or at least a song,' Amelie said with a wry smile, 'one song?'

'Okay, I had their second album,' Frankie said, shrugging, 'but I was, like, twelve!'

'Ha!' Amelie giggled. 'See?'

'Wow, I can't believe it. This is just so cool that you know him. I wonder if there's a way—' She stopped herself. Did she need to leverage this? Amelie had already helped them so much. She couldn't possibly pull any more favours, could she?

'I'll def put in a word,' Amelie volunteered as they walked back to the studio.

'Oh man, thanks,' Frankie said.

'You know,' Amelie said, stopping by the door and turning to Frankie, 'one of the other reasons that things moved quickly for me was that I had quite a lot *out there* already. Like a SoundCloud or Bandcamp. I mean, I already had a bit of a following. Ugh, I hate talking about this stuff.'

'I know, I online stalked you with Haruna.'

'Oh God.' Amelie blushed, shaking her head.

'Look, it's not my taste per se,' Frankie began, 'but I really loved it.'

'Thanks. I'll take that.' She grinned. 'The guitar on the two later tracks? That's Maxx. My boyfriend.'

Amelie was half blushing as she talked about herself, though she was forthright and clear about everything else. Even a little sassy at times. But for all her talent and hard work, Frankie just couldn't picture her actually on stage performing. If she was *this* shy talking?

'Anyway, you can send the demo to Geoff. But really – do some stuff online. It really helps. I've seen your website and it looks like you've had a gig or two? But there's not much else.'

'I don't do Twitter,' Frankie said plainly. 'None of us are that into social media. Aimee gets harassed for being a lesbian, Haruna's stepdad wouldn't let her do social media – I guess she could do now, though. I mean, I have Facebook? But my bloody mum's on there, so . . . '

'What about doing something for Instagram or something? Like some videos? A photo shoot? I dunno, I'm just thinking out loud. There's a girl I know who runs social media for bands – for Falls Records, in fact – it's her job – I could see if she'd maybe give you some pointers?'

'Oh man, anything like that would be great.'

'You have to kind of create a buzz. When's your next gig?'

'We don't have one booked.'

'What are the record company going to come to, then?'

'I need to book one,' Frankie admitted. 'It's hard, though, like, to book one. You have to *do your time*,' she moaned.

'You should try to support someone. That way you get their crowd. Give you lots of atmosphere. Do you know anyone with your kind of vibe?'

'Kind of. There is one guy I know. He said he could help. But ugh, I don't want to ask him for help.'

'Well, you should find some way to get into support gigs. But you will need to sort out the online stuff—' She stopped. 'You know what, I'll just call this girl Greta and see if she'll help you.'

'Aww! Thanks so much, Amelie; that would be amazing.'

'No sweat, Frankie,' she said, smiling. She pushed the door to the studio open. 'The tracks should have all exported now, so you're good to go.'

Aimee was curled up on the sofa, her head in Haruna's lap. Everyone was completely exhausted. Haruna looked up and held her phone to Frankie. 'Cheq's on his way. He's going to drop us all home.'

Frankie yawned. She was also exhausted, and absolutely ready for her bed.

'He's a keeper,' Frankie said with a smile and Haruna nodded back. Their third song, a moody, slower number called 'Fuck Your Feelings', was all about her life and her isolation at home. Frankie was relieved her friend was out of that shit situation, but Haruna was far from saved. She had become more withdrawn and sad. She slept a lot and wasn't eating properly, and Frankie was worried. Her mum and dad could help maybe.

She vowed to take Haruna for some warm family time soon.

In the meantime, the band seemed to be the only thing keeping Haruna buoyant, and Frankie wanted to keep the momentum up. She decided to take the plunge.

'Can I make a quick, um, private call in the studio, Amelie?'

'Why not pop into my dad's office?' Amelie said, nodding to the door behind the kitchen.

'Okay – give me, like, two minutes, Haruna.'

Frankie snuck into the small office, plonked down on the office chair behind the desk, and searched through her call history for Jules's number. She was nervous about calling him. It was one thing to chitchat with him about demos and to get the name of the studio, but now she was going to ask him for a slightly bigger favour. She felt bad. She was using him because she thought he would likely say yes.

'Frankie,' he said, the sound of his band stopping mid-track in the background. 'How's it going?'

'Good. Hi, Jules.'

'What's going on?'

'Um, I wanted to ask you something. A favour, really.'

'Shoot,' he said. She could hear the clang as his amped guitar was lifted off and rested down. 'Let me just pop out of the practice room ... Hang on, guys, I need to take this call.'

Frankie frowned. *Why was he so goddamn nice?*

'So, I haven't seen you since my gig,' he said. 'How's things?'

'Oh, your gig was cool. I mean, though, once again, I can't remember much,' said Frankie.

'Shame you didn't stick around,' he said, 'it was great to chat, briefly anyway.'

'We did? Yikes. I'd taken an *e* that night and honestly I can barely remember a thing,' Frankie said sheepishly. 'I'm sorry if I was weird or anything. Not my finest hour.'

'It's okay. You were pretty hilarious really,' he said, before pausing for a moment. 'Also met your boyfriend, what's his name?'

'Doc. But, ah, he's not my boyfriend.'

'Oh, I thought he was,' he said, surprised. '*He* said he was!'

Ugh, this was a disaster. 'He's *really* not.'

'Okay,' he said, unconvinced. 'Well, I'm sorry about the whole song thing. I'd never have done it if I'd known you were there with someone. But look, it doesn't matter anyway. What can I do for you?'

What song? She racked her brain, but it was like someone had wiped her mental hard drive. Did he play a song for her?

'Jules, he's not my boyfriend. He was once. But it was a while back now. We were just catching up,' she said hurriedly. *Why am I explaining myself to you?* 'He was even more wasted than me. Anyway, look, the reason I'm calling is, um, our band needs a gig and I wondered if you guys would let us . . . '

'Support?' he said quickly. 'Sure. We're kind of quiet this month, though. Ramps up again after recording. I'll check with the guys and we'll see which gig would work. I'm sure you can do a short opening set. No worries.'

Frankie was taken aback. 'Um, okay. Gosh. Thank you.'

'The Roundhouse, maybe, next month. Would that work?'

The Roundhouse. She thought back to the bullshit story she'd told Doc about playing a gig there. If she cared what he thought any more, this would have been a jackpot.

'Yeah, that sounds cool,' she said, sitting on the edge of the desk, chewing on her thumbnail, 'really cool. Thanks, Jules.'

'Shall I call you back when I've confirmed?'

'Sure, that would be great.'

When Frankie returned to the room, the girls were already outside in the car with Cheq and Amelie was zipping up her coat.

'Why did *you* help us?' Frankie asked, as Amelie opened the front door and motioned her towards it.

'It's practice. I like engineering,' she said simply. 'Julian's waiting for me, I have to split.'

'But you must get tons of bands calling up here every day. Why us?'

Amelie thought for a moment. 'Because this industry isn't particularly good to women. Because I know what it's like to want something and not have the tools available. And also,' she said with a smile, 'because I had time.'

Chapter 25

Cannonball

Haruna sat in the chair of the salon, while Frankie's Aunt Di flapped about with a bunch of plastic dishes, brushes and tin foil. She looked at herself in the mirror – her longish hair around her shoulders, with a pale grey T-shirt of Frankie's that had become one of her wardrobe staples. She had that poker-straight dark hair from her dad, and although it had always annoyed her when she was younger at school, how it wouldn't fall about her shoulders in a soft wave like the other girls, it was going to be perfect for the look she had in mind. If only she were in the mood.

'Makeover day!' said Frankie, spinning around in the chair next to her. 'We need to look perrrrfect.'

Somehow Frankie had done it again, hustled another thing for nothing for the band.

This time it was press shots. A girl called Greta and her

photographer friend were going to come and take photos of them on the canal by Victoria Park and overhaul their social media presence (whatever that meant). Their first band shoot. With that and the demo, it was starting to feel, like, real.

First, Haruna needed a makeover. She knew she did. She wanted one. But not with all this Frankie fanfare. But it was free, and with almost all her money gone, she didn't want to rock the boat by being picky about the day – or the hairdresser.

'I feel like we should be playing some eighties makeover track or something,' said Haruna as Di wrapped a plastic cape around her. 'Thank you so much.'

'So, I'm going to dye it first and then we'll do the cut, okay?' Di explained. She was a big, round lady with a very warm and open smile and one of those middle-aged ladies' hairstyles – one colour all over, slightly too dark for her complexion. Oozing warmth and motherliness, just like Frankie's mum.

'Okay. Did you see the photo?' Haruna asked, holding up her phone with a picture of the cut she was after.

'Yes, I did. Definitely going for a blacker black?' she asked for, like, the hundredth time.

'Definitely,' Haruna said, smiling at Frankie who gave her the thumbs-up and a big supportive grin.

As Di began to paint dye in long strokes artfully along the length of her hair, Haruna and Frankie ran through the day.

'So, is Aimee going to meet us here?'

'Yep. And Greer is going to style us,' Frankie said. 'I think she'll do great. She's bringing a bunch of outfits, so we can get changed here and then walk down to the canal. It's only five minutes. There's a pub on the corner – Pub on the Park, we're meeting the photographer there. And the social media girl.'

'What's she like?'

'Greta is hilarious,' Frankie said, 'proper Londoner. She had loads of ideas for the band and was super excited to help. I don't know the other one – Alex, I think? She does mostly video stuff but she takes photos too.'

'And are they really doing this for free?' Haruna asked dubiously.

'Um, yes. Mostly,' Frankie said, leaning into the mirror in front of her and inspecting her face for blemishes. Frankie was one of those girls who was an incessant pimple squeezer, even when she didn't have any, and especially when she was being duplicitous.

'Mostly?'

'Don't worry, Ru. It's not much. The photographer wanted some money, but it's a total bargain really,' Frankie said, brushing it off.

Haruna felt a stab of embarrassment, and guilt. Frankie was paying for everything, and Frankie didn't have much money. Sure, she was the only one with a job, but she was also the only one paying rent. Haruna owed her money for the drum kit, bills, including her mobile, which Frankie had been topping up for her, she'd also topped up her travel card, food, and now also everything to do with the band, including this haircut.

The debt owed, both emotional and financial, was weighing

heavily on Haruna, making her feel ... somewhat trapped again.

'Frankie,' Haruna said, 'you know how grateful I am. You're a great friend.'

'Cool, cool.' Despite wanting to always be the centre of attention, Frankie didn't like it when people actually showered her in it.

'Aww, you two,' said Di. 'Makes me need to go out back, call my bestie Marie and have a little cry.'

Once she'd finished with Haruna, she put down the dye and turned to Frankie. 'You just want a style, right?'

'Yes please.' Frankie had stuck with her blonde, shaggy look for a while now and it suited her. In fact, her whole look had settled into something very cool and effortless. She was just so *Frankie* now.

By the time Di had washed and blow-dried Frankie's hair, and then Frankie had demanded to use the hairdryer herself, emptied half a bottle of spray and teased her hair with a fine-tooth comb, Haruna's hair was ready. She lay back and enjoyed the feeling of Di's expert fingers massaging shampoo and then conditioner into her head.

Frankie, meanwhile, had pulled out the world's most enormous make-up kit and was fishing through it for black kohl to line her eyes.

'I can't wait to do your make-up. Look what I borrowed from the studio,' Frankie said, waving a dark red lipstick in front of her. 'I mean, it's not like you haven't worn it before but today we can really go for it. I think we should put some posters up around town? Don't you? Imagine if your mum and Greg saw them. Oh man, I'd love to see their faces.'

Haruna bit her lip. Thoughts of her mother had been weighing on her more and more recently. Her hand instinctively came up to her heart and then it ran down and rested on her belly.

Fifteen minutes later, Frankie was ready and Di was putting a towel around Haruna's head and walking her back to the mirror.

'Ready?' she asked, about to take off the towel.

'No! Don't show her till it's all done,' Frankie cried.

'Frankie, no, no, no; this isn't *Top Model*,' said Haruna, 'and it's not going to look *that* different – just slightly blacker.'

'Please. I'm paying!' Frankie said. She was teasing. Playing. But for Haruna it felt controlling, although there was no way to express how she felt without creating a whole *thing*. She wondered about telling Frankie the whole truth, but didn't want the attention back on her. *Poor Haruna* in need of saving again.

Haruna force a smile. 'All right, all right. I'll play along.'

Frankie rolled over in her chair and as Di moved swiftly behind her, cutting her wet hair, Frankie pulled out the makeover kit, perched it on the stool next to her and started on her face.

'You're going to look amazing,' Frankie said, looking up at her hair. 'Holy shit, my friend. Cheq's going to die.'

'I'm so grateful. You know how long I've wanted to do something different with my hair. I mean, since I was, like, thirteen, I think.'

'I know, I know. So I'm thinking, dark dark purple lips, almost black, and not much else. A bit kind of goth?'

'Oh, I dunno, Franks.'

'Shh,' Frankie said, applying powder from a huge pillowy puff to her whole face. 'Fixing powder. My God, the things I learned at the dance studio.'

'I don't want much make-up, though, Frankie; it isn't me.'

'When I'm done, you'll hardly know you're wearing it. I promise.'

Haruna was dubious, but she figured she'd let her friend have a stab – she could always make a secret visit to the bathroom later. Haruna looked at Frankie, who was literally fizzing with excitement about today, and felt more guilt. She could barely muster a grin. She loved being in the studio, she loved practice, but she hated all this stuff.

As Frankie burrowed around in the make-up kit, Haruna decided to ask about Doc. She'd been avoiding it because Frankie had been avoiding it, which likely meant *something* had gone on since they last spoke.

'Hey, Franks. I want to ask you something that's been on my mind for ages to ask, and I don't know why I haven't. About Doc,' Haruna started carefully.

Frankie glanced up at Haruna and pulled a face. 'Dick?'

'Dick Doc,' Haruna smirked. 'You're calling him that now?

What happened? Last time we spoke about him he'd sent you a message, and you never said whether you replied – did you write him back?'

'Um. Okay, you're going to freak out, but you have to listen to the very end,' Frankie said seriously, holding up some silvery eyeshadow as a suggestion. Haruna shook her head.

'Like, you've got to listen to all of it before you freak out. Do you promise?'

'Oh no,' Haruna said, sighing, wishing she'd never asked. 'I'm now absolutely dreading what's coming.'

'Well, probably fair enough. We went on a date,' Frankie announced, letting the weight of the revelation hang in the air for a moment.

'YOU DID WHAT?' Haruna shrieked!

'Stop moving!' Di ordered, pushing Haruna's head forward so she could cut the back evenly. The cut was blunt so precision was key.

'Hear me out,' Frankie said. 'I didn't want to worry you. Anyway, I was weirdly not very into it, but then I kinda slept with him, after taking an *e*.' Frankie knew how to shock. 'Don't tell Mum,' she directed at Di, who giggled nervously.

'What? Start from the beginning! Please!' Haruna begged.

'Well, it's weird because after I got his text, I was going to reply, you know, then there was stuff going on with the band, and then that day I met the Falls Records people, and I don't know, I just forgot.'

'Okay, that's definitely a bit of a change, considering you were basically his stalker at Christmas,' said Haruna. 'So, a good sign.'

'I know! And then I just kind of met up with him anyway. I don't know why really, curiosity. I think because I felt strong, like I had the upper hand or something. And, God, he looked pretty rough. I mean, almost sick, you know? Grey complexion. And he had *zero* money. I mean, not that I mind that, but it was just a bit dull having to pay for everything, and then he pulled out some MDMA and I was, like, "Jesus, anything but another hour of this", and the next thing I'm wasted at this gig – that's where I saw Jules . . . "'

'Oh god, Jules muttered something about you having a boyfriend,' Haruna interjected.

'An unfortunate side effect of the whole mess,' Frankie winced. 'But let me finish. I was at this gig and then for some dumb reason I go home with Doc and we shagged.'

'But why did you sleep do it if you didn't want to?'

'It was like an exorcism. Like I had to go back there one last time to get rid of him for ever. Anyway, it was all pretty grim the next morning. And you know he's not even in his band any more? Oh. And get this. Please don't tell anyone, though, he got really touchy when I mentioned it . . . '

'What?'

'He's been smoking heroin.'

'Ugh. That's too much.' Haruna said. 'Cheq's friend Oli smokes it all the time and he's so boring. And he's been stealing,' she paused, realising what she was saying before adding, 'off his *friends*, I mean.'

'I know, right? Don't get me wrong, Ru, I loved being high, it was amazing, and I'm not going to rule out doing it again, that's for sure, but heroin is just kind of ... I dunno, losery.' Frankie leaned forward. 'Don't move,' she said, putting a line around Haruna's lips.

Di turned on the hairdryer and pulled out a large round brush. 'You done?'

'Yep,' Frankie shouted back over the noise. 'And there is something else. Just seeing the way Cheq treats you, it's like, how could I ever have dated a loser like that?'

'He's got his charms,' Haruna said, feeling a tug on her heart, while Di tugged at her hair, adding the final touches. 'But I struggle with him too. I sometimes feel like I can't breathe around him. Move in. Do this. Do that.'

'Really?' Frankie said, surprised. 'I mean, I used to think that, but now I look at him and he seems really ... attentive and kind, maybe?'

'Yes. I guess.' Haruna shrugged. 'I don't know if I feel suffocated because he's suffocating or because I'm ... '

'What?' Frankie asked gently. 'Not in love?'

'I definitely love him,' said Haruna. 'He *is* awesome in so many ways ... but ... '

The front door of the hairdresser's flew open and Aimee was standing there holding two enormous plastic carrier bags.

'It's wardrobe time!' she shrieked. She was pure perfection

from head to toe. Fresh-faced and virtually make-up free, strawberry hair, undercut, black jeans, white shirt, thin leather tie – all slightly distressed – and Beatles-style military jacket. She looked the bomb.

'Haruna, your hair!'

'I haven't seen it yet.'

'You look great. But you always look great,' Greer chimed in, dragging in another huge bag of clothes. 'Kind of robot punk.'

'She looks ah-maze!' Frankie enthused. 'We're going to do the big reveal.'

'No! Let's dress her first,' Aimee said, 'get the whole look down.'

'I feel like a social experiment,' Haruna said, pouting, 'but I'm cool with it.'

Di finished, then gave Frankie a kiss on the forehead and made herself scarce at the other side of the room by the till. Haruna was ushered to the back of the hairdresser's where there was a bit of privacy while Greer fished around in the bags looking for something very specific, before pulling out a hot pink corset. 'Hear me out . . . ' she started to say. 'It's kinda kinky but it will look really cool with—'

'Black. I want all black,' Haruna said.

'Not even a splash of colour?' Greer asked, holding up a cherry-red vintage blouse.

Haruna shook her head.

'Small splash?' Greer held up a lime-green scarf.

'Sorry, I just want to wear black,' Haruna said. 'I dunno why.'

'Okay, well, I like these black leather leggings for you. And for a top – maybe a simple slogan tee?'

'No slogans,' Haruna said, taking the leggings. 'I just want to be in black. Love the leggings, though.'

'We get it. Black. We get it!' Frankie said, rolling her eyes at Haruna. 'Can't you be a bit more adventurous? This is your chance to be you.'

'I am being me,' Haruna said, rifling through the T-shirt choices.

'I know, but can't you be a bit *more* you?' Frankie said. 'You know, for the shoot?'

'No,' Haruna said bluntly. This makeover was starting to lose its charms.

'You be you,' Greer said, nodding, 'but do you like the military theme that Aimee has going on, because I have this hat?' She pulled out a blue felt army hat with a red ribbon and a black peak. 'Just we need to find a way to link you all together if we can.'

Haruna picked up the hat, and fondled it before looking for the toilets to change in. 'I like it.'

'Don't look in the mirror! I want to see your face when you see it!' Frankie shouted.

'Yeah, I got it,' Haruna said, hiding her *shut the fuck up* look. She pulled open the door to the toilets, and scooted inside, arms full of clothes. She felt lighter with all that hair gone, and could see the edges of her black hair brushing around her shoulders. She turned on the light, caught a flash of herself in the mirror and looked quickly away. And then she pulled on the leather leggings, and fished through the various black tops, settling for a sleeveless men's office shirt with frayed edges. Before she slipped it on, she glanced down at her shoulder to her new tattoo. A black, spindly, wintry tree that crept down her back and around her upper arm. On one of the small branches a solitary pink blossom clung to the edge just by her forearm.

Not even Frankie knew. She'd got it done a week before she left her mother's house with money she'd stolen from Greg. Perhaps she'd known what was coming.

Instinctively, and mostly because thinking about her parents made her allergic to any kind of control, she looked in the mirror. She looked first at the blue-black hair, cut into a long, blunt, fringed bob. She put her hands up to touch the silky strands and marvelled at the way they slipped through her fingers. The edge of the fringe set off her thick, poker-straight eye-brows. And where Frankie had used what felt like a ton of make-up, all that was visible were her deep, dark purple, almost black, lips.

She moved her head from side to side, and a small smile crept on to her face.

'You better not be looking!' Frankie shouted, rapping on the door. 'I wanna see your face!'

'No, no, hang on!' Haruna said. There was something she needed to do first. Something she'd been avoiding for a couple of weeks, but had become unavoidable. A big something. She looked back in the mirror and nodded at her reflection. *You can do this, Rooney. And whatever happens, you got this. You do!*

She reached into her bag and pulled out the box from Boots. Then she opened the cubicle door and squeezed inside.

She looked at the little box in her hand. *Rapid detection Clear Blue pregnancy test.* She slid out the long blue and white stick. After she read the instructions she pulled down the leather leggings and her knickers, slipped the cap off the stick and did the thing.

'Haruna!' Frankie was banging on the door now. 'Come on! Don't deprive me of this excitement!'

'I'm having a poo!' she shouted back, looking down at the stick as the water line moved down from the control window to the result window. It sure was rapid. She already knew what was coming, though.

Positive.

She double checked, holding the stick up next to the instruction sheet.

Definitely positive.

She sighed with relief at the knowing.

She'd guessed for a few weeks now, but it had been easier to ignore, push aside. There was so much else going on, it was easy to pretend it wasn't happening. But it was.

Positive.

It was eight weeks since she last had a period, about six weeks since the night she'd slept with Cheq, and about three weeks since she'd started feeling the tiredness and the nausea. She sat for a moment, putting her head in her hands, looking down at the toilet floor. In her heart, she knew what she wanted.

She collected the bits and pieces, shoved everything back in the Boots bag and thrust it to the bottom of her bag. She wasn't ready to tell anyone yet, but she needed to get moving.

She felt surprisingly calm. That probably came down to the decision being easy. There was no decision, really. But also, she felt no emotion. No joy. No fear. No attachment. Nothing. She was sure she was supposed to feel something. Some connection to the thing in her belly, but she didn't. The only trepidation was the how to do the next bit. But the internet could help with that.

When Haruna emerged, she looked at Aimee, Greer and then to Frankie and bit her lip to try to stop herself from giving anything away. But they were absolutely distracted by her appearance, and it was easy to get lost in the jubilation of the moment.

'You looked!' Frankie said, clearly disappointed, yet still beaming at her. 'I can *so* tell you looked. You can't hide anything! Oh well. You look so awesome. I love the hair. Love it. Adore it. It's perfection. And . . . ' Frankie gasped when she saw the tattoo. 'When did you get this?'

'A while back. While I was still at Mum's. It took ages.'

'Why just one flower?' Aimee said, coming over to admire the work. 'I mean, it's glorious . . . so sweet, that little blossom.'

'Maybe one day I'll get more.'

'Did you run out of cash?' Aimee asked, confused.

'Something like that,' she replied, catching Frankie's eye for a moment and then looking away, ashamed at the secret she was keeping from her.

'Look at us all in the mirror!' Aimee said, squeezing next to Haruna and pulling Frankie in for a squeeze. 'We look like a band, right? Our future awaits, gals! We're unstoppable!'

Chapter 26

Hot Topic

The scene on the canal was chaotic but super fun. The three band members stood in moody, slouchy poses by a bench next to a bin, while photographer Alexia ordered them around, regularly stopping for dog walkers, cyclists and joggers.

'So many joggers,' complained Frankie, as Alexia dropped her camera and stood back for the third time in a minute.

'I know. *Jogging*. Ugh,' said Alexia, as they shared a mutual irritation.

Though the park behind them was starting to show hints of spring, they managed to find a corner that looked bleak and grubby enough to shoot an up-and-coming punk band.

'Frankie, is it?' Alexia said, in her cool, unruffled New York accent. 'Could you move back a little? Just you're much taller, and we're losing Haruna.'

'But I'm the singer,' Frankie half-joked, pouting.

'Ha. Well, it's just for this set-up.' Alexia smiled. 'And you're going to have to be much more annoying and demanding than that if you're going to be a famous singer.'

The other girl, Greta, burst into an infectious high-pitch giggle at that, and the two glanced at each other as if sharing a private joke.

Despite being just shy of a year older than the girls, they were both very organised. Alexia was an earnest budding film-maker type, which made the whole thing feel far more serious and professional. Also, she only had two hours till she needed to be at another shoot so time was ticking.

'Oh man, when we're famous,' Frankie joked with Haruna and Aimee, 'I'm going to make the world's most demanding artist, I tell you. I just want dudes running around after me all day, answering my ridiculous demands.'

'Aimee, can we try you at the front?' Alexia called out, changing lenses, as Frankie pretended to be even more put out.

'Working in TV must be fun and super busy,' Frankie crowed, as she took her position for the hundredth time next to the bin.

'Yes, well, we really are,' Greta said. 'Well, I don't work in TV any more, but I used to do music TV and it was really busy. Lots of waiting around to actually be busy, though. So much waiting. All the time.'

'Haruna, can you look over there, towards the bin?'

'Of course,' Haruna replied, before whispering to Frankie, 'How long is this going to take? I feel uncomfortable.'

'Oh come on, you look amazing. Stop that,' Frankie chirped back.

Snap Snap Snap. Alexia was going a hundred miles an hour, making the most of every second, while Greta sat atop one of the canal boats behind her, her laptop open, pouring over Seven's website and social feeds.

'What's the Instagram password?' Greta shouted to Frankie.

'lovedoctor,' Frankie said, 'all lower case, same as Twitter and Facebook.'

'Jesus,' Haruna scoffed under her breath, 'seriously?'

'You must be feeling better,' Frankie said, as they moved a few feet to the left, 'since that snarky tone has returned? I guess the makeover did its trick?'

'You haven't posted even a picture since January!' Greta called out. 'Guys, you need to get on to this stuff! Thank God for me.'

'I never know what to post,' Frankie replied. 'None of us like being on social media. It's like the worst of high school online. It's just more of that shit. And also, when I first signed up for Facebook, my mum kept commenting on my posts, and signing everything with her name. Humiliating.'

'No no no; you need to just find your boundaries and your brand and go for it,' Greta said earnestly.

'We're a brand now? I thought we were a band . . . ' Haruna muttered under her breath.

'I heard that!' Frankie said, frowning at her. 'Come on, this is important. We need this.'

'Do we? I thought we needed some gigs.'

'I already spoke to Jules. It's arranged.'

'Have you heard from him, though? I thought he needs to confirm.'

Frankie held her hand up to Alexia for a moment to stop the snapping. 'Just a sec,' she said, smiling politely. She turned to Haruna, her voice dropping to a whisper. 'Are you okay? You've been all weird since the hairdresser's. Are you trying out a new persona? Like angry goth? Because it's too much. Even for you.'

'Sorry, I've got a lot on my mind,' Haruna said, looking glum. 'I'm sorry. I'm grateful.'

'It's okay, I was just checking,' Frankie said, vaguely irritated. She was finding herself starting to get fidgety with Haruna.

She was down. There was no denying it. Maybe even depressed – lethargic, moodier than usual, morose. And she was *always* home. Frankie should have expected that, given she was actually living with her right now – but she *did* think Haruna would spend the occasional night with Cheq, but it wasn't happening. Even when he picked them up from the studio, she insisted on going home with Frankie. And every bloody day after work, Frankie would heave herself up the stairs to her little bedroom to crash out, and Haruna would already be there, binge watching *Drag Race*.

It's not that she wouldn't do *anything* for her dearest friend, but occasionally she would have liked a bit of s p a c e.

'Your website needs a bit of work,' Greta was saying now. 'Can I take it home and redo it? I mean, it's hard to make out that you're actually a band. It doesn't even say band. If I didn't know what you were I'd struggle. And you've no SoundCloud. No Bandcamp. Guys! Let me redo your website please.'

'Oh, Greta, that's really kind of you but we can't afford it,' Frankie said, brushing aside the embarrassment at her dreadful marketing.

'Oh, I won't charge you. Pleeeeeease let me,' she begged. 'I've got time and I've never built up a band from nothing. Well, not nothing; I mean, you're already a band and stuff. You're obviously not *nothing*, but you're really just starting out. I built up a social feed once and had over a million followers. Are these reviews real? Cos, like, I can't find the full review anywhere online.'

'I made them up.' Frankie shrugged. '*Over a million followers. Wow.*'

'Leave it with me, and I will make you internet famous,' Greta replied, grinning as she continued tapping away on the keyboard.

'But still cool,' Frankie said with a cautionary tone. 'Like, I don't really care what you do, but don't post memes and dumb shit like that.'

'Memes are not dumb!' Greta said, aghast. 'Anyway, I'll stick to promotion, I won't speak for you. But you will need to post some stuff now and then or it's not authentic. Anyway, we can go into that later,' she went on, realising Alexia was waiting with her camera poised for their conversation to finish.

Frankie's phone tinkled in her pocket. 'Shit, sorry, Alexia, I have to take this.'

'No worries, I think we should put you guys on top of Greta's boat now anyway, for a change of background,' Alexia said, checking back the photos on the screen on her camera. 'That brick wall behind the boat is super cool.'

'Barge!' corrected Greta. 'It's a barge.'

'This is yours?' Haruna was saying as Frankie walked away down the canal to take the call from Jules.

'Hello, Jules, this is Frankie,' she said nervously. 'How's things?'

'We're on!' he said cheerfully. 'Sorry I didn't call sooner, but it's been ... busy.'

'Oh wow!' Frankie exhaled, some anxiety from the last few days floating away. 'Jules, this is just the *best* news.'

'Good,' he said, 'I'm glad too. It's gonna be fun playing with you. You need to call my manager; I'll give you all the details for that via text. He'll arrange everything for you; I've told him you might need some extra support.'

'Extra support?'

'Well, because you don't have a manager yet or anyone working with you, so ... '

'We do just fine,' she said cheerfully, looking back at the photography set, where Alexia was directing the girls on to Greta's boat. Haruna was standing at the edge of the canal waiting for Aimee to climb on, arms folded, pouting. *Something's up with her*, she thought, with frustration.

'I've no doubt,' Jules was saying. 'Um, I guess I'll see you there, then? Or fancy catching up before?'

'See you there!' Frankie replied, distracted by Haruna, who was now sitting on the boat, blanket wrapped around her bare shoulders, looking nineties-emo levels of glum.

'Okay then,' Jules said. 'Speak soon.'

'Oh, Jules,' Frankie said quickly, just as the line went dead on her. *Shit.* She groaned. *That was rude.* She thought about calling him back for a moment, and then saw Haruna climbing back off the boat and pulling on her coat on. *What now?* she thought, irritation growing. She hurried over to Haruna, who definitely looked like she was leaving.

'What's going on?'

'I have to go, I'm sorry,' Haruna said. 'Alexia said she probably has something she can use.'

Frankie spun around to Alexia who nodded. 'I think so. There were a bunch straight off the bat that were cool.'

'Where are you going, though?'

'I have to see Cheq.'

'I have to see Cheq,' Frankie repeated.

Haruna pulled her bag around her shoulders and lowered her voice. 'It's important, please. Don't make a thing. You have to trust me. Please.' With that she turned to leave, but as she passed, Frankie grabbed at her arm, jerking her back.

'Wait!' Frankie said, her voice sharp and high.

'Hey.' Haruna pulled her arm back. 'What the hell?'

'What the hell are *you* doing? What's up with you?' Frankie shouted.

'Nothing, Frankie, please. I need to go. We're finished here. I've been doing the band stuff for hours now and I have something important I need to do.'

'No!' Frankie said defiantly.

'No?' Haruna said. 'Excuse me?'

Frankie stared at her, brow furrowed, leaning in, spoiling for a fight. 'You're so ungrateful. I've done so much to organise this. Alexia and Greta came along at short notice. Even bloody Greer did something for us with half a smile. Sorry, Greer,' she said, glancing across at the other girl. Greer looked furious, but Frankie was on a roll. 'They're all here because I pulled these favours. All because of me and you're, what, bailing? To go see a fucking dude you could see anytime you wanted?'

'Please, Frankie, don't be a dick. You don't know what you're talking about.'

'Don't be a dick?' Frankie said, aghast. 'How can you say that? I put you up in my own house. I pay your rent. If it wasn't for me, you'd have nowhere to go.'

'So what, I owe you? You're in charge now?' Haruna challenged. 'You're looking after me so I have to live the way you want me to. Sounds familiar.'

'Oh, fuck off. It's not like that and you know it.'

'What's it like, then?'

Haruna stared at Frankie for a moment, with a look she had never seen before. It was cold. Damn cold. Frankie felt a chill run through her as she became aware of Greta, Greer, Aimee and Alexia behind them listening.

'Fine. Go.'

'I don't need your permission,' Haruna said, marching off down the canal, her perfectly symmetrical bob swaying like a pendulum behind her.

Chapter 27

Spare Me

Haruna didn't really have a plan, other than going to see Cheq with a fifty per cent intention of telling him her news. She had a ninety-nine per cent idea of what she wanted to do next, and the chance that Cheq would feel differently scared her.

As she walked along the glassy shop fronts of Mare Street she kept catching flashes of her refection in shop mirrors. It was a strange feeling, not recognising your own reflection, and it made her uneasy. Too much change. Too much she couldn't control. She felt a knot in her stomach, different from the mild nausea that had been plaguing her for weeks now; this was an angry, vengeful, twisting knot, something that she'd been growing since she was ten.

She arrived at Cheq's flat, marched up to the front door and banged four times firmly. Sometimes the guys were asleep or playing Xbox in the lounge and didn't hear the door, but a moment later Jules was standing there, holding a mug of tea, looking surprised.

'Haruna,' he said, smiling at her. 'Cheq's not here. But do you want to come in?'

'Yes. Thanks, Jules. I'll come in,' she said, looking longingly at his cup of tea.

'Can I make you one?' he asked gently, eyeing her. Jules was intuitive, and he had clocked her attempt to hide her distress immediately. 'Come in. I just turned the heating on, and believe it or not, we have a cleaner now.'

Haruna hesitated, looking at Jules nervously, before stepping into the warm hall.

'Cool hair,' he said, helping her with her jacket, which she let him do. 'Come through. Jump on the couch. I'll make you a tea and leave you to call him or wait or whatever you need. Netflix? Xbox?' he added with a grin.

'Thanks,' she said, her voice starting to waver a little. She swallowed, the taste of bile rising in her throat. She needed to eat. Eating helped. 'Do you have any bread? Or something?'

'Sure do. Want a toastie? I was just making one for myself,' he said, before adding, 'I got sourdough from 54.'

'I don't know what that means,' she said.

'It means it's your lucky day.'

'Is it?' she replied sourly.

'Take a seat. Have you called Cheq? He can't be far away, we were going to go out tonight.'

'Oh.' It was the only answer she could find.

She walked slowly through to the lounge, which, despite the old furniture and absolute lack of interior design, was warm and welcoming and clean. She curled up on the couch and pulled out her phone.

There were several angry messages on WhatsApp from Frankie, which she promptly ignored, and she dropped Cheq a quick note.

At your house, we need to talk.

And then, because she didn't want to freak him out, she added:

Nothing serious. Just hanging out. Jules making me a toastie.

Jules came through a moment later with a toasted cheese sandwich and a tea. Nothing fancy, but it was just what she needed. He flicked on the TV and handed her the remote.

'You know how to find Netflix?' he asked. 'Help yourself, okay?'

'Thanks, Jules,' she said, and then, as he went to leave, 'Jules?'

'Yes.'

'Can you sit with me?' she said feebly.

'Sure. You wanna talk? I've got three big sisters, I'm a good listener,' he said, laughing. 'What's up? This isn't about Cheq, is it?'

'No. Not really,' Haruna said quietly. 'Everything is connected somehow, though, isn't it?'

'Yeah, I guess so,' he replied, studying her face for a moment, before putting his toastie on the coffee table in front of him. 'Did Frankie tell you we're definitely doing the gig together?'

'Oh. No. She didn't. When did you—'

'I just called her, like, an hour ago.'

'Oh, that's great news,' Haruna said, feeling more guilt. She brought her hands up to her face, resting her forehead to her palms. 'She's amazing.'

'She is,' he said with a sigh. 'Maybe drinks a bit too much, but yeah, she's amazing.'

'You like her.'

'Yeah. I can't hide it,' he laughed. 'But I surrender. She's not interested. I won't push it any more. No means no. I don't want her to feel uncomfortable.'

'I don't know,' Haruna said, 'she's uncomfortable being adored. Though anyone can tell just by being with her five minutes, it's all she really wants. It's a riddle.'

'Adored?' he said. 'I just fancied her. I mean, I do fancy her, still. I was hook, line and sinker after I saw that messed-up show you did at the bingo hall.'

'Oh God, you were our only fan.'

'She was … incredible on stage. Like, she really has this electricity.' He sat back, shaking her head. 'She was super-hot. And I know she's a bit full of shit, but I can't help finding it pretty funny. She told me Falls Records were coming to see you. I mean, come on? You guys have only played one gig! She forgets I live with Cheq.' He burst out laughing before shaking his head at the memory. His face full of affection.

'Falls Records are coming to see us,' Haruna said, 'at least I think so. She did a deal with one of the A&R guys when she auditioned for a girl band.'

'What? She auditioned for a girl band?'

'Frankie makes a lot of stuff up. But I do think Falls Records promised her they would come to her gig if they liked her demo. You wanna hear it? I haven't even played it to Cheq yet.'

'I'd love to.'

Haruna handed him her iPod. 'It's on there. There're four tracks. We recorded them at The Church. Listen to the first … That's kind of the single, I guess?'

'The Church? That's where we're recording.'

'Probably where she got the idea.'

'How did you pay for it?'

'They did it free,' Haruna said, biting her lip. 'I know, I don't know how she does it either.'

'Okay. I'm still really into her,' Jules said, putting the headphones in. 'She's such a hustler, it's really attractive.'

Haruna picked up the remote and turned on the TV while Jules listened. She glanced over a couple of times, nervous of his reaction, but he smiled and nodded in her direction. After three minutes and twenty-three seconds he took off the headphones.

'Wow,' he said, 'it's punk as. Makes me want to drink booze and mosh. Awesome. Can I listen to the rest?'

'Sure. I can email them to you. Don't tell Frankie, though. She's all "keep them secret" and shit.'

'She's really not with that Doc guy?' he asked, as if assessing whether he could try one last time.

'I don't think so. As you can see, I'm never a hundred per cent sure of anything with Frankie,' Haruna said, looking over at him. He was so calming to be around. So easy. 'I think you would be good for her. Doc, he was . . . ugh.'

'Oh yeah, I met him. I've seen him around Wick Rooms too, I think. He's in that band Blood, something something.'

'*Was*,' she corrected, sighing. 'He's such a loser. She makes me so mad sometimes.'

'Did you two have a fight today? Is that what this is about?'

'Kind of,' she said, feeling vaguely disloyal.

'That's the bitter-sweet inevitability of friendship,' he said thoughtfully, 'there's always bad times. But you stick around because of the good.'

'She's been so good to me.'

'Well, I'm sure you've been good to her too.'

'Maybe . . . ' she said, her voice trailing off. 'Mostly I think I've been a drain. Sorry, you don't need this.'

'It's okay. You know, when I saw her on the night of my gig she was talking about you for ages. Saying how much she loved you. I mean, I know she was high, really high, but she couldn't stop talking about you. She said you were her sister from another mister.'

'What happened that night?'

'It's a bit embarrassing,' he said.

'Oh, you have to tell me now.'

'I played her that Sleater-Kinney song – "I wanna be your Joey Ramone".'

Haruna bit her lip, suppressing a smile. 'Oh dear.'

'I dunno, she was moshing. She kept smiling at me. I thought—' He stopped. 'Well, I thought she might be into me. I got carried away. But we met after the gig and chatted and I don't think she even knew the song was for her. And then there was Doc there and, well . . . Whatever. Own goal for Jules.'

Haruna giggled a bit. 'She *does* get too wasted. She knows it, though; I think she's aware she needs to knock it on the head.'

'Probably should. At least a bit.'

'And then she makes dumb choices,' Haruna continued, 'but then, she makes those dumb choices sober too, so . . . '

The front door opened and Haruna stiffened a little, Cheq's arrival home sending her back to her reality. She heard him shake off and hang up his coat, and call out, 'Haruna?'

'In here!' she called, as Jules stood up, shaking the crumbs off his shirt and on to the floor. *Thank you*, she mouthed to Jules, who nodded and made himself immediately scarce.

'Hey, babe. What's happening? Everything okay?' He stopped suddenly, taking in her new look. 'Ru, your hair. It looks . . . wow.'

'You like it?' she said, feeling all those annoying girlie insecurities come flooding back. She touched the back, suddenly feeling shy about the dramatic change.

'It's great. You look older . . . ?' He paused. 'Can I say that?'

'Yes,' she grinned.

His concern was arresting. She didn't uncurl, offering only a tight-lipped smile. The kind that meant there was a conversation coming.

'Has something happened?' he said, his concern turning to confusion as he sat on the other end of the couch, leaning towards her, a hand on her leg. 'Are you okay? Is this about your mum. Or is it school?'

'School? What about school?'

'Well, you haven't been going and Frankie said that social services might start asking questions. I don't know. You're suddenly not there. What if your mum tells the police you're missing?'

'Oh.' Haruna shook her head.

'It's not about that?' he asked nervously.

'No,' she replied, 'sorry you've been worrying. I should really look into what I need to do to formalise my life in some way. I need to drop out of school, I guess.'

'You can't do that!' he said. 'What do you mean? You've only missed a couple of weeks, you can go back. Say you were sick. You should really finish.'

Haruna let out a long sigh. More life direction. 'But I've had enough. I don't need to be there. I don't even know about uni any more.'

Cheq sat back. 'Ru, what's going on? Something is definitely up, babe.'

'What's up? Let's see. Shall we start with the fact I want to go to Japan to see my dad. But I don't have any money because my mum gave it all to Greg. Or the Church or whatever.'

'Have you spoken to him?'

'Who, Greg?'

'No, not that fucker.'

'My dad?'

'Yes.'

'No.'

'Okay,' Cheq said, looking at her curiously, 'is that what you wanted to talk about?'

'No.' Haruna looked down at her hands, cupping them together protectively. She wasn't sure what she wanted to do. She was scared he would complicate the situation. Make her think things she didn't want to think. Her mind wandered to the night they slept together. She had contained the memory to snapshots. Him leaning over her, topless, his dark skin beautiful in the soft light. The pain and the pleasure of the moment it happened. At times she felt like she was standing back, watching her, watching him – a weird detachment that came from being too focused on what was happening. She couldn't let go. She had a kind of internal commentator: *Is he enjoying it? Should I move? Why won't he look at me?* But she still liked it. It wasn't what she'd expected, but it was sweet. Intimate. And he told her he loved her, right after. When his heart finished pounding against the skin on her chest, he whispered it to her. *I love you.* She didn't reply, but she knew he knew how she felt. She put her hand up on the back of his head and stared up at the ceiling.

She still got a warm flutter up her spine when she remembered.

But then there were the hours afterwards, when the feeling of intimacy turned to fear. It started as a slow creeping feeling inside her; a deep regret at her vulnerability, at her loss of control. Control. It was something she had so little of.

When they discovered the split condom, Cheq had tried to comfort her. It's probably fine. *So unlikely*, he'd said. He'd even joked, 'Wouldn't be so bad, would it? A little baby Cheq one day.'

'Sounds frightening,' she'd joked in return, and vowed to go get the morning-after pill just in case. But didn't. She tried to get the money together, and then find a way to sneak out from the house, but she kept putting it off, convincing herself that Cheq was right, it was one in a million. And then ... the window closed. It was only a few days later she discovered she could have got the pills free at the pharmacy around the corner. It scared her that she was so unprepared, and so clueless.

That fear seeped into all corners of her like a virus,

distorting her perception and confusing her. It chipped away at her trust of the relationship, and her trust of him. *Her feelings.* Did she even love him?

Cheq wanted more than she could give. And that wanting *more* of her was suffocating.

This same fear ate away at her feelings for her mother. That her mother had chosen *Greg* over her. That she'd stolen that money from her. Her future. And *the fear* was why she had grown resentful of Frankie. The fear that she was in her way – putting her out – causing pain, being an inconvenience.

'Ru,' Cheq leaned forward again, 'you need to speak to me. I'm doing my best here, but we've got to talk. You're living at Frankie's, you've dropped out of school, you're different.'

'Different?'

'You're ... I don't know. Like, not yourself. One minute you're clingy, the next you're pulling away. Ever since that night at my brother's, I feel like you've been angry at me—' He stopped himself. 'Are you still into this?' He pointed to her and then back to himself.

'Yes, I guess so,' she replied.

'You guess so?' he repeated. 'Did I do something?'

'No.'

Cheq sighed and put his head in his hands. 'I'm trying, Ru.'

'I know,' she said, looking down to her belly. And there she was, pregnant with Cheq's baby. It was the size of a grape or something now, but she felt nothing. No attachment to it. Nothing. Was that how her mother felt about her? Was there something wrong with her that she felt nothing about this pregnancy?

There was an undeniable truth that she couldn't shake. She had lived for so long in a state of oppression. Her entire self, hidden away from her mother, living a rebellious half-life built of stolen afternoons and secret memories. She was clipped. She didn't know who she truly was. She needed to find out.

'Cheq, I want to break up,' she said quietly.

Chapter 28

Close Up

Frankie's phone went again: Aimee for the third time that morning. She put down the parcel with the USB stick containing their demo and the press photo that Alexia had sent her that morning. The image she chose was cool, breezy and weirdly one where they all looked happy, despite the rumbling discord that was, in retrospect, so obviously present that day. The angry punky ones just didn't feel like them, although today perhaps, that was more apt.

She needed to send it right away if there was any chance of getting Geoff to come to their gig. She doubted he would chase her for it again.

Everything had got urgent at the same time it was falling apart. Greer called yesterday to say that she'd found all their stuff back in storage at Wick Rooms. Whether the room had finally been rented or not, she didn't know, but it had put practices on hold for now. Not that it urgently mattered, what with their drummer missing.

'Hi, Aimee, no news I'm afraid.'

'Well, she's not at her parents',' Aimee said bluntly. 'Her mother was totally weird, by the way. She wouldn't open the door to me properly. And she was all "I don't speak with Haruna any more", and "she has chosen her own path now". I mean, wouldn't you care that your daughter had gone missing?'

'I guess she's been missing from her mum's life for a few weeks now, so it probably didn't make as much of an impact. If she didn't care then, she ain't gonna care now,' Frankie said grimly.

'What are we going to do, Frankie? We kind of need to hit the streets.'

'Haruna isn't sleeping rough or anything like that, I can promise you. And she's only been gone a few days. I bet she's going to be back here soon.' Frankie was trying not to worry Aimee any more than she already was. But the truth was, Frankie was really worried. 'But yeah, I might go and check a few places out. I know someone who might be able to get a car. I'll call you, okay? Call me if *you* hear anything?'

'Yep. Love you, Frankie,' Aimee said softly. 'I hope she's okay. I have a bad feeling.'

'Don't worry. Frankie's here,' she said. 'You know me. I'll sort it.'

Frankie hung up, racking her brains for where Haruna could be.

She hadn't returned on the day of the photoshoot, when she'd stormed off to see Cheq about *something important.* She'd broken up with him. That much Frankie knew. When she called to ask after Haruna, Cheq spoke to her for about thirty seconds before abruptly hanging up. He was angry. But it didn't make any sense to Frankie. Why? Why would she break up with Cheq? Had he done something?

Frankie sat on the edge of her bed, looking over at the cardboard box of things Haruna had brought back from her mother's house. She walked over and flipped through the contents, but there was nothing in there that would give anything away, except the fact that she hadn't taken anything with her. It can't have been planned. She tried her number again, but the phone was still off.

She returned to the envelope and slipped the USB inside, licked the gluey seal and then taped it – just to make sure – and pulled out a pen and scribbled the address on the front. She needed to get to the post box asap.

But as she neared the front door, she pulled her coat off the rail and stopped. Why was she doing this? She looked in the hall mirror at her reflection. Her eyes were tired.

This whole thing started because of a guy.

Doc. She wanted to be in a band so badly to impress him. She wanted to be as cool as possible so he might like her. Before Christmas it was just a bit of bullshit. She carried her guitar around mostly so people (or, Doc) could see it – not because something in her *ached* to play. Not because her very soul depended on it like Haruna's did. But in the last months, something had changed. The band had transformed her in a way, given her a focus.

And it was the performing that grabbed her first. That night at the bingo hall, when she stood there in, basically, her underwear, surrounded by her best friends, belting out those messy, under-rehearsed rock 'n' roll songs. If this was something she could actually do with her life – like, for a living – she wanted to try. No, not just try. She wanted to give it everything she had.

She bent down to tie up her boots and remembered the afternoon in the recording studio with Amelie when they'd reworked that first song, and how it had evolved into something that made sense. Something that was a part of all of them. Haruna couldn't be gone. She wouldn't walk away from that, would she?

She pushed open the door, tucking the envelope into her pocket, and headed towards the post office. She was determined. This band was going to take off, and Aimee was going to defer med school and Haruna was going to come back and that was that.

She pulled out her phone and dialled her mum, who picked up almost immediately.

'Pet,' she said, 'I was just with Anya at work and she said you stayed late and helped clean out the back store last night.'

'Hi, Mum. Yes, but only cos I need the money,' she said more sharply than she intended. 'Sorry, Mum. Listen,

I'm just covering all bases but Haruna has kind of … gone missing.'

'Gone missing?'

'Yes. We had a fight … '

'What did you do, Frankie?'

'Why is it that I had to have done something?' Frankie said, irritated. 'Anyway, we had a fight and she's gone and I just wondered if you'd heard from her, but you obviously haven't.'

'No, I haven't.' Her mother let out a deep sigh. 'Oh, I always worried it would come to something like this.'

'Something like what?'

'Haruna running away or being … hurt, or something.'

'Something?'

'I liked Linda very much once, as you know. But that man, Greg. Something was always off about him. Made her give up work, and go to church. Her! *Church*. She was never religious when I knew her. What kind of a bloody church lets a mother turn their back on their child?'

'That's bloody right!' her dad boomed in the background.

'Tell Dad hello,' Frankie said, suddenly wanting to be home in the tiny lounge watching *Bargain Hunt* with him.

'Oh, this is all just such a worry, Frankie,' her mother fretted. 'Do we need to call the police?'

'Um. Maybe. I don't know. It's been a few days. I thought the first couple of nights she just stayed at Cheq's to cool off. I was kinda glad really because she's been sharing my bed. But then when she didn't come back the next night I called him, concerned. And he was, like, "Duh she broke up with me", and I was, like, "What? She totally loves you", and he was— Hang on, Mum, I'm at the post office.'

She hung up and made her way to the cashier.

'I need this,' she said, fishing out her envelope, 'to go to Soho as quickly as possible.'

'Bakerloo line to Oxford Circus,' the chubby bespectacled man replied, chortling.

'Can it get there tomorrow? First class or whatever?'

'Absolutely.' He grinned, sensing Frankie was in no mood for chitchat.

Twenty minutes later and Frankie was on the overground to Hackney. She jumped off at Hackney Central, stopping for a minute by one of the charity shops, remembering the days she'd spent after school hunting the racks with Haruna who couldn't really get anything. *She had had it really hard.* Sometimes when Frankie really thought about it, she felt an ache so big, so overwhelming, she couldn't bare it.

Rounding London Fields she headed down the path towards Cheq's place, and dialled Jules's number. He picked up in three rings. It was refreshing to not have to wonder if someone was going to answer. He always seemed to.

'Frankie,' Jules said, surprise in his voice, 'you calling about the gig? Is there a problem?'

'No, no. Not really. I'm calling about Haruna.'

'Oh,' he said, 'is she okay? Cheq's a mess.' He sounded bummed. She was bummed too. She had grown to like Cheq a lot, and he was good for Haruna. Just enough wild for her rebellious side, just the right amount of stable, and of course, pretty talented and hot.

'He's not heard from her?'

'No, she's totally ghosted him. I think he tried to call a couple of times, but I'm trying to distract him now. He's playing Call of Duty, which I think has been therapeutic.'

'Jules, can you borrow his car and take me for a quick drive somewhere? I need to find her.'

'Where is she?'

'She's missing, we think,' she said carefully. 'I'm sure everything is okay, but I need to check some places and I can't do that quickly on foot.'

'I can come pick you up, for sure.'

'Oh, you're a lifesaver. But, I'm actually outside. Look out of the window!'

Jules appeared at the second-storey window and Frankie waved at him from across the street. 'Okay, that's creepy. You'd make a good stalker.'

'Like you wouldn't believe . . .' Frankie felt the pressure drop as she let out a giggle. 'Sorry, I didn't knock as I don't want to freak Cheq out. Oh God, it's my mum on the other line.'

'Give me five, I'm on my way down,' he said.

Frankie switched lines. 'Hi, Mum! Sorry I hung up on you.'

'Darling, I've spoken to Haruna's mother. And the police.'

'You what?' Frankie's jaw dropped. 'Mum!'

'Well, the police won't do much as she's near enough eighteen. So, then I called her mother. Your father and I discussed it, and we decided to speak to her as parents. And, well, I feel utterly heartbroken at this business. How that girl turned out as wonderful as she did is beyond me.'

'What happened, Mum?'

'Haruna *has* been home. Two days ago. She turned up asking for money.'

'God, I would have given her money,' Frankie tutted, feeling like she'd let her friend down once more.

'You shouldn't be supporting her, Frankie; you're just a bloody kid yourself. I know what you earn, and I know how much rent you pay. You can't afford to look after Haruna.'

'All right, all right. I just hate the idea of her begging her mother for anything,' Frankie said.

'Look, Haruna's mother is a victim here too, Frankie. It might not seem that way to you right now but that is a fact. I wish I'd been more of a friend to her, but it all became too hard and you make your decisions, don't you? All my intuition was firing. She was a lovely woman and a sweet mother before that Greg. *Ugh.* Makes me shiver just thinking about it. Anyway, seems Haruna has a plan at least. She wants to go to Japan,' her mother said, 'and apparently, she was fine. Well, according to her mother, anyway.'

Frankie sighed. 'Did she give her any money?'

'She did. She gave her some cash, I believe. But she didn't have much.'

'Funny, she took all of Haruna's . . . ' Frankie huffed.

'What you must understand is that Haruna's mother is scared too, Francesca. She managed to find her a few hundred pounds or so, I think. She said she was – and I quote – "afraid of what she might do if I didn't". I told her I would keep an eye on Haruna as best I could and I will honour that.'

'Oh my God, she's trying to get to Japan,' Frankie wailed just as Jules jogged across the street to meet her. 'Mum, I have to go.'

Jules was holding the keys in his right hand, and he reached out to usher Frankie towards Cheq's car. He gave her a nod. He was calm. He was calming.

'He let you take it?'

'Yeah, he doesn't know why, though,' Jules said, shrugging. Frankie pulled a worried face, before Jules quickly reassured her. 'It's cool, don't worry. And I'm happy to help. You can't drive?'

'You don't know me very well if you think I should be in charge of driving a motor vehicle. I had one lesson once and took out a stop sign.'

'You took out a stop sign? Why doesn't that surprise me?'

He laughed. A gentle laugh that relieved the soberness of the situation. They jumped in the car and as the door slammed, Frankie said, 'She was at her mother's looking for money. I know she wants to go to Japan but she doesn't have a passport so . . . Well, I doubt she's gone yet anyway. Can we drive around a bit?'

'Sure,' Jules said without hesitation. He turned the key

and expertly pulled out of the park, drove round the one-way system and out on to Mare Street. 'Victoria Park way first?'

Frankie nodded. *Where is Haruna and what the hell is going on?*

They took Well Street and darted around the back streets to Victoria Park Village, Frankie gazing out of the window looking for any sign of her. They pulled up outside a café that Haruna used to visit, Hackney Library and the Picturehouse – memories of their friendship apparent on every street corner, under every stone.

'Does she have any aunts? Uncles? Other family besides her mum?'

'No. They're all in Japan. No one on her mum's side.'

'I can't imagine. I've got such a big family.'

'Same. An uncle on every corner.'

'Same here,' Jules laughed, 'can't get away with anything on the bad streets of Notting Hill.'

'That's where you're from? Notting Hill? God, I never go west.'

'West is best.'

'West sucks. It's full of snobby rich kids and tourists.'

'And east is full of city bankers.'

'I wondered why you spoke so posh,' Frankie said, prodding him.

'Notting Hill used to be pretty cool, you know. It's where punk originally came from. The Sex Pistols. Vivienne Westwood lived in Chelsea.'

'No, that's impossible,' Frankie replied, shaking her head at him.

'She did. And the Roundhouse, where you're gonna play; The Pistols played there too. And the Damned, Patti Smith, the Ramones . . . The Clash.'

Frankie gulped. 'Wow. I love the Ramones. I'm so amped for this gig.' *Oh my lord, this has to happen.* It was scary and big and beyond what they were ready for but it had to happen. 'But we currently don't have a drummer . . . so?'

'We'll find her. If there's no family, what about school?'

'No. Oh, hang on!' Frankie said. 'Hackney Wick!'

'Wick Rooms?'

'Yeah, she's got the key, we should definitely try there.'

'You got it.'

'I'm a genius,' she said, as Jules pulled into the next drive and turned the car around to head east.

Minutes later, as they pulled up outside Wick Rooms, Frankie started to worry. *What if Haruna didn't want to see her?* She looked at Jules. 'Can you just stay here? I'll call you in a few minutes if she's there.'

'Hang on, I'll need to let you in, right? You don't have a key?'

He jumped out of the car and fished through his own key chain and stuck the key in the lock. 'Good luck. I hope she's there.'

Chapter 29

Hey Baby

Haruna tried to roll over on the sofa in the corner of the practice room, but it was awkwardly lumpy and shallow. She pulled the coat up over her to try to keep warm. The cramps were gentle, but the doctor had said they would get worse and last about six hours. She looked up at the ceiling. It had been painted brown, but was peeling at one corner. Her eyes trailed down to the wall, a half-torn-down poster revealed about eight different layers of posters underneath. Next to it, some graffiti was scrawled in thick black pen.

WE GO THROUGH LIFE. WE SHED OUR SKINS. WE BECOME OURSELVES. PATTI SMITH.

We shed our skins.

We become ourselves.

She closed her eyes and felt the peace in her decision and the relief that it would soon be over. She had no emotional connection to what was happening, but it didn't mean she didn't feel grim. And alone.

She felt bad for Cheq, but she didn't want to tell him. She didn't want things complicated by his feelings. And she needed to be alone.

She heard Frankie clomping down the corridor long before she shoved the practice-room door open, hands on hips, leaning forward looking for a fight.

Haruna tore her eyes away from the quote on the wall. She stretched and rubbed her tired eyes. She longed to sleep. To curl up in Frankie's bed next to her.

'What the hell is going on?' Frankie said, in a tone far gentler than her words. 'You broke up with Cheq? You left my house? Your phone's off? Where have you been? Jesus, Haruna, it's been terrifying. Mum even called the police, although they wouldn't do anything.'

'Hey, Frankie,' Haruna replied, 'I'm sorry I worried everyone. I don't know what happened really. I just wanted to be alone.'

'Your mum says you got money to go to Japan.'

'Yeah, that's what I told her.'

'*What you told her*?'

'Yeah,' she said, slowly pulling herself up into a seated position. 'Sorry, I'm . . . a bit . . . '

'Are you sick?' Frankie said, looking at her again.

'Kind of.' Haruna put her head in her hands. 'Frankie, please don't give me a hard time. There were some things I had to do. But I also made some mistakes. I can't think about them now, but know that I know and I'm sorry.'

'What? What did you have to do? What have you done? Can't you just tell me?'

'Can't you respect that I want to keep something private?'

Frankie sat on the edge of the sofa and put her hand on Haruna's leg. Haruna stiffened at first, then reached her hand up to touch Frankie's.

'I want to go home. With you,' she said. 'To your home. Can I come, please?'

'My home is your home, Haruna,' Frankie said, frowning.

'Can you take me?' Haruna said. 'I need a shower, I think . . . '

'Of course. But Jules is outside,' Frankie said. 'Do you mind? He doesn't need to know anything.'

'I don't mind Jules,' Haruna said, with a small smile. 'I just need to go to a home. I was supposed to be with someone, the doctor said.'

Frankie looked at her again, and then her eyes trailed down to the floor where she saw a shopping bag with pads, and ibuprofen.

'Why were you at the doctor?' Frankie said. 'Please tell me, Ru. Are you pregnant?'

'Yep,' she said quietly, '*was* pregnant. I don't know if I still am. It takes six hours.'

She looked up at Frankie again, glancing over at her quote once more and, steady and assured, she asked, 'Can you take me to yours?'

Frankie stood up and held out her hand for Haruna.

'Come,' she said. 'Come home with me. I know what you want. I'm going to help you.'

Chapter 30

Bad Apples

Frankie kicked her guitar case out in front of her, and tossed a few coins on to the top to encourage the busy commuters of St James's Park to offer up a couple of their millions of pounds. How hard could busking be, really?

She took a deep breath and rubbed at her eyes. She was tired. Bone tired, really. The last few nights with Haruna had been rough. It wasn't the recovery from the abortion that had weighed them down – physically that was all mostly over by the next morning – it was holding Haruna afloat generally. Since then, they had been discussing the events at her mother's house, her decision to break up with Cheq, and to keep him in the dark about the pregnancy, almost from dawn to dusk. The same conversation over and over. Every time Frankie thought she could steer the conversation forward, towards the looming gig at the Roundhouse, or to practising again, Haruna would pull it back. Frankie could feel herself losing patience.

'But we really need to go over the songs, just practise. It will do you good, I promise,' Frankie had said.

'I need more time, Frankie, please,' Haruna had replied. 'All I can think about right now is getting out of this place. Getting on that plane.'

'Well, why don't you bloody email your dad?' Frankie had said too sharply. 'Tell him you want to come and, like, ask him for the money to go.'

'I can't do that,' Haruna had said, looking sullenly out of the window. 'I don't feel like I can do that. Not right now, at least.'

'What about your mum? She said there was *some* money left, didn't she? Do you think what she gave you was all of it?'

'That's going to need a whole lot more time, that one.'

'You know,' Frankie had said, taking a deep breath, 'I think you should really consider calling her. Mum was pretty adamant she was, I dunno, *trying*.'

'No chance,' Haruna had answered, with a bitterness that both broke Frankie's heart and made her frustration start to boil.

'Okay.' Frankie had taken a deep breath. 'Well, why don't we try to raise some money for you somehow? Or we could speak to Dad about a loan or something?'

'Frankie, you don't have to fix me. I'll get there. I just need—'

'Time. Yes. I got it,' she'd snapped.

Then yesterday, time was suddenly up, as Frankie got the call she'd been waiting for.

'Hello?' she said brightly, grateful the call had interrupted the dreary atmosphere in her room.

'Is this Frankie Taylor?' said a gruff voice.

'Yes it is . . . and you are?'

'Well, I'm not impressed.'

'I'm sorry, who is this?'

'Geoff, Falls Records.'

Frankie's heart started thumping. *No. This can't be. He called!* She had to remain super cool.

'Oh, the girl band guy?' said Frankie, with a pretend laugh. *I'm cool. I'm cool. I'm cool.*

'Yes. That's me. The fucking girl band guy,' he snorted. 'Listen, I'm calling because your bloody demo caused all sorts of shit.'

'It did?' Frankie said. 'That doesn't sound good.'

'I did some bloody digging right after we spoke, not that I had the fucking time, but my boss raked me over the coals for indulging you at that audition. I had a feeling about you, and I wanted to give you a go and he just thought you were a snotty-nosed little East End rat. A bloody shark, more like.'

'Excuse me, I—' Frankie started before Geoff's bellowing voice shut her down.

'You made out that you were an established band, but I put out a few calls and no one has even heard of Seven. Your website was a bloody mess. It was clear you'd never really done a gig, despite a few ropey snaps at what looked like a school hall? No Bandcamp. No SoundCloud. A fucking waste of my time.'

'It was a bingo hall,' she said sheepishly.

'Whatever, anyway, so I tossed your bloody computer stick in the bin—'

'USB stick,' she corrected, getting annoyed. 'What are you, like forty?'

'Easy, kid. I'm not the one who had a website designed by a five-year-old.'

'Okay okay.' Frankie cringed. 'Look, if you're ringing to give me a hard time for wasting your time, hands in the air. I'm sorry.'

'Well, you know what's *not* better than a crappy manufactured girl band?'

'A band that has been together for five minutes?' Frankie said, sighing.

'Exactly. And James, my boss, who by the way *rarely even* comes to those auditions and will probably never come again after meeting you, said you were arrogant and that I got taken in because of some nostalgic lust for guitar music. Anyway, fuck him. His taste is terrible.'

'Sorry?' Frankie said, confused.

'I listened to your demo.'

'I thought you threw it in the bin?'

'I did. And then curiosity got the better of me. It's good. And so are your sodding press shots.'

'Oh. Okay.'

'And so then I go back online and in what, like, three weeks, you have suddenly got a flash new website, and social media presence, and managed to get Amelie at The Church to record some demos for you?'

Frankie gulped. *A flash new website? Social media presence?* Greta had been hard at work. Oh my God, all this work that Frankie had done. All this investment. She'd been so tied up in Haruna she'd not even checked.

'So when's the gig?'

'Next week, Thursday.' For a moment Frankie faltered. She could convince Haruna, couldn't she? She was sure of it. 'Thursday. We're on before Giants of Earth.'

'Oh, I know them. *The saviours of guitar music.* Apparently.'

'Hmm. Well,' said Frankie, 'I think Seven will save it first.'

Geoff laughed. 'Okay, Frankie. I'll see you there. Put me on the fucking door, okay?'

'Okay.' She'd hung up the phone and screamed.

Frankie *had* to get Haruna back into a good place and on board with this gig. Somehow.

It was 7:45, so Frankie had to get cracking. She unfolded the rickety music stand she'd pinched from her brother and stacked her music book on it, and then slipped her dad's acoustic guitar around her neck and checked the tuning. *It'll do*, she thought, as she readied herself.

In front of her, people in black and navy and crisp white cotton pushed hurriedly past, making their way to some bland firm with a bland name like Wanknut and Associates, or, worse, some dreadful desk job at parliament. She wasn't nervous playing in front of them, especially since she had help.

'Frankie?' Jules said, looking confused as he ducked and dived his way through the heaving field of suits to reach her.

'Oh, you made it,' she said with a big smile.

'What's going on?'

'Oh my God, guess what? I told Haruna but she didn't exactly burst with excitement. But it's so cool . . . Falls Records are coming to see our gig!'

'Yeah, you told me that already.'

'I did?' Frankie said, racking her brains.

'Yeah, weeks ago,' he said, shaking his head with a slight grin. He'd caught her out on a bit of a lie.

'Oh yeah, they said they'd come if they liked the demo, and they *did* like the demo. So, it's true *now*, anyway. They *are* coming.'

'That's great . . . really really awesome news, but . . . ' He paused, looking at the music stand, the guitar and then back up to Frankie, side-stepping a rushing commuter who was glued to his phone, 'but what is *this* about?'

'Oh, right, now, I know I didn't exactly tell you on the phone, but I need someone to busk with me,' she said, grinning.

Jules burst out laughing. 'What? What do you mean?'

'I need to raise some money, and although I can play Seven songs adequately, when it comes to bashing out well-loved busking hits such as,' she paused, flicking through the chord book she'd stolen from school, '"Wild Wood" by someone called Paul Weller, or "How Deep is Your Love", by the Bee Gees, I'm a little out of my depth. Only a little out of my depth, mind. Anyway, I thought it could be fun.'

'When you texted and said come and meet me this morning and bring your acoustic, I thought it meant we were going to go for coffee and then maybe jam?' Jules said, putting his guitar down on the ground and folding his arms. 'Busking isn't really my thing, Frankie.'

'Oh pleeeeeease,' she said, painting on her most precious smile and clasping her hands together under her chin, shaking away the creeping feeling that she might have taken one liberty too many with him this time.

'Ugh.' Jules looked around him, perhaps for an escape route as Frankie touched his arm gently.

'Please, Jules. Just for a bit.'

'You're something else,' he said, rubbing his face with his hands.

Frankie frowned, and bit her lip. 'Sorry. I dunno, I thought you'd find it fun.'

'Did you really?' Jules said dubiously. 'Why do you need to raise money so urgently?'

'It's for something important.'

Jules sighed. 'Okay. I'm really happy to help you out, Frankie, and maybe I would have been happy to busk with you, but I just wish you'd be straight up sometimes.'

Frankie pulled off her guitar, rested it against the wall of the station and took a step towards him. 'I'm trying to get some money together for Haruna,' she said, lowering her voice. Telling him even *that* felt like a betrayal.

'Haruna? Why?'

'It doesn't matter,' Frankie stammered, embarrassed, 'I feel like I shouldn't tell you. I'm sorry I called. I was kind of on this roll of asking for favours and I just didn't think.'

'Do you want to borrow some money?'

'No. No,' Frankie said, shaking her head, 'I don't borrow. It's just … look, please keep this to yourself. I feel like I shouldn't tell anyone, but she wants to go to Japan and I thought maybe if I could raise the money for her—'

Frankie's voice cracked. She battled hard to suppress the tears that were fighting their way through. 'I just thought that if I could buy the ticket then maybe she would be happy and we could do the gig next week and maybe Geoff would like us, and then she could see her dad, but she'd have something to come back for, you know? She's just so fucking sad and I don't know how else to fix it.'

She lost the battle: a single tear rolled down her cheek and then the floodgates opened and she was suddenly openly sobbing. Jules put a hand on her shoulder and squeezed it gently, and with that one gesture she leaned into him, burying her face in his armpit. She felt the warmth of his arm lift up around her and hold her gently around the shoulders and she let the tears flow.

He stood completely still and just held her. The slightly

sweet smell of his sweat was good. She closed her eyes and felt the rush of deep, soothing affection blanket her. The last week had been exhausting, and for the first time, Frankie wanted someone to share the mental load – just a little bit.

'Hey, that's really a cool thing to do,' he said after some time had passed, and her sobs had slowly subsided.

'It's fucking mental,' she said, sniffing and subtly wiping the snot from her face with her T-shirt.

'Nah, it's cool. I'll help.'

'No, Jules, you've done enough. I shouldn't have asked you. I'm an asshole.'

'You're pushy,' he said, 'but I can take it.'

He pulled back and picked up his guitar, unzipping the case and sliding out a beautiful dark wood, steel-stringed acoustic.

'Really?'

'Really. I'm just playing guitar, though. You can sing, okay?'

'Fuck off, I'm playing guitar,' she said, giggling through her tears, picking up her guitar as well. 'This was my idea, remember?'

Chapter 31

Wild is The Wind

Frankie's mum was making crumble again, but this time it was Haruna opposite her helping to cut and core the apples.

Diane hadn't stopped her chattering since she opened the door an hour ago and pulled Haruna in for an enormous hug. 'This will always be your home, pet,' she'd said, before launching into a huge tirade about how the dance studio was losing money and the owner, Abigail, didn't want to modernise. It was just the kind of inane chat Haruna needed after the last few days.

The night Frankie had found her, she was overwhelmed with relief.

She was so grateful Jules had driven them home. Frankie sat beside her in the back, her coat over Haruna's knees, Haruna's head on Frankie's shoulder. They drove down through Lee Roundabout and under the Blackwall Tunnel in silence, the only interaction in the car was the stolen glances between

Frankie and Jules in the rear-view mirror. The radio was turned down low, but not low enough that they couldn't hear soft-rock classic 'Dream Weaver'.

Back at the flat, they crept up to the bathroom, where Frankie made Haruna take a shower and ready herself for the coming hours.

There was pain. Blood. So much blood. And finally exhaustion.

She had sunk into the bed next to Frankie, rolled over to face the window, and let the tears of relief fall. This was not the right time. Not even close.

A few days later, Haruna felt some sense of calm return. She had spent the time in bed, reading a book by Kim Deal, listening to Big Joanie, a Brixton punk band Cheq had once recommended, and had even found some paper and pens and was sketching again. She couldn't face the drums, though. There was something about that instrument that was stirring, and she wasn't brave enough to face whatever was coming.

Frankie sat next to her, plucking away on her guitar. She was excitedly chatting about the gig. Haruna felt like the band had become a freight train, driven by Frankie, and she was tied to the front like in one of those western films. She couldn't stop it. She didn't know how. But all she wanted was room to breathe.

Today was her first outing, and it felt good to be up and about again. The fog was beginning to lift, and she felt strong enough to start taking her next steps.

Frankie called out to Haruna from the hallway. 'Ru, come here! I want to show you something!'

Diane smiled and nodded for her to go, collecting the unfinished apples from her. Haruna wiped her hands on a tea towel and went through to Frankie.

'Look at these pictures from the dance studio.'

Frankie had a shoebox of old photos out and was flicking through them. There was Frankie and Haruna outside the dance studio in full tap costumes – Frankie posing and Haruna rolling her eyes. Haruna in a purple tutu looking fraught. Frankie and Haruna eating chips on the studio floor. Probably her mum had to work late, and Haruna was allowed to stay with her. 'Look at us – we must have been, what? Eleven there?'

'Oh man, remember that show? You were a tree,' Haruna said, grabbing the photo from Frankie. They looked so cute and happy, Frankie with her tongue out and Haruna standing next to her, cracking up.

'And you were a woodland fairy,' Frankie said. 'I was never allowed the good parts cos Mum worked there, so I always had to be the damn tree.' She grabbed the picture from Haruna and tossed it into the box.

'You outperformed everyone as a tree, though.'

'And you were always the best dancer.'

'Frankie, I wanted to talk to you about the band.'

'Well, since Geoff loved the demo, we're basically full steam ahead. As soon as you're ready,' Frankie said, grinning. She was brimming with optimism, and it made it even harder for Haruna to do what she had to do. She needed to shut it down.

'You did so much work, and I love the band ...' Haruna began.

Frankie looked panicked. 'I love the band too, Ru. It's become a bit part of me. For the first time I really feel like there is something maybe I am good at. Maybe I was meant to do. I don't want to lose it.'

'You're not going to lose it,' Haruna said, 'but, Frankie, it doesn't have to happen like right now. Today. We're all just eighteen, we've got years to get going. Jules is only just signed now and he's twenty. And so is Cheq. I mean, he's taking off now but he's been at it for years.' Her voice faltered at the mention of Cheq, but she took a deep breath and continued. 'I can't do it right now. The gig. I just can't.'

'Really?' Frankie said. She looked resigned. Like she knew it might be coming. 'I was all organised. I wrote a set list for us. The four tracks from the demo, and then, maybe, I wrote this new one I'd like to try and then ... "Hound Dog", for old times' sake?'

'Six tracks would've been good,' Haruna said with a tight smile. 'Gosh, you really were so amazing, Frankie. I feel like that week in the studio with Amelie was this massive turning point for us, you know? I do feel like something could happen and I'm sorry to let you down, but right now I just need some peace.'

'It's okay. I've been too pushy. Classic Frankie. I know

that,' Frankie replied. 'I know it sounds all cliché and shit, but working hard at something you love didn't feel like working.'

'But we shouldn't give up. I just need to drop the pace for a little while, okay?'

'I know you do,' Frankie said. 'I realised it when I found you in the practice room. You need some time. I understand. I pushed everyone too hard. I just wanted it all now, now, now. You know? I'm impatient.'

'Well, that's certainly true,' Haruna said, putting a hand on her shoulder.

'Anyway, don't think I'm not going to be back on you at some point. This isn't a forever break, got that?' Frankie paused for a moment and then turned to her friend. 'Well, I think this is probably the right time to do this. I've got something for you.' She put the last photo back in the shoebox. 'A birthday present.'

'It's not my birthday!'

'Well, whatever. Let's say it's for that.' Frankie stood up and walked over to her bag and pulled out an envelope.

'I know you have no money. And let's face it, it's going to take you the rest of your teens to save up enough money, and I really want you to go do this thing ... '

She handed her the envelope. Haruna stared at her, and then ran her thumb under the fold and tore it open. Inside there was a small card. A voucher of some sort with a huge blue and yellow logo: *From Roman Road to Rio (and BEYOND)*. Haruna looked at Frankie and then back at the voucher, *This voucher entitles the bearer to £800.00 worth of travel and accommodation at From Roman Road to Rio (and BEYOND). Happy Wandering, friend!*

'It should get you there at least. Maybe you'll get a job in Japan or something for the summer . . . or—'

'Frankie.' Haruna looked down at the envelope and gasped. 'How did you get the money? It's going to take for ever to pay you back.'

'I don't want you to worry about where it came from. It's not all from me, anyway, and obviously that's Mum's cousin's shop so we got a good deal.'

'Did other people chip in?' Haruna said, looking a little mortified. 'Oh God, I feel like a charity.'

'It's totally not like that, don't worry.'

'Did Cheq chip in?' she said tentatively.

'No, he didn't, I didn't talk to him about it. I hardly spoke to anyone. Don't worry. Maybe you could give Cheq a call, though? Will you tell him?' she said, before adding, 'I mean, do you want to?'

'Yes and no. Maybe. I need some distance from him,' Haruna said. 'My feelings for him are not as strong as my need to be on my own, and that's the only thing guiding me right now. Oh Frankie, this is such a wonderful gift, but you've done so much already. I can't take it.'

'You can. And you will,' Frankie insisted, 'bloody night-mare arranging it, so just take it or I'll be pissed off.'

With that she smiled at Haruna, and Haruna realised there might be more to it. 'There's a catch, though, right?'

'Of course there is,' Frankie said, before pausing and looking at Haruna thoughtfully. 'Actually, no catch. Just take it. Go meet your dad or do whatever you want. Whatever *you* want.'

'I wanna see my dad so bad,' Haruna said breathlessly. 'I want to see the spring, and the sea. And do all the rotten touristy things. I want it so badly.'

'Well, you'd better hurry,' Frankie said, sniffing.

'Thank you, Frankie,' Haruna said, smiling. 'Oh, I'm going to take it because I could really use this right now.'

She cried as she held on to Frankie's arm, then pulled her in for a hug. She gripped her tightly, with everything she had. And for a moment she didn't want to let go.

'There's one more thing. It's not a huge thing, but it might help a bit. Dad spoke to Uncle Ben, and he's cleared out the basement area of the flat in Peckham. They're going to paint it while you're away and get it set up for you to use as a base. I should really let Dad tell you, he's so proud of himself; I mean, he's been crowing about it all day. Anyone would think it was his bloody place. Anyway, Ru, you don't have to use it. You don't even have to come back,' she said, her voice cracking a little, 'but if you do, it's yours.'

'But what about your flatmates? Jesus, I only met one of them once, in the bloody bathroom. Don't they care they're getting a new flatmate forced on them?'

'They're fine. The rent goes down with an extra person. It's only my cousin that really mattered anyway, and she's always at her boyfriend's house. Like, I literally never see her.'

'I can't believe it,' Haruna said.

'Well, I was a bit worried you wouldn't come back so it wasn't a totally altruistic move. Consider it a little investment in your return,' she said, 'if you want to return.'

'There's the catch,' Haruna said, hugging her one more time.

'Girls!' Frankie's dad called from the lounge. 'Come quick, it's *The Voice* final!'

'Your dad likes *The Voice*?' Haruna asked, clutching the envelope to her chest.

'Yes, but he thinks it's completely rigged, which makes it a bit boring to watch.'

'I'm not going to keep going on about it, but this is without a doubt the greatest gift of my life.'

'You go on through. Get Mum to give you a beer. I've to make a quick call.'

'Okay, Franks.'

Haruna made her way through to the lounge. There were new beginnings ahead, a first burst of hope had blossomed in her heart.

Frankie waited until Haruna was out of earshot and dialled Jules, but this time he didn't answer.

'Jules, I never leave voice messages so consider yourself special. The thing is, I wanted to thank you so much for your help the other day. Well, all your help really. I've decided to never tell Haruna where the money came from and keep all the glory for myself – but only because I think she'd feel a bit embarassed. So, yeah. It was kind of you to make such a big contribution, even if you'll barely notice it's gone from your account. Bloody trustafarians. See, I knew your West London upbringing wasn't to be trusted. Anyway, I'm blathering. Maybe I could pay you back by busking outside your bedroom for a month?' Frankie stopped to laugh heartily at this thought, and continued, 'Anyway, about the Roundhouse. I'm gutted but after everything, we need to cancel . . .'

She knew it was the right thing to do, but it still stung to say. She took a deep breath and hung up the phone. *Jules.* She closed her eyes and thought back to the way he'd held her, and relived the sweet feeling she'd felt.

Jules, who after four, painful hours of busking and earning £152, had pretended to 'sneak off to the toilet' and come back with a small handwritten note which he'd tossed in the hat for her. She had stopped playing and fished it out while he watched her, arms crossed, smiling. It read: *I have the money, let me loan it to you. You can pay me back when you can. I hate this. The public hate us. Let's give everyone a break and stop. Please. I beg you. Do it for me.*

Frankie looked down at her phone and readied herself for the next call.

'Hi Geoff, it's Frankie from Seven here.'

'Yes?'

'The gig is off, I'm afraid.'

'So, when's the next gig, then?'

'Ahh ...' Frankie paused, remembering Haruna, the trip to Japan. She closed her eyes and against all her own desires, forced out the words, 'Ahh, we don't have any more booked.'

'Well, book another. I'll need to see you live.'

'I'm not sure that we can.'

'Why not? What is wrong with you millennials?'

'I'm sorry. Seven are on a hiatus.'

'What? Why? You broke up?'

'We're on a hiatus,' she repeated, attempting to sound confident and assured. 'It's indefinite. But I'll get back to you if that changes.' She bit her lip, knowing she would probably never hear from him again. She felt sick to the stomach with disappointment, and just as she was about to mumble a long, heart-felt explanation, Jules called back on the other line. 'I have to go,' she said meekly. 'I'm really sorry, Geoff. It's out of my control.'

'Hello, Jules?'

'Frankie, just heard your message. You're cancelling? You can't do it? Haruna still doesn't want to?'

'The band needs to take a break for a bit. Haruna's going to go to Japan. I gave her the voucher. You should have seen her face, she totally died.'

'I'm glad. But can't you play before she goes?'

'She's definitely not ready and I need to respect that. Also, as you know, we kind of have no practice room now. Greer's a bit annoyed about it all. Anyway, I think it's best we take a step back for a moment, as much as I loathe saying it.'

'Wouldn't it be good for her to play live?' Jules said. 'Ha, now it's me being pushy. I just feel bad for you, I guess.'

'Right now, Haruna needs zero pressure from anyone. She has some stuff to do.'

'Okay.'

'How's Cheq?'

'He's okay. He's confused. I haven't told him anything, though I don't like keeping this from him.'

'You can tell him Haruna is going to Japan, I suppose,' she suggested. 'Ugh, I feel bad for him, I wish he knew everything that was going on, but then, it's probably best he doesn't.'

'Hey, Frankie, I've got to go, but, you know, I'll cancel the show,' he said, 'and if you want to rebook with us another time, please just ask.'

'Thanks, Jules,' she said, before taking a deep breath. 'And Jules, I'd like to take you for a drink. Not because you helped me, but because I'd like to,' she paused, 'like a date or whatever. I hate that word.'

'Well,' he replied, 'that would be cool.'

Chapter 32

Bad Girls

Summer had finally arrived, and Frankie was taking two weeks off her job to enjoy some of it. She was waiting by the edge of the park, in her shortest shorts, with an I Heart Peckham T-shirt on, just to wind up everyone in London Fields as much as she could. She fidgeted with her hair, freshly touched-up blonde. She was also nursing a new, painful tattoo on her forearm. It was a crazy decision to get one, and really, the place should probably never have let her get one when she'd had a couple of beers, but she loved the way he'd written SEVEN so small and neat.

She had a new job. It wasn't anything fancy, just a small café in Peckham where she waited tables and made coffees and bantered with the customers – who were all basically south-of-the-river versions of her dad. On Sundays she worked at Groove – a record store round the corner from her house.

She was saving as best she could, and practising her guitar and writing songs, and she and Aimee were still meeting up regularly to practise 'unplugged' when they could. Haruna's drum kit was now set up in her huge basement room at their Peckham flat, waiting for her return. And that return was imminent.

She'd spent three months with her father. She'd been keeping Frankie updated with sporadic Skypes and the odd email. It hadn't been a perfect, fairy-tale meeting with her dad. He opened his home immediately, but was angry and regretful about losing touch with her and seemed to find it difficult to overcome all that guilt.

He blamed her mother a lot, for everything, something that bothered Haruna at first – but on the last Skype with Frankie she seemed to have made peace with the difficulty of his situation. Her father had thought, when her mother remarried, that it was better to step back and let Haruna live her new life. He had sent letters now and then. He said a part of him found it easier to let go than to keep trying to include her in his life. He regretted that.

'I don't know how hard he actually tried,' Haruna said to her during one Skype.

She learned he was an artist as well. Fine arts. He lived alone in an apartment in Tokyo, which was apparently large by Tokyo standards. He was from money, although he earned very little now himself; he had savings to sustain himself and his painting. He was furious Haruna's money was gone, and offered her a little while she was there to keep her afloat. But it wasn't much.

She saw the coast. She met her grandmother, who had held her in her arms when she was born. She met two cousins, Niko and Juno. She ate out almost every night. They travelled into the lush mountains, went to see some live music.

They also fought. The close quarters of the apartment meant they got very little space and he, apparently, needed a lot of it. He was moody. And sometimes irritable with her. But mostly they rubbed along okay.

'Jules!' Frankie said, running down the cycle path and straight into his arms, not caring in the slightest about the oncoming traffic.

'Hey you,' he said, kissing her on the mouth. 'Shall we?'

She hooked her arm through his and they headed down Broadway Market and across to the little pub just off the canal.

'Last place in Hackney that does pints for under a tenner,' joked Jules, as they walked into the main bar area and took a seat at the only available table in the far corner.

'Make mine a double,' Frankie said, as he headed to the bar. She watched him go, and felt a warmth radiate through her. Her boyfriend? Nah, fuck that, she would never call him that.

'What time are we expecting her?' Jules said as he slipped down into his stool, and handed her her pint.

'Half an hour,' Frankie said. 'God, I feel sick with excitement.'

'Well, don't dump all the band stuff in her lap right away, please.'

'I won't. Jesus,' Frankie said, grinning, 'I just . . . I don't want to audition for a new drummer. Aimee and I are adamant she is the only one that will do, and if she doesn't want to do the band any more, then that's that. I'll call Geoff and see if he'll still have me in his all girl pop band.'

'Now that I would pay to see.'

'Punk Spice.'

Jules put his arm around her and pulled her in tight. 'Don't be nervous.'

She felt bad about all the people she'd pulled in favours from who she'd ultimately let down, particularly Greta who had, despite Frankie's insistence that Seven were on a hiatus and she should stop working on their stuff, continued to build them up online. Their demos were quite popular on SoundCloud as it turned out, and Greta sent her regular messages:

TO FRANKIE: I've had another few requests this week for when you might play live.

TO FRANKIE: Did you see that Amelie's boyfriend just tweeted your track?

The last one was particularly amusing since, it turned out, Amelie's boyfriend was the ex-singer of a huge, superstar boyband called The Keep. The band that Frankie had been so disparaging of to Amelie. She cringed at the memory. His tweet read:

> Check out the new demo track by @seventheband, produced by the awesome @callmeamelie

The result of his tweet was, after about four thousand retweets, they gained a ton of new followers online, all wanting to know more about this mysterious and enigmatic punk band from East London. As marketing whizz-kid Greta excruciatingly put it, 'The hype train is going to leave the station if you guys don't jump on board.'

And Frankie was good on the guitar now. Not amazing. She would never be as good on the guitar as Haruna was on drums, but she was *fierce* and she understood how to make music.

Jules finished his beer and looked to Frankie who had hardly touched hers.

'Sorry, Jesus. Why am I so nervous?'

'Do you want me to go?'

'No. Well, yes. Afterwards! I want her to see you and me together. She didn't believe I'd finally hooked up with you,' she said. 'I feel so sad about Cheq.'

'Don't. He's doing okay now. He even went out on a date

the other day. Think he's going to struggle to find someone who'll keep him on his toes like Haruna did, though.'

'They were an okay couple,' Frankie said with a smirk, 'I admit.'

'Do you think, maybe, she might even go back there?'

'Hmm.' Frankie bit her lip. She couldn't tell him, but it was hard to make him understand what had happened. She looked him in the eye. 'You know I can't tell you the full story, but if I could you would understand that it won't be that easy. Even if she wanted to.'

'Did she cheat? That's what he thinks.'

'God, no. She loved him.'

Just then the pub door flew open and in walked Haruna. Hair messy and grown out. Crazy, layered clothing, all in black. She was beaming. BEAMING.

'Frankie!'

Frankie jumped up and ran across the pub to hug her friend.

'Let me get my pack off.' Haruna said. 'Wait.'

As she dropped the huge pack to the ground with a thud, she threw her arms around Frankie again.

'You look like a goth and a backpacker had a baby. A gothpacker!'

'Ha! Yes, I got a right going-over at security.' She laughed. 'Where the hell is my delicious English pint of lager?'

'Coming up, darlin'!' Frankie said, beckoning to Jules.

Haruna looked at him and then back at Frankie with huge excited eyes. 'Oh man, you did it. YOU WENT THERE.'

'He's okay. Bit too fucking happy all the time,' Frankie said, as Jules walked over to join them and heaved Haruna's pack into the corner by their table.

'And she's full of shit,' Jules joked.

'Well, she always has been,' Haruna laughed.

'Oh, piss off, you two.' Frankie shook her head.

They fell straight in. Stories of Japan, and her father, and food, and gigs, and a girl she hung out with (who Frankie was instantly jealous of). Haruna was so bright. So beautiful. So back.

After an hour, Jules excused himself. 'I'll leave you guys to get to the real stuff now, without me hanging around.'

'See you soon,' Haruna said before looking thoughtfully at Jules for a moment. 'Is Cheq, um, like, does he know I'm back?'

'I don't really talk to him about you. It's easier for him. Frankie's seen him a bit, though, you know, when she's been over to visit me.'

'He's still there, then?'

'Yep.' Jules looked over at Frankie, and gave her a nod, flicking his hair out of his face in that sexy way he did now that it was longer. 'Speak later?'

'Maybe. Haruna's my priority. First I want to get her home,' Frankie said.

Haruna looked at Frankie and reached out her hands and grabbed both her wrists. 'It's good to see you. To be home.'

'How did your dad take it? That you were leaving?'

'He was fine. I think he was happy to have his apartment back. I mean, we got on and stuff, but he didn't *love* having me there twenty-four/seven. We didn't really know each other. It was the strangest thing.'

'That must be weird. Looking at a parent and not really knowing them.'

'I know. In my mind there was this father – you know, like yours. A big, kind, open person who was everything that was missing in my life – but in the end, he was just *a guy*. A man who was my dad. Who gave up on me too easily and probably thought he'd never see me again. It was so great to see him, but, really, it wasn't what I'd imagined.'

'I'm sorry.'

'No don't be. Don't get me wrong, parts were great. His art was pretty amazing. He was always sketching. Like, way more than I do. He knew some amazing places to eat. Like, really eccentric little noodle bars. He was really sarcastic and a bit rude to people, which I found a quite funny.'

'Just like you!'

'Whatever.' She pushed her shoulder.

'But I missed you. And Aimee. And London,' she said, lifting her eyes up to meet Frankie's. 'I don't know how I'll ever thank you for the opportunity to go, though. It really helped ... fill out my corners.'

'Well, I'm not going to lie. I had to start seeing Jules because there was no one else to hang out with,' Frankie teased.

'I also missed Cheq,' she said. 'I didn't let on to you quite how much I missed him, but I have already called him and he's agreed to meet me "at some point" in the next few weeks. I don't know what will happen. It's probably too much to expect he might forgive me, but maybe . . . we can put it to rest.'

'Well, look,' Frankie said pragmatically, 'whatever is meant to be, right?'

'Right,' she said. 'I realised while I was away what the problem was. I wasn't ready. He was so full on – loving, really – wanting me to move in, and all those things, and I just needed some time on my own.'

'I get it.'

'And so I heard the amazing news that Aimee is staying in London. She's going to med school here, right?'

'Yep, I'm so relieved,' Frankie said, holding her breath – was this the right moment to ask? 'She got a place at Nottingham too, I think. But she's going to UCL.'

Haruna grinned. 'Awesome. Because there's also something really important I need to ask you. Are we still a band?'

'Yes. Oh my God, yes,' Frankie said, finally breathing out. 'Thank God.'

'Good, I can't wait.'

'Yep, we've been practising all the time. Me, every day. We've got tons of new songs. And Aimee is so much better on bass now! And wait till you see what's been going on online! Greta has been amazing. You saw the website, right? And a massive superstar tweeted about us. Greta said that Peaches followed us online. And MIA. I mean, shit. We're already world famous! We just need to pick up and go and tear shit up.'

Haruna did a little jig in her seat. 'We've been totally manufactured, you realise.'

'What do you mean?' asked Frankie, confused.

'Well, you managed to somehow create a band out of almost nothing, and look at us. The most hyped punk band of the millennium, and we've barely played a gig.'

Frankie laughed. 'Oh my lord, you're right. It's the greatest Frankie scam of all time.'

Chapter 33

Top of the World

Frankie pushed past the heaving crowd of people gathered by the door. She was sweating, her heart was thumping in her chest. Behind her, bouncing off the walls, Haruna was basking in the glory of Seven's debut gig at the Sebright Arms. The venue wasn't huge, but the crowd was thick, and thanks to Greta's incredible work, it was one of the hottest tickets in town.

The atmosphere was crazy. And it was so loud at times Frankie couldn't hear anything but the driving, distorted, chaotic mess that was her guitar and the crashing boom of Haruna's kick drum.

'*More more more*,' the crowd were shouting as Haruna lingered for a moment on stage, holding her sticks up high.

Drunk. Wild. And so fun. She went absolutely nuts on stage. It was like all the most crazy parts of her combined to be this loud, proud and magnetic performer. Everyone was moshing. Girls, *just like them*, knew their songs. Every one was a fellow searcher, freak, outcast, non-conformer, curious, kick-ass woman. They were home. A bottle was thrown. People got hurt. It was madness. Someone jumped on stage and knocked over Haruna's cymbal.

When they finished, buzzing with excitement, Frankie leaped off the stage and threw herself into Jules's arms. He was glowing. She planted a big kiss on him, and whispered into his ears, 'I've got to find out what he thinks.'

'Go,' Jules said as Frankie pushed on towards Geoff, who was stood right by the back, chatting to Amelie. As she approached, Amelie gave her a big grin and disappeared into the crowd. Geoff watched her curiously as she wiped the sweat off her brow and rested her hands on her hips.

'Well, what do you think?' she shouted above the noise.

'I think it's a goddamn mess,' he said.

They both looked at each other and for a moment it seemed like he was going to say something disappointing, until his face cracked, and a smile spread across it.

'A goddamn mess,' Geoff repeated, 'but the crowd seemed to like it.'

'More, more, more,' they kept shouting, as Frankie grinned from ear to ear.

'It's good. It's exciting, actually,' he said. 'I'd like to work with you.'

Frankie grinned, and slapped him on the shoulder. 'I'll let you know.'

'Fuck off,' he said, momentarily smiling back, before resuming his usual grumpy face. 'Go back to the other children and have a good night. I have to get home. I'll be in touch.'

Frankie squealed with delight as he made his way out, then she turned back to the room. Haruna and Aimee were stood nervously, waiting for her by the stage. Aimee waved to Frankie to come over and she came running back.

'We fucking rule,' she said, throwing her arms around them both. Frankie buried her face in Haruna's hair and shouted in her ear, 'We didn't need his fucking approval but we got it.'

'*more, more, more,*' shouted the crowd.

'We don't have any more songs,' said Aimee, 'but it feels kinda rude not to?'

Frankie looked at the crowd, and then back at her friends. 'Let's play.'

Have you read the rest of Rebecca Denton's *This Beats Perfect* series?

Out now.